TEMPEST

Kiki Clark

SILVER OAK PACK

Inferno
(Riggs & Myles)

Tempest
(Cash & Ore)

Fervor
(Saint, Jorge, & Walker)

TEMPEST

When duty and desire clash, fated mates are caught in the middle.

Cash's loyalty to his pack is unwavering. He'd sacrifice anything to protect his packmates. Do anything to keep them safe. Put their needs above his own—always.

It is the life he was born for, and the one he's worked years to achieve. As an Enforcer, he swore an oath to his alpha: pack before self.

Not once has he regretted his choices.

Until an injured eagle shifter lands in his lap, and his protective instincts get torn in two.

He knows he can't risk the safety of his pack—no matter what his panther demands. Once the little bird is all healed up, Cash will have to send him on his way.

For the good of his pack.

But dark, frightened eyes and a sweet smile call to his cat in a hungry, possessive way and challenge everything he's ever thought he knew.

For the first time in his life, he might just have to put himself first.

Tempest is the first book in the Silver Oak Pack series, set within the Kincaid Pack Universe but able to be read and enjoyed completely on its own. It features an overly protective panther trapped by his own responsibility-driven morals, an eagle who can't remember much but knows the surly cat makes him feel spine-tingling safe, magical tattoos, skinny dipping, a delicious age gap, gobs of scenting, and a swoon-worthy happily ever after.

AUTHOR'S NOTE

Hi there!

Thank you so much for picking up *Tempest*. I hope you truly enjoy Cash and Ore's story. Starting the Silver Oak Pack series is so fun and something I've been thinking about since I stumbled upon them while writing *The Enforcer and His Heart*.

There are a few mild content warnings if you'd like to check those out below. I would consider some to be **SPOILERS** so proceed at your own risk.

Oh! And please forgive me for the scene with Nero and Nico. 🙈 When I named our sassy vamp in *The Mobster's Mate*, I forgot to take into account he might appear in scenes with KP members. Both starting with N and ending with O? What was I thinking???

-Kiki

CONTENT WARNING:

There are mentions in this book of a main character having experienced childhood abandonment by parents into grandparents' care; a (fictional) slur is used against a main character; there are mentions of past experiences of stalking/unwanted advances; and a main character has experienced medical torture while being held captive but doesn't remember for most of the book.

Plus a death—but not descriptive and not one of the good guys.

Please be kind to yourself and proceed with caution if any of these topics are triggering for you.

If you have questions or would like more details, please don't hesitate to email my PA at admin@kikiclark.com.

CHAPTER 1

"Come on, Jorge. Fern is being ridiculous. Just point me in the right direction."

Cash raised his eyebrows at the scene in front of him.

He'd stopped by his buddy Jorge's house to get a charge up on one of his spelled tattoos and was met with something unexpected. He closed the door behind him and smiled a little as he watched Jorge—all five foot six of him—try and contend with the newest member of their pack, a human named Myles, who towered over him at six foot.

The Silver Oak Pack didn't have a lot of human members, and their territory was isolated enough that the closest human town was half an hour away. Exactly how they liked it.

But Myles had crashed into their lives and refused to leave.

Cash didn't mind that much. He knew from firsthand experience what being so isolated and exclusionary was doing to them, but he didn't make the rules.

Crossing his arms over his chest, Myles tipped his chin up defiantly. It exposed the mating scar on his neck from Riggs, one of the pack's betas. The two had been friends their whole lives, but it had taken Riggs moving away and then Myles coming for a visit for his tiger to recognize his fated mate.

Since joining the pack, Myles was doing his best to learn all about the parahuman world and what it had to offer, which meant he had a lot of questions and drove some people crazy with them. Just the other day, Cash had been at the Alpha House when an older packmate had come storming in to "have a word" with Liam about Myles's incessant questions.

Cash figured some of the pack had just forgotten what it was like to have someone new learn about their world. Or maybe they'd never lived through it. Either way, Cash understood why Myles was so dogged in his pursuit of answers.

He was just trying to find his place.

But there was one aspect that had gotten Myles into some real trouble, which was why he was at Jorge's, pleading for his help. Jorge was a member of the pack's coven, and Myles wanted to learn about magic and how to use it.

Some people had a problem with that.

Their pack was small, but their coven was even smaller. Six witches and a single seer made up the group, and they were led by a tiny but terrifying woman named Fern, who was adamantly against Myles learning anything from the coven.

It was probably because of how they'd all met Myles, when he'd accidentally cast a spell on Riggs and sent him into a spell-induced heat.

Which was *not* something they usually had to deal with as shifters and had come as a bit of a surprise to folks. Especially because it could have killed Riggs.

Fern had been less than impressed, to say the least, so Cash could understand why she didn't want Myles anywhere near magic again. The rest of the coven—as far as Cash could tell; he tried to stay out of their internal politics—didn't hold quite as much of a grudge but agreed with her that it was probably for the best. Myles wasn't a natural-born witch, and that would limit the amount of magic he would actually be able to do anyway.

Though, as Myles liked to argue, because he was part of a fated mate bond, he had direct access to magic through the shifter he was mated to. He couldn't understand why they wouldn't teach him how to tap into the bond to fuel spellwork.

Fern remained unconvinced.

Cash thought Myles had a point, but he wasn't about to get in the middle of the fight. There was no way he would ever cross Fern. The woman looked sweet as a button, but if you pissed her off... He shuddered at the thought.

Some of her curses were legendary, and he wasn't about to be on the receiving end of one.

But since Jorge was less scary and less firm in his denial than Fern, Myles had turned his attention on him, trying to convince him that it would be a good idea to just give him some tips and that Myles could teach himself.

Which seemed even scarier than him learning magic to begin with, in Cash's opinion.

Jorge didn't stop what he was doing, basically ignoring Myles and his demands as he used a mortar and pestle to mix the ingredients for the spell for Cash's tattoo. His kitchen was full of plants and sunlight, but the scent of magic was so strong it was tickling at Cash's nose.

"Fern said no. Until you convince her, I'm not going to help you."

Myles slumped dramatically. "Seriously? I learned my lesson when my mate almost *died*. Why is she still punishing me?"

"Seriously." Jorge looked up finally, giving Myles a hard look. His amber eyes could be intense when they were pinned on you. "And she's not punishing you. She's protecting you, the coven, and our pack. You'd do well to remember that."

3

Oh damn.

Cash crossed his arms over his chest and leaned back against the counter behind him. Jorge wouldn't be ready for him for a few more minutes, so he'd just wait for them to acknowledge him. He didn't have anywhere to be until his evening patrol later, and things were getting good.

"You're right. I'm sorry," Myles said quickly, holding his hands up in surrender. "But come on, man. I know now not to just say random spells. I'll be careful. Isn't it better to train me than to be worried about what I'm learning on the internet behind your backs?"

Jorge sighed and pinched the bridge of his nose, the black-and-gray rose on the back of his hand catching Cash's eyes. "¡Dios mío! You just won't quit, will you?"

Cash did his best to suppress his amusement. He was honestly glad they weren't paying much attention to him because he didn't want to have to give his opinion. Technically, as a pack Enforcer, he had the authority to overrule Fern, but he would never do that. None of them would. The only person in the pack who could really tell Fern what to do was their alpha, Liam.

And even then, their relationship was more of a partnership than him dictating to her. Liam trusted her and sought her advice quite often. She'd been a part of the Silver Oak Pack long before Liam had moved there and taken over and was very protective of all of them.

"Magic, spellwork, and being a witch are more complicated than just getting to say a few fancy spells to make your life easier," Jorge said, staring Myles down, but he wasn't giving up.

"I know that. I promise," Myles said urgently. "I read the books that Fern gave me. I understand. You have to be respectful, and I am. Please, Jorge. At least help me convince her to give me another chance."

Cash looked away.

Now he wished he wasn't there to witness what was happening. He could scent the desperation on Myles. For whatever reason, this was important to him, and Cash's panther wanted to soothe their packmate.

Maybe he could gently suggest to Fern that she should ease up on the poor kid.

He was just thinking he'd slip out, maybe go and get some lunch before coming back to get Jorge to recharge his tattoo, when his phone started vibrating in his back pocket. Pulling it out, he saw Liam's name on the screen and frowned.

He'd just come from a meeting at the Alpha House.

Glancing up, he caught Jorge's eyes and tipped his head toward the back door he'd come in through. Jorge nodded and waved him off, but Myles barely even glanced at him as he slipped back out into the late-spring heat.

"Alpha," Cash answered, instincts prickling and raising the hair on the back of his neck.

"I need you to go check something out," Liam said, his voice carrying a barely perceptive urgency.

Cash jogged toward his truck. He'd parked on the street since Myles's car was taking up the extra space in Jorge's driveway, but it only took him a few seconds to get there and wrench the door open. "What happened?"

"Fern just texted me. There was a breach through one of the wards."

His heart lurched. It could be nothing more than some stray hikers, but his instincts were rarely wrong. "Where?"

"She's going to send you the location," Liam said as his phone vibrated against his face, "but I know it was the western border, somewhere deep in the woods."

Cash nodded as he jumped into his vehicle. "Okay. Does she know what broke through?"

They kept their borders locked down tight. Unexpected visitors were not welcome and were usually sent back the way they'd come. Whoever it was, Cash would deal with

5

them. It was his main job as an Enforcer. He shared the responsibility of patrolling the territory with the betas, but border security fell to him and the coven.

"She's not sure," Liam said, "but she thought that it was probably a shifter. At the speed they passed through, she thinks they were flying. It's possible they might not have realized they'd trespassed into our territory until they hit the warding."

Breaking through it would have hurt like a bitch too. Humans could pass through without issue, and it would just alert Fern of the intrusion, but parahumans had to counteract the repellant aspect of the spells used in the protective warding that encircled their territory.

Though maybe a bird shifter could fly through fast enough to beat it? He'd have to ask Fern about that.

Cash fired up his truck and started down the street. Jorge lived close to the center of town, his house attached to his tattoo shop, so it was a straight shot for him to head west. "All right. I'll check it out and let you know if I need any backup. They probably just need to get turned back around. I doubt it'll take much to scare them off."

Liam chuckled in his ear. "That is the reason I'm sending you."

Cash rolled his eyes and hung up. He didn't think he was that scary-looking, but the other Enforcers and betas disagreed. Whenever somebody needed threatening or scaring out of their territory, Cash was the one they sent. It usually worked too. A hard stare and stern growl and the intruder was on their way again.

Silver Oak, Kansas, was a bit off the beaten path—just the way they liked it—but their tiny town had grown on a small peninsula that jutted into Silver Oak Lake. It drew humans who thought it'd be a nice place to camp or hike. Most packs wouldn't bother driving them off—hell, the little bit of tourism would probably be good for them—but their pack laws were clear, so Cash shooed them away.

Whenever he thought about suggesting they update the law, he reminded himself that the cubs in the pack liked to run around in their shifted forms as soon as they learned how. That alone was reason enough for him to get on board with keeping nosy humans away.

He took the main road out of town, heading straight for the western edge of their territory. When he reached it, he pulled his truck over to the side of the road and turned it off.

The text from Fern showed a location a couple of miles north of where he was. There weren't any roads near that area, so he'd have to go the rest of the way on foot. Just to be sure he was still headed in the right direction, he sent Fern a quick reply.

Cash: *Has their location changed?*

Fern: *No. For some reason they haven't moved at all.*

Cash frowned and tucked his phone away. That seemed... odd. There was no way whoever it was hadn't felt it when they'd gone through the warding, so why hadn't they left if they weren't going to keep moving toward town?

He didn't have to use the map on his phone to lead him to the spot, knowing their territory like the back of his hand. Several times a week, he ran the whole perimeter, and each night, he went through a section of woods that surrounded them on three sides. Whatever sections he didn't take, the betas split up and covered.

He used to only check the perimeter a couple of times a month to make sure nothing had disturbed the warding, calling Fern or Jorge to come and fix it if need be. But since last year, they'd tightened their security in reaction to the upheaval in the parahuman world.

His whole life, all parahumans in the country were ruled by the shifter Council, a group of retired alphas who made laws and heard disputes between packs. Once, when he was a

7

cub, a Council member had visited his Pops for help with some persistent medical issue, but otherwise, they hadn't seen or heard much from the Council as far as he knew.

But then the largest pack in the country asked for his alpha's help, and a Council woman, two strange witches, a powerful Enforcer, a distractingly beautiful lioness, and a child had landed in their territory. Cash hadn't spent much time with any of them except Ericka, the lioness who stayed longer than the Enforcer and Council woman. She'd laughed in his face when he'd suggested they get dinner while she was there, and he'd liked her even more for it.

The strange visit by the group had only been the beginning of changes though. Not long after everyone had finally left, they'd gotten word that Rick Kincaid and his pack had taken down the Council and those aligned with them. It had shocked the entire parahuman community and caused massive confusion and chaos for months.

Many had said Kincaid had led the coup for selfish reasons, wanting even more power than he already had and to control shifters throughout the country. Cash's own pack hadn't been sure what to believe, but Liam had calmed them, reminding them of the rumors they'd been hearing for over a year about unprovoked attacks against anyone who dared to stand up against the Council, reports of hideous beasts made from magic and evil, and the truths that had been shared with him when Rick's Enforcer had been in Silver Oak.

While tension had eased throughout the pack, Cash and the other Enforcers and betas were staying alert. The elected governmental body Kincaid was building from the ground up was taking far longer than anticipated, leaving the parahuman world without proper leadership.

And where there was a power void, there were unsavory people willing to fill it.

They'd been hearing new rumors the last few months. Shifters going missing. Roving groups terrorizing small, unprotected packs. Alphas being overthrown and replaced by brutal outsiders.

It had been enough to have them stepping up their own security as a precaution. They were a small pack, but they weren't weak or unprotected. Still, Liam wasn't about to risk anyone's safety, and Cash couldn't agree with him more. Protecting the pack was his number one priority, and he took the job seriously.

He didn't know what this shifter who'd crossed into their territory was doing, but he'd find them and send them on their way. Since they weren't moving, the only thing he could figure was that maybe they were injured or were resting and thought that being on the edge of their territory would be a safe spot to stop.

Either way, the shifter couldn't stay.

Trudging through the thick foliage of the woods kept the sun directly off his shoulders and neck, but the heat and humidity were ratcheting up as summer neared. It was going to be a hot summer, but he didn't mind. He loved to lie in the sun as his panther, his black fur soaking in the warmth.

He also didn't mind going for a swim in the lake with the pack cubs. As far as he was concerned, making sure the water was safe for them was part of his job too.

At least... that's what he said whenever Liam teased him about it.

A light scent of avian shifter drifted toward him, and he paused just as a large twig broke beneath one of his black boots, the sharp snap ringing in the air around him. He ignored it since he hadn't been bothering to hide his approach. This was his territory; he wasn't skulking through the woods to find one little bird.

The scent was faint, but his nose pinpointed the direction, and he followed it, noting absently it was a nice scent. Almost floral in its sweetness, but he couldn't quite pinpoint what kind of flower. He followed it around trees and fallen branches, mulling over the different notes as he went. There was something… strange just beneath the floral fragrance.

He tracked the scent to the very edge of the territory, exactly where Fern had said they'd be. The scent of magic was thick here, burning his nose and almost covering the bird's. Focusing, he closed his eyes and inhaled deeply, ignoring the magic and concentrating on the stranger.

They were hiding in the trees, way up above him.

He opened his eyes and peered up. Whoever they were… they smelled fucking delicious, riling his panther into alertness. It didn't matter though. An alluring scent wouldn't save them. It was his job to expel whoever it was, and he would do it.

He took his duty very seriously.

"You might as well come down," he called. "I know you're up there."

He stared up into a big bushy maple, just able to make out the shape of a dark-colored bird perched near the top.

"You can either take off now or come down and tell me what it is you're doing in our territory and then leave. Either way, you can't stay."

The bird cocked his head at him, wings twitching. Cash sighed, about to start removing his clothes to scale the tree, when the bird swooped down to land on the ground in front of him.

He was a golden eagle. Large, with dark brown feathers that lightened toward the ends and a couple of spots of white near the base of his tail feathers. Under Cash's scrutiny, he ruffled his feathers and clicked his beak irritably.

Cash ignored the noise, narrowing his eyes and inhaling deeper. Now that the bird was right in front of him, he could tell what was off in his scent. It was… hot, like a burning fire. He also smelled strongly of fear and pain, even as he stared Cash down in his most primal form.

Cash took a step closer without thinking. "Are you okay?"

He hadn't meant to ask that.

It wasn't his business whether this eagle was okay or not. He wasn't Cash's responsibility. His only job was to send him on his way.

Even if the very idea made Cash's panther growl in protest.

The eagle cocked his head, made a squeaking chirp, and then began to shift. It took longer than it should have. Longer than anyone Cash knew, except maybe a cub trying their first time.

Even though it shouldn't, the slowness worried him. He knew it wasn't a good sign and indicated the eagle had grown weak from injury or exhaustion.

When he finally finished, a tiny man with olive skin and black hair groaned and dropped to one knee. He took a few deep, heaving breaths, his muscles twitching beneath his sweat-slicked skin, a dark flush between his shoulder blades.

Cash wondered how long he had been flying that he was so overheated even in his human form.

Eyes so dark they looked black peered up at him, and Cash took half a step back. The man was breathtakingly beautiful, his features delicate in a way Cash had never seen before. His dark rose lips looked supple despite being chapped.

All the blood in Cash's body headed south as the eagle's tongue swiped out, trying to wet those tempting lips.

"Please," the man gasped out. "Help me."

"Help you with what?" Cash asked.

The eagle opened his mouth, but then all Cash could see were the whites of his eyes. He darted forward, but he was too far away to catch him before he hit the ground.

CHAPTER 2

C ash's knees hit the grass next to the eagle, but his hand hovered above all that exposed skin.

He was hesitant to touch him, some instinct telling him that it was going to be a life-changing experience. There was a tugging in his gut, driving him to snatch up the tiny man and take him somewhere safe so Cash could protect him until he was better.

Except his instincts didn't control him. Cash listened to them, but *he* made decisions. He weighed options and went with what was most logical and best for his pack. Neither his panther nor his most base impulses were in charge of him.

And yet…

Growling at his own ridiculousness, he shrugged off the notion of some stranger disturbing his well-ordered life and laid a hand on his shoulder.

A small zap of electricity sparked where they touched, shooting up Cash's arm.

He jerked back and stared at his own hand, feeling betrayed. What the fuck was that?

Ignoring the fact that it was humid as hell, he told himself it was just static electricity and refocused on the young man.

He looked like he was maybe in his mid-twenties, a good ten to twelve years younger than Cash.

Not that that mattered. Nothing about the eagle was his business. He just needed to get him out of their territory and get back to Jorge's. It didn't matter how desperate he'd looked when he'd begged for Cash's help.

Clenching his jaw, he gave the small man a rough shake, his head moving with the force of it, but there was no reaction or sign of him coming to.

Cash leaned forward and tilted his head to listen, frowning at the odd rhythm of the eagle's heartbeat. The burning scent was overwhelming so close, worrying him even more than his off-beat pulse.

He sat up straight and stared at the man's face. His cheekbones were sharp and flushed with exertion... or maybe fever. He had dark, thin brows, long lashes, and a cute little rounded chin that made Cash think it was probably adorable when the man tried to look serious.

He swallowed roughly. This man wasn't his responsibility. The safety of the pack was all he should be worried about, and some strange shifter with an unknown illness posed a potential threat.

Cursing himself, he slipped his hands underneath the man's body, his weight barely more than a feather as he lifted him and started jogging back toward his truck. He couldn't leave him. He just... couldn't.

He kept having to remind himself to watch where he was going, even though he could probably traverse the forest around their town with a blindfold and not get lost. But that didn't mean he needed to spend the entire trip back to the main road staring at the unconscious man.

That just seemed creepy.

When he reached his vehicle, he carefully opened the passenger door and set him inside. The guy just flopped over, sprawling across the bench seat since he couldn't support himself. Cash hurried around the hood and carefully climbed in on the driver's side, lifting the eagle's head so he could rest it on his thigh.

He knew it was inappropriate, but he couldn't stop himself from running his fingers through that messy black hair. It was so soft, like downy feathers. He wondered if the eagle was as soft in his shifted form and if he'd let Cash touch him one day.

He frowned at the road as he headed back into town. That was a weird thought. Why was he thinking about that? They were just going to make sure the guy would be all right, and then he'd be going on his way. He wouldn't be staying, so Cash wouldn't be touching him in any way.

Grabbing his phone, he called his alpha, preparing himself for Liam's displeasure.

"Did you find them?" he answered after only a single ring. Cash heard Fern in the background say something about the intruder moving farther into their territory and grimaced.

"I found them," Cash confirmed, eyes darting down before he could stop himself from running over the smooth olive skin that would be haunting his dreams. "It's an eagle shifter."

"What does he want?"

"I don't know. He passed out. And... he doesn't smell right."

"What do you mean?" Liam asked, sounding concerned. Fern demanded he put the phone on speaker so she could hear too.

Cash licked his lips, dragging his gaze back to the road. "There's something off in his scent and heartbeat. I'm not sure if he's sick or injured in some way."

"Where are you right now? I'll come to you."

"I'm bringing him to Pops," Cash said, bracing himself for Liam's reaction.

The lion didn't say anything for a long moment. Even

Fern was silent, waiting for their alpha to rip him a new one for not following protocol. Finally, he said slowly, "You're bringing him to your grandfather's house?"

"Yes, sir," Cash said, hoping the extra sign of respect would help remind Liam that Cash wasn't usually such a dumbass. "He needs a healer."

"He needs to get out of our territory," Liam said, voice still carefully level, but even over the phone, Cash could feel the edge of *alpha* coming through. The only real indication that he wasn't happy with Cash, and it was enough to upset his panther.

"I know," Cash said quickly. "It just... It felt *wrong* to just leave him outside the warding while he's sick and unable to fend for himself."

Liam sighed heavily, but Cash knew he would agree with him. Liam was wary of outsiders, just like all of them, but he wasn't heartless. Far from it.

Compared to their old alpha, Liam was a damn pushover.

"I'll meet you at Pops's," Liam said and hung up.

Cash's panther stirred restlessly in his chest, unhappy with upsetting their alpha but also thrilled at the nearness of the eagle. Ignoring what that could mean, Cash turned south on a road half a mile outside of Silver Oak.

He and Pops lived in an A-frame cabin a little way away from the rest of the pack. His grandfather had built it for his nan when they were first mated, keeping it updated over the decades. There was a small outbuilding Pops used to see patients from the pack, but otherwise, it was just them and the trees. When Cash had moved in with them when he was eight, it had become the only real home he'd ever had.

He knew Pops would be there, even though it was the middle of the day, because it was right in the middle of his favorite soap opera. Pops never missed it, not since he'd retired a few years ago. He'd owned a veterinary clinic in the next town over for decades, his grandmother running the reception desk and keeping the schedule—and his grandfa-ther—on task.

After Nan passed away, Pops had said it wasn't the same anymore and had sold the business to a human, deciding to retire. He couldn't fully stop working though. Pops was the only healer they had in the pack, which Cash knew was just one of many concerns on Liam's plate.

While a lot of the pack liked keeping their size small, it was proving... problematic. The median age of their pack members was rising; not enough young people were coming to the area to help replenish those aging and retiring like his Pops. Too many members were avidly against opening their pack to non-cat shifters or even just actively trying to encourage new cats to move to the area.

If they didn't though, within a couple of generations, there wouldn't be a pack left to protect from outsiders.

Their A-frame came into view, the top peak visible over the tops of the trees nearby. Turning onto their driveway, he rumbled up the rutted path and parked next to Pops's older sedan.

When he turned the truck off, the eagle stirred, turning his head into Cash's thigh and rubbing his face against his jeans, making a faint, confused sound.

"Hey, can you hear me?" Cash asked quietly, running his fingers through that soft hair again.

The eagle made another noise, smashing his face harder into Cash. His panther rumbled happily at the scenting, even though it was obviously accidental.

"Can you tell me your name or what happened to you?"

He didn't say anything, and his body went lax against Cash's a moment later. Sighing, he carefully slipped out of his truck and moved around to the other side to grab the bird. He was walking up onto the porch when the front door opened, and Pops stared at him, his bushy gray eyebrows raised in question.

"Now, who's this?"

"I don't know." He looked down at the eagle, his grip tightening a fraction as a protective instinct flared inside him, but he stomped it out. "He flew through the warding along the western edge of the territory. When I found him…"

Cash hesitated. Should he tell anyone the little bird had asked for help? Would that make a difference once he was awake and able to move?

Probably not.

He wasn't a part of their pack. He wasn't their responsibility.

And yet…

His panther growled at the very idea of sending the eagle on his way without helping him.

"He just said he needed help, and then he passed out."

"Well, bring him in, bring him in." Pops stepped back and pointed with his cane toward the living room. "Lay him on the couch."

Cash maneuvered himself and the unconscious man through the door and past his grandfather, but then he headed toward the kitchen instead. "The couch is too low for you to examine him, Pops."

He huffed behind him but didn't argue, limping as quickly as he could toward their small rectangle kitchen table and clearing the few things sitting on it. Cash laid the man down, surprised at how little of the bird's legs hung over the edge.

He really was a tiny thing, and it just made Cash want to protect him even more. He lingered, not wanting to stop touching that smooth skin or leave him undefended. Goddess, what was this man doing to him?

"Go and grab my bag, son."

He did, hurrying into his grandfather's bedroom and grabbing his medical bag. Pops had just started examining the eagle when there was a knock at the door. It opened before he could do more than turn to look, Liam coming through first but Fern right behind him. Their alpha towered over her at six foot five to her five foot. Her sweet, freckled face was set in a serious expression as she zeroed in on Pops and the bird and hurried forward, pulling her long, wavy hair up into a messy bun as she moved.

"What are we looking at, Terry?"

"I'm not sure," Pops said, frowning. "He's definitely not well, but I'm not sure what's wrong. There's no visible wound or injury."

"Wolfsbane poisoning?" she said, dropping the small duffel she called a purse on a chair and pulling it open. "I've got some antidote in here."

"Maybe. It's usually introduced through a wound though," Pops said, studying the soles of the eagle's feet for some reason. "I suppose it could have been slipped into something he ingested."

Cash's heartbeat thumped heavily in his ears as his eyes found Liam's all on their own, looking for reassurance from his alpha. Liam beckoned him over, and Cash didn't hesitate, only stopping once he was right in front of the lion. They were about the same height, but the power radiating from Liam made him feel small and safe, easing a little of the tension inside him.

"I know what you're going to say," Cash said quietly, averting his gaze and tipping his head to the side to expose his throat out of respect. When Liam didn't respond, he chanced a quick glance and saw the side of Liam's mouth was tipped up in a small smile.

He clasped the side of Cash's neck, using his big palm to scent him and calm him further. "No, you don't. You did the right thing. He might not be our responsibility, but that doesn't mean that he doesn't deserve our help."

Cash nodded slowly, relieved that his alpha wasn't actually upset with him.

"He didn't say anything to you?"

Cash shook his head. "He just... He asked me to help him and then passed out."

Liam nodded, eyes on the table behind Cash. His palm moved against the side of Cash's neck, gently sliding up and down to leave his scent behind. The gesture was common among close shifters, especially family, but it felt different coming from an alpha. Even more so from one Cash respected and trusted.

"We'll do what we can," Liam decided, giving his neck a squeeze and dropping his hand to his side. He shifted his attention to Cash. "If need be, we can help him get to another pack if he's running from something."

Cash's panther snarled at the idea, but he kept himself contained. His panther needed to fucking chill. "Yes, Alpha."

The two of them stood there for a while, watching Pops and Fern work without seeming to make much progress. After nearly an hour, Fern sighed and came over to them. Pieces of her strawberry blonde hair had escaped her bun, but she just swiped at them irritably.

"Something is preventing him from healing," she said, glancing back at the eagle. "Something I've never seen before."

"Okay. What does that mean for him?" Liam asked, crossing his arms over his wide chest.

Cash unconsciously mimicked his stance, watching the witch as she rubbed at her face.

"I don't know. He's definitely been dosed with something," she said, her tone a little frustrated, though not with them. She didn't like not knowing the answers to problems. Her scent was thick with worry too, and that made Cash's apprehension grow. "Whatever it is, it's not wolfsbane because it's not reacting at all to the antidote. Even if it was some strain we hadn't seen before, the generic antidote would have some effect. So it's something else, something that has..."

invaded his body and is suppressing his healing or stopping it from kicking in somehow."

"Will he wake up?" Liam asked.

Cash's heart jumped into his throat.

Fern shrugged. "We're not sure. If we can figure out something to help his body fight it, it might be enough of a boost that his healing will be able to overcome whatever it is. But we need more answers."

Pops shuffled over behind her. "I can run some tests on his blood here, but a proper lab will be able to tell more."

Liam nodded. "Do what you need to do to try and keep him alive and get him feeling better."

They both nodded and moved back over toward the table, Fern telling Pops she was going to call in some more coven members to come and help. Pops pulled out his phone to call a friend who worked in a lab. Liam clasped his shoulder briefly, and then he headed out the door, telling Cash to update him frequently.

Cash's eyes stayed on the profile of the eagle, his feet unwilling to move from their spot of vigil.

Where could he have come into contact with something neither Fern nor Pops had ever seen before? Something that was preventing his parahuman healing from kicking in and fighting off the infection? He wasn't sure, and he didn't like that.

"Is it contagious?" he asked once Fern and Pops finished their calls.

Fern looked over at him and shook her head. "I doubt it. I think it was done on purpose to hurt him specifically."

Cash's fists clenched at his sides. "To kill him," he clarified.

"Yes," she said without hesitation. "To kill him."

CHAPTER 3

*L*avender...
    There was something...
Safe... He was... safe now...
Lavender... The lavender was safe...
He had to remember... He needed to tell someone...
Goddess, he hurt...

ORE STRUGGLED TO FOCUS, his body burning from the inside out. There were voices around him, some close, some farther away, but he couldn't understand what they were saying. Fear began to build inside him, his limbs too heavy to move, and then it shot up to terror when a hand grabbed his shoulder.

He screamed inside his head, wanting to fly as fast and as far as he could to get away. He was in danger. He needed to get help. He needed—

Lavender.

He tried to turn his head toward the scent, but he couldn't move. Not at all. But it permeated through his nose and into his brain, seeping all the way through his body and calming him. It was so strange. He had never been ruled by scent before. Birds weren't. Their sense of scent wasn't as strong as canine and feline shifters. It was their eyes that were most advanced. But just having the smell of lavender surrounding him wherever he was eased his panic and fear back down to a manageable level.

A low, husky voice said, "You're all right. I've got you."

When that hand on his shoulder squeezed, it felt so big, like with just that one hand, Ore could be scooped up and held high up into the sky. It made him feel safe, just like that lavender scent. He wanted it closer. He wanted it coating all of him. He knew that he could trust whoever belonged to that scent. His eagle knew it, and he always trusted his eagle.

He tried to speak, but nothing came out, his mouth barely parting. He knew there was something he needed to say, but the longer he fought against the drowsiness tugging at him, the harder it was for him to remember. He needed to warn someone. He needed help... but what did he need help for?

Goddess, everything was so foggy, like his brain was out of fuel. No matter how hard he tried to turn over the engine, it just wouldn't catch. Maybe after he got some more sleep, he'd be able to focus and remember.

As he drifted off, that firm hand was still gripping his shoulder.

Keeping him safe.

ORE WOKE UP SLOWLY.

He wasn't sure where he was or what had happened, but he wasn't afraid. He probably should be, but all he felt was cozy, his body a little heavy from having been asleep too long. Shifting his limbs, he found there was an ache in his joints he wasn't used to, but it wasn't too bad.

Maybe he'd flown too far? But to where and why?

He racked his memory, but there was… nothing. Did he live here and he'd just forgotten?

He looked around the room and was pleasantly surprised by what he found. Nothing was familiar, but it was a lovely space. There were huge windows on the back wall, letting in a ton of sunlight. The ceiling above him came together at a steep angle, making him think he was in a loft in an A-frame house.

Being up off the ground level made him feel a little better, but nothing in the space felt like *his*. The bed he was in was soft, almost too soft, so that his body sank into it in a way that almost felt like a cocoon. He could imagine falling asleep very easily once more, but he forced himself to sit up.

The walls were painted a very pale yellow, and the sheets were soft and white. It smelled a little like lavender, leather, and the way the air smelled high up when he was flying across the sky and everything beneath him was so tiny. He didn't know how else to describe it other than it smelled good and safe. He felt it in his gut, but he wasn't sure why.

He still wasn't sure where he was. Nothing looked familiar. He could tell that two cat shifters lived there, but that didn't tell him anything. Did he know them? Had they rescued him from something so terrible his brain was protecting him from remembering anything?

He knew his name. He knew he was a golden eagle shifter. He knew he was twenty-five and that he hated brussels sprouts.

But everything else? Like where he lived or his parents' names… it was just blank. That scared him more than anything else.

He rose from the bed and looked down at himself, his eyebrows scrunching together in confusion. He was wearing a T-shirt that was so big on him it went down to his knees. Whoever it belonged to was a giant compared to him. That wasn't exactly abnormal, though, since his five-foot-two frame was shorter than most avian shifters too.

Wait. How did he know that?

There was an unmade cot on the floor a few feet away from the bed, and that lavender-leather-air scent was on the pillow and blankets too. Whoever's bed he'd stolen, they must have slept on the cot. Staying close but giving him space. Warmth spread through his chest as he lifted the collar of the shirt he was wearing and inhaled deeply. As he'd suspected, it was steeped in the alluring scent as well.

On the wall opposite the bed, there were dozens of framed photos. He stepped closer on light feet, his eyes widening. Not photos, pictures—some painted and some crayon, but all terrible in that cute way only kids could do. As he neared the wall, he noticed that most of them had different names written on the bottom right-hand corner in neat, black ink.

There had to be at least a dozen different names. How many cubs did this family have? And why was it so quiet if there were supposedly a dozen kids running around somewhere?

On the floor, right at the base of the massive windows on the back of the room, was a fluffy-looking pallet. He stared at the indent right in the middle and smiled. He didn't know if he'd ever met a cat shifter before, but he somehow knew that the owner of this sunshiny bedroom liked to curl up in their shifted form right there in the afternoon light. It reminded him of the way he enjoyed going for a flight just to stretch his wings when he was restless.

Instead of a regular banister separating the loft space from where it looked down at the floor below, there were ten feet of bookcases creating a half wall. *All* of the shelves were full.

There didn't seem to be any rhyme or reason to the organization though. Some of the books were even facing the wrong way, their dull, tanned-with-age pages the only thing showing instead of the title on the spine. His fingers twitched, but he resisted the urge to go over and rearrange them alphabetically... or maybe by color... definitely at least by genre.

Shaking his head, he tiptoed over to one of the two doors the loft had. Finding a bathroom, he quickly did his business and washed up a bit, then went to check the other door. The walk-in closet looked only half full, but he checked the built-in drawers too. Nothing. He definitely didn't live in the happy, yellow room. There wasn't a single piece of clothing small enough to fit him. Everything was giant-sized, like his current T-shirt.

He stepped back out in the bedroom and paused at the top of the stairs. He could hear someone moving downstairs and wondered if he should just go down and see if they knew what had happened to him. His nose wasn't strong enough to detect if it was the lavender-leather cat or the other one who he guessed was elderly, his scent mostly just a lingering odor of menthol from a pain cream he must use.

Before he could decide what to do, a kind male voice called up to him, "Whenever you're ready, you can come on down and I'll feed you."

Ore's stomach growled just at the idea. Goddess, he was starving. When was the last time he'd eaten anything? He glanced again at his bare legs and shrugged, hurrying down the dark wood steps. If they wanted him dressed in something else, they'd have to provide it.

The stairs ran down the side of the house, the wall to his left decorated with family photos that he didn't allow himself to linger on. Reaching the bottom, he grabbed the large, round cap on the last post on the handrail and used it to skip the last step and spin toward the rear of the house. He blushed as an elderly man with a cane grinned at his antics. His once wide shoulders were stooped, and there was a large bald spot at the crown of his head.

Ore could tell immediately that he was kind—and definitely not the man from the loft. There was a short hallway behind the kitchen that he'd guess led to another bedroom and bathroom.

The rest of the first floor was one open space full of large windows and comfortable-looking furniture facing a huge TV mounted on the wall above a fireplace. The kitchen was updated but lived-in, some dirty dishes in one side of the sink and two overly ripe bananas on the counter next to where the older man worked at putting together some sandwiches.

There were already place mats set at the rectangular table that separated the kitchen from the living room. He shuffled forward a few steps, unsure what to do in the strange situation he found himself in. Should he offer to help finish the food? Jump right into questions about what had happened to him? Beg the man for details on the other feline inhabitant of the house?

The other man's bushy mustache—the same shade of gray as his thick brows and hair—twitched in amusement, though he was obviously trying not to show it. His light blue eyes were positively twinkling though. "Go ahead and take a seat, son."

Ore grabbed the back of one of the chairs. "Are you sure I can't help?"

"No, no, I've got it," the man insisted. He went over and opened the refrigerator door, disappearing from view for a second. "Do you want water, juice, or milk? We don't have soda, but I could have my grandson get some if you want."

"Water's fine," Ore said, sinking into the wooden chair. His fingers fussed with the edge of the T-shirt he was wearing. It was black with faded lettering he couldn't really see anymore, but it was soft. And even though it was thin, it made him feel protected.

The man's face popped back out from behind the fridge door and studied him. "Hmph. I'm going to give you orange juice. You could use the vitamins and electrolytes."

Ore raised his brows. "Um, okay."

The man disappeared for a second again before reemerging with a bottle of orange juice.

He studied the man as he moved around, filling two glasses from the bottle, returning it to the fridge, then bringing them over to the table one at a time. Ore was pretty sure he was a black panther—though he wasn't sure how he knew that or the fact that they were pretty rare.

Picking up his glass, he took a sip of the cold juice and then couldn't stop himself from chugging down the rest. Goddess, he was parched. The sweetness was also hitting him fast, waking him up a bit more.

"Mhmm," the older man said knowingly, setting a plate with a roast beef sandwich and some potato chips in front of him. He took Ore's empty glass right out of his hand and went back over to the fridge, pulling the juice out once more.

Ore barely paid attention, his mouth watering at the scent of meat and cheese hitting him in the face. He wanted to wait for the other man to sit to dig in, but he couldn't stop himself from snatching it up and taking a huge bite.

Good Goddess.

He'd eaten half of it before his second glass of juice was set in front of him. Embarrassed at his lack of manners, he put his sandwich down and wiped at his mouth with the plain white paper napkin next to his plate. "Sorry."

"Don't be," the cat said firmly. He placed the second plate full of food right next to Ore's first one. "You need the fuel after the last few days. I'll make another for myself."

"No, I'm fine," he said quickly, horrified at the idea of taking food from this elderly man.

"Nonsense," he huffed, using his cane to tap on the floor twice in emphasis. He'd left the sandwich makings out on the counter, so Ore wondered if he'd anticipated needing to make more for him.

"I'm sorry," he said softly, even as he took another bite. "I don't know why I'm so hungry."

"You've been unconscious for three days," the man said gently, his kind face sobering.

"Three days?" Ore repeated, nearly dropping the last of his sandwich in his shock. "That's not... What? Three days?"

He couldn't wrap his head around it. What had happened to him?

The cat hummed, quickly put together another sandwich, and then brought it over to the table. He lowered himself slowly into the chair opposite Ore with a soft sigh. "You gave us quite the scare."

Ore started eating his second sandwich, but more slowly, his appetite having nearly disappeared as his mind spun. "I can't remember anything," he admitted softly, watching the other man through his lashes.

Those bushy brows rose a millimeter before the man cleared his face and smiled gently once more. "That's not altogether surprising. You were injured when you got here."

"Where is here?" he asked, ignoring for a second the fact that he'd been so hurt it had taken him three *days* to heal. He had to have been near death for his healing not to have worked faster than that.

"Silver Oak. Kansas," the man added when Ore just looked at him in confusion. "You flew into our territory a few days ago, and it set off our coven's wardings."

"You have a coven?" Ore asked, surprised. He knew it wasn't completely uncommon for packs to have a coven of witches living within their territory. He wasn't sure *how* he knew that, but it was there in his mind, even though he couldn't remember what his parents looked like or if he had siblings.

"We do. It's not large, and neither is our pack." He shrugged, taking a large bite of his sandwich and chewing slowly. "We're all cats. A lot of us have been here for generations, keeping to ourselves and minding our own business."

He said it without much inflection, but Ore could read

between the lines. As a bird, he wouldn't be welcome to stay. They were an isolationist pack, not interested in growing or diversifying their numbers. For some reason, that made him sad.

He frowned down at the crumbs on his plate. For all he knew, he had a family waiting for him. What did it matter if he couldn't stay in Kansas?

"How badly was I injured?" he finally asked, looking up and meeting the man's serious eyes.

"Badly," he said, taking another bite. "We weren't sure if you were going to make it for the first day or so."

"But I was able to fly here?" He didn't really understand. Had he been shot by a hunter? Poisoned with wolfsbane? What could have prevented him from healing for so long?

The older man eyed him speculatively. "You were, though I suspect it nearly killed you. I'll leave it to our alpha and the head of the coven to explain what we were able to figure out."

He frowned. Why couldn't— Wait, what was this guy's name? "I'm Ore, by the way," he said awkwardly, leaning over the table and extending his hand.

"Terry," the cat said, smiling a little more easily as he shook it, "but everyone calls me Pops. I used to be the healer for this pack."

"Is that why I'm here?" He wasn't sure how much Pops was allowed to tell him, but he was still kind of confused as to what had happened while he was unconscious.

Pops nodded, finishing off his own sandwich. "We don't have a new healer yet, so I'm only *technically* retired."

Ore returned his grin, wondering if it was hard for a pack so small and isolated to find someone to fill such a vital role. Sure, shifters healed pretty much on their own—except when dosed with certain things like wolfsbane or they encountered certain kinds of powerful magic—but they also had witches in their pack, and they were human, without the same healing ability.

The pack healer was an extremely important role, and based on how old Pops looked, one that they needed to fill sooner rather than later.

"When do you think—"

He stopped, his spine straightening as his eagle trilled happily in his chest.

Craning his head around, he watched the front door open, a massive man in blue jeans and a tight gray V-neck filling the entire width of the doorway. There were black tattoos trailing down his arms and up to the side of his neck. One of the ones on his right arm was glowing faintly, but Ore could barely focus on that.

All of his attention was caught on the glowing blue eyes staring right at him as he was hit with a fresh, overwhelming wave of lavender, leather, and fresh air.

"Oh."

CHAPTER 4

He froze in the doorway.

It wasn't that he hadn't known the bird was awake. His grandfather had texted him twenty minutes ago to let him know he'd heard him stirring upstairs and was going to try to feed and talk to him.

Cash had finished with Jorge and hurried home. He told himself it was because he didn't trust some stranger alone with his frail grandfather, but his panther didn't buy that, prowling in his chest and eager to lay eyes on the beautiful eagle again. To see his dark eyes once more and not just stare at his listless face as he slept in Cash's bed.

And yet the second their gazes connected, his whole body locked in place, at war with itself.

He had always been protective of his family. As he'd gotten older, the instinct had expanded to his pack, driving him to look for ways to help wherever he could. He'd become a beta when he was only twenty, under the pack's former alpha, and he'd taken pride in working hard to keep every single member of his pack safe.

That need to care and defend had only grown stronger as

he'd gotten older. When he became an Enforcer, the drive only increased. Every day, he woke up with purpose and a sense of responsibility that kept him grounded. He'd never found someone he wanted to mate and settle down with more than he wanted to dedicate his life to his pack. They were his first priority. Always.

But his panther, the part of himself that he trusted to know what was best for his pack, was at war with his logical mind, urging him to forget everything he'd worked for and all his responsibilities, grab the pretty little eagle, and drag him up to the loft to claim in such a way no one would ever question who he belonged to.

He squeezed his hands into fists and sucked in a deep breath, immediately regretting it when that light, teasing floral scent invaded his senses, dragging him further under its spell.

His panther—and his fucking cock—needed to chill the fuck out.

No matter what his haywire instincts were telling him, the chances of the eagle being allowed to stay in Silver Oak—assuming he would *want* to—were as close to zero as you could get. Not only did their pack distrust outsiders and rarely allow anyone new to join, but there hadn't been a non-feline shifter in their pack in over two generations.

Liam hadn't started the policy, but he hadn't put an end to it either. After he drove out the old alpha and took over, he'd held a pack meeting. At first, he'd talked about making changes, helping the pack grow and thrive once more, but he'd gotten so much pushback, he'd dialed things way back. People hadn't wanted things to change any more than having a new alpha and his strange second-in-command had already done so.

It hadn't mattered much to Cash either way. Whether they were all cats or a menagerie of parahumans, he would do his job to the best of his ability. But now that he stared into those dark brown eyes, his panther itching to spring forward? He cursed the pack law that wouldn't allow him to keep the little bird.

Then he scoffed at himself. Even if the policy wasn't in place, what were the chances that a handsome young shifter like him didn't have a family of his own? Maybe even a mate.

His stomach churned, his blood heating with outrage.

There wasn't another shifter's scent on him, but that wasn't uncommon for birds and prey animals that didn't exchange bonding bites. The magic of the bite mixed mates' scents, but it wasn't an urge all shifters had. It was mostly just canines and felines, their predator instincts more heightened than other species.

Depending on how long the eagle had been flying and what had happened to him before he came into the territory, the lingering scent of a mate could have been washed off.

His panther didn't care.

It yowled inside of him, refusing to accept the idea that there could be another that the eagle would choose over him.

He knew what this feeling meant, and while it made his heart soar, he couldn't forget the agony fated mates had brought his family before. He needed to protect himself from experiencing that pain again since it was very likely the eagle would be leaving shortly, no matter what his reaction to him was.

There was no point in him trying to convince him to stay. There definitely wasn't a reason to work on wrapping his head around the idea that maybe his mating could be different than his parents'. And he certainly saw no point in begging his alpha to make an exception to the law.

It didn't matter. Protecting the pack was what mattered.

That was his job, his purpose.

He dismissed the way Pops was grinning at him behind

the bird's shoulder, his scent full of amusement. Clearing his throat, Cash stepped into the house and closed the door behind him.

"Grandson," Pops called. "I'd like you to meet Ore."

He nodded at the bird but kept his distance, ignoring the way his panther happily rumbled at the sight of him in Cash's T-shirt. It was so big on him he was swimming in it. He had a feeling Ore wouldn't even reach his pecs when he was standing, and he had to fight back a shiver at the image.

"Hi," Ore said, voice soft and a little shy. His olive skin flushed a gorgeous red on his high cheekbones, his gaze darting away for a second before coming back.

Cash nodded and looked at his grandfather, eyebrows raised in question.

Pops rolled his eyes and pushed to his feet using his cane. Cash had to stop himself from stepping forward to help, knowing it would only annoy Pops, and he'd be just as likely to whack him with the cane than to accept the help.

"Ore, this stoic young man is my grandson, Cash."

"It's nice to meet you," Ore said, climbing to his feet as well.

Cash bit back a groan. He'd been right. The man was so fucking tiny Cash's shirt hung down to his knees, mixing their scents in a way that pleased him. He'd known it would. It was why he hadn't asked anyone in the pack for something that would fit the younger man better. He'd simply cleaned him up as best he could after Fern and Pops had finished working on him and then slipped an old shirt on him. It was the softest he owned—the urge to pamper and care for the little bird had been so strong he hadn't been able to resist.

"How are you feeling?" Cash asked, his voice huskier than normal.

"Pretty good," Ore said, his slim fingers playing with the material of Cash's shirt. "Kind of achy in my joints," he added softly, eyes downcast.

Cash wasn't sure if he was embarrassed about having been injured or admitting to some sort of weakness, but it didn't sit right with him. He took a step forward before he could stop himself. "Understandable. You're lucky to be alive."

Ore's eyes darted back up. "Am I? Pops didn't really say what had happened, and everything is a blank."

Cash glanced at Pops.

"Amnesia isn't... uncommon with certain types of injuries," Pops said carefully. Having been raised by the man most of his life, Cash recognized the tone. His grandfather was a spectacular veterinarian and healer, but he didn't know why Ore didn't remember what had happened and was surprised—and worried—by it.

The eagle's scent didn't say he was lying, but Cash knew from personal experience shifters could learn to suppress their scent to protect themselves or to hide their intentions. He didn't know Ore that well, hadn't learned the nuances of his heartbeat and scent, so it was possible he was making it up.

Though his panther grumbled at him at the harsh insinuation against the man he was convinced was their mate.

He reminded himself for the hundredth time that it didn't change anything.

"We should go talk to Alpha Amato," Cash said, running a hand over his short hair. "I let him know you were awake, so he's waiting for us."

"Oh yes, of course," Ore said. "That makes sense. Let me just go—" He looked down at himself and grimaced, his cute little nose scrunching. "Never mind. I don't have anything to change into."

"I'll ask around," Pops said, smiling gently at him. "I'm sure someone has something that'll fit you a little better."

Cash ground his teeth together but didn't protest.

L ̲IAM A ̲MATO HAD BEEN alpha of the Silver Oak Pack for a few years, and while he'd made some changes to things for the betterment of the pack, Cash was always a little surprised that he'd barely touched the Alpha House after he'd moved into it. He knew for a fact that some of the guest rooms upstairs were decorated rather... eccentrically, but he didn't question it.

It wasn't his job to question his alpha.

For the most part though, the place met their needs. There were public areas in the front of the house where Liam or the Enforcers could meet with emissaries from other packs, members of their own pack who had problems or questions, or someone visiting from out of town. On the second floor, there were four bedrooms—Liam's and three spares for guests. And then there was space in the rear of the house for them to use for holding the beta and Enforcer meetings and an office for Liam.

That's where he brought Ore, knowing that his alpha was in there waiting for them. As soon as he stepped in the house, he scented the other Enforcers and Fern, and his panther prickled a little at the fact that the little bird would no doubt be intimidated by such a gathering. Cash wasn't sure if the show of force was the point or if Liam wanted additional ears to listen for indicators that Ore was lying about anything.

Fern's presence was expected. He'd known she was going to be joining them so she could explain—as best as she could —what had happened to Ore after his arrival in their territory.

Ore followed behind him, gaze darting all around like he was worried he'd be quizzed on a paint color or something. As they neared the closed door of the office, Cash paused and turned to Ore.

"Don't be nervous," he said, unable to stop himself from

providing some sort of comfort. He wanted to put a hand on his slender shoulder, showing he was there for him, but that wouldn't be appropriate for a number of reasons.

The top one being that he *wouldn't* be there for Ore. Once they stepped into that room, he would be Enforcer Lawson. It would be his job to help Liam interrogate the eagle, not protect him.

Ore nodded slowly, gaze glued to the door. Even though his nose wasn't as good as a cat's, there was no way he couldn't *feel* the power emanating from the room with all of the Enforcers, the head of their coven, and their alpha waiting for them.

Liam alone could be intimidating. He was as big as Cash —which could be enough to scare a tiny little bird—but he also radiated the strength he received from his pack. They might not be large, but they were a tight-knit group. Their close bonds gave their alpha even more strength.

He waited another second, though he wasn't sure what he expected from Ore, then dropped his hand from his shoulder and pushed open the door. When Ore hesitated in the hallway, Cash let himself touch him one more time, placing his hand on the small of his back and guiding him through the door. As soon as he was over the threshold though, he forced himself to drop his arm to his side again.

Liam was sitting behind his desk, feet propped up on the edge and crossed at the ankle as he looked at something on his phone. He didn't glance up as they came in, a furrow etched between his brows as he started typing. His scent wasn't worried, only a little frustrated, so Cash assumed he was texting with his older brother, Quinten.

Fern was perched on the front of Liam's desk, hands folded calmly in her lap as she studied Ore with her sharp hazel eyes. Her curls were looking particularly wild, and her scent was satisfied in a way that made him realize immediately she must have been with one—or both—of her mates just before coming to the Alpha House.

In the two chairs directly in front of Liam's desk were Saint and Rachel. They both craned their heads around as he and Ore walked in and had very different reactions.

Saint raised his scarred brow, a grin spreading across his wide, bearded face. He was handsome, in a rugged way, his white skin a warm sand color combined with his dark brown hair and beard and diamond stud in his right ear giving him a dangerous appeal. Cash had seen it work on unsuspecting human men and women since they were eighteen-year-old idiots. The scar was something he'd accidentally given himself when he was a cub, but Saint liked to tell people he got it in a bar fight.

Cash had been best friends with him his whole life; he knew all the truths behind his bullshit.

Rachel's narrowed honey-brown eyes were locked on Ore's bare legs. When Cash stepped up next to him so he could close the door behind them, she turned her unimpressed face on him. He avoided her gaze, feeling heat rush to his cheeks. Rachel's family owned a small boutique clothing store, and the way she dressed showed it. Despite it being an impromptu and unofficial meeting, her thick curves were wrapped in a navy blue dress that perfectly complemented her tawny skin. Her long, dark hair was also perfectly styled into loose waves, and she wore a pair of big gold hoops in her ears.

The sight of Ore in Cash's shirt was definitely offensive to her sensibilities.

Doing his best to ignore her judgment and Saint's lecherous grin, he pointed Ore toward the only remaining seat in the room. A chair from the meeting room across the hall had been brought in and set to the right of Liam's desk. Halfway across the room, Ore froze, and Cash knew he'd realized who —or rather, *what*—the last person in the room was.

The pack's second-in-command stood in the corner of the two bookcases in the room, leaning casually against a shelf and watching the room with an impassive stare. Ore's tiny body was stiff and unmoving, but Finlay didn't react, completely unperturbed by the common reaction.

"Um." Ore glanced back at him, eyes wide.

"Yup. Vampire," Saint said before Cash could say anything.

Ore's surprised face turned to the tiger, and Cash nearly snarled out loud. He wanted those eyes on him, looking only to him for guidance.

"He's harmless though. It's cool, little man." Saint smiled even wider and fucking *winked* at Ore.

Cash was going to rip his eyelids off.

Rachel rolled her eyes at him, and he realized he was projecting his feelings all over the place. Taking a deep breath in and then slowly letting it out, he pulled himself back under control, locking down his emotions. When he felt less volatile, he leaned back against the closed door and crossed his arms over his chest. His movement caught Ore's attention once more, and he gave the little bird a nod of encouragement.

Before Finlay had joined their pack, Cash had believed—like most others in the parahuman world—that vampires were extinct. Over a century ago, they had been hunted down and killed by human hunters who had deemed them *too dangerous to exist*. The hunter clans had joined forces and tracked down every vampire enclave on the continent, massacring everyone they found without hesitation.

Because vampire enclaves were so isolated—they kept themselves removed even from other parahumans—it had taken too long for anyone to realize what the hunters were doing. By the time they did, it was Cash's understanding that no one actually cared enough to attempt to protect them from eradication.

Even the shifter Council hadn't taken action, arguing that

as vampires, they didn't actually fall under their purview or protection.

Which was utter bullshit. The Council never had any issue dictating to witches and seers, creating laws to hold them in check, or using them to attack those deemed *enemies* of the Council.

One of many reasons why Cash hadn't exactly cried over the Council getting overthrown last year.

It had turned out, though, that vampires hadn't all been killed by the hunters—despite their best efforts. Some had managed to flee across the ocean, hiding alone or in small groups in Europe, Asia, and Africa. In the last decade, they'd begun to slowly come back, oftentimes being smuggled into the country by Liam's mobster brother, Quinten.

Cash didn't know what had changed that had drawn them back to North America since Finlay was pretty closed-lipped about his past and vamps in general. Until last year, the Council had still been ruling the parahuman community with total authority, and while hunters had lost some numbers—some clans even moving toward killing for money rather than fanatical beliefs—they were nowhere near being considered not a threat.

He had no idea how Finlay and Liam knew each other either. Liam hadn't shared much when he'd introduced his second-in-command to the pack. He'd simply stated that they had known each other for a while, that he trusted Finlay, and that he had agreed to come and serve as his Second.

The only other vampire that Cash had met since then worked for Liam's brother up in Chicago. The elder Amato had recently declared himself alpha of his own pack, despite the fact that he was human. It hadn't *exactly* been a surprise, considering the man surrounded himself with parahumans and had been leading them for years, but it was still unprecedented.

Nero, the vampire who worked for him—and was now

officially one of his Enforcers—came down to Silver Oak sometimes to check in on Liam, though he never called it that. He'd show up every few months, hang around the Alpha House, flirt shamelessly with everyone he encountered, then disappear once more.

Cash had asked Finlay once if he and Nero were friends, and the vamp had just shrugged and said, "Of a sort."

When he'd pressed for an explanation of what that meant, Finlay had told him, "He slaughtered half my family a decade ago, and I've owed him a debt ever since."

And then just walked away.

Like that was a completely normal thing to say.

Vampires were so fucking weird.

And while he was far from harmless, Cash had grown to trust him and knew he wouldn't harm Ore unless he proved to be a threat to their alpha. It was frustrating sometimes the number of things his alpha and Second kept to themselves though. He knew it wasn't fair to compare, but everyone else in the pack he'd known basically since birth. Everyone knew everyone else's business—there weren't exactly secrets in a pack as small and close-knit as theirs.

He hoped one day Liam and Finlay would feel comfortable enough to share more about themselves. It would be hard for some pack members to fully trust them until they did.

As soon as Ore's cute little ass hit the chair next to his desk, Liam tossed his phone over his shoulder at Finlay without looking. The vampire caught it with a twitch of an eyebrow.

"If my brother gets his head out of his ass, let me know. Otherwise, hold that for me so I don't throw it across the room."

"Again," Finlay murmured, tucking the device in the pocket of his jeans.

Liam curled his lip at the vamp, then focused on where Cash still stood at the door.

Answering the unasked question, Cash said, "Alpha Amato, this is Ore. He's having some difficulty remembering anything from before he woke up inside our territory."

The scent of surprise and disbelief filled the air around him, but no one spoke. Liam turned to the eagle, his wavy, blond hair just short of his shoulders and giving him a rather pirate-esque look. The faint scars at the base of his neck didn't help and were another subject Liam didn't talk about.

"Ore. Interesting name. Is that short for something?" Liam asked, dropping his feet from his desk and sitting upright.

"Forester, sir," Ore said quietly, tugging at the hem of his borrowed T-shirt.

Rachel caught the gesture and threw him another look, but Cash ignored the leopard, keeping his full attention on Ore so he could pick up any discrepancies in his heartbeat or scent.

"I see. But you prefer Ore?"

"Yes, sir."

"Do you think it's strange you remember that but not what happened to you?"

Apprehension spiked in Ore's scent, and he licked at his lips before shrugging. "I couldn't say, sir. Pops said I was hurt p-pretty badly."

The small stutter ripped at Cash's heart. He had to clench his hands into fists to keep ahold of himself, his panther already getting pissed at the fear and dismay Ore was displaying, his fingers twisting so hard in Cash's shirt it was a surprise it didn't rip.

"So you don't remember what brought you to my pack?" Liam said. His voice was calm, but there was a thread of disbelief.

Ore shook his head. "No, sir. It's all just... missing. I don't know what happened, how I was hurt, or why I came here."

Liam leaned back in his chair, scratching at his short beard. "Where are you from? Who's your alpha?"

Ore swallowed audibly, and even from across the room, Cash could see his eyes getting glassy before he dropped his gaze to his lap.

"Ore," Liam prompted, "where is your pack?"

"I don't know," he whispered. "I can't remember that either."

CHAPTER 5

O re's knuckles began to ache from how tightly he was squeezing his hands into fists. Despite that, he thought he was doing a pretty good job keeping his voice and demeanor calm as he answered the same question for the fourth—no, fifth—time. Alpha Amato just kept circling around, asking the same things repeatedly.

Ore's responses didn't change.

No, sir.

I don't remember that either.

I don't know.

I'm sorry, no.

I can't remember.

Over and over and over again.

Alpha Amato switched up their order and changed them just enough to try and trip him up. He knew they were trying to catch him in a lie, that they didn't believe he couldn't remember anything beyond his name and the generic information any parahuman would know. He also knew it wasn't personal.

It still sucked.

He hadn't felt that bad when he'd left Cash and Pops's

house, but after an hour of sitting on the hard chair and being grilled relentlessly, he found he was growing increasingly tired. That was more concerning to him than anything else. Even after three days of healing, he was still so weak from whatever they'd done to him. His joints were aching so badly he'd have to clench his teeth to hold in whimpers every time he shifted his weight.

He just wanted to go back to the cozy loft in the homey A-frame where he'd woken up. He wanted to curl back up in the sheets that smelled like lavender and leather and fresh air. He wanted to bask in the sunshine and the feeling of safety that permeated the whole house.

But he knew he couldn't leave until they were done with him and that even if they ended up believing him, they could still send him away.

He shuddered at the idea of going off on his own without knowing anyone, without any clothes or a phone or money. But it would be well within Alpha Amato's right to remove him from his territory in the name of protecting his pack.

The only thing that made it tolerable was the fact that he could tell Cash was upset at the intense questioning as well. The panther didn't say anything—he never interrupted or protested—but the longer it went on, the more Ore could feel his temper rising. It was like a pull at Ore's insides, a hook in his guts, connecting him to the Enforcer. Pushing him to move closer, even though he knew he couldn't. Knowing Cash didn't like how he was being treated was enough to ease some of his own discomfort.

The only person who spoke to him was Alpha Amato. The other Enforcers—whom no one had bothered to introduce—sat or stood around the room, watching silently. The one who'd winked at him had turned serious as soon as the interrogation began, not offering any more reassurances or encouragement.

The intimidation factor was at an eleven, and combined with everything else, he was at his limit.

Before Alpha Amato had really dived into his questioning, the sweet-looking woman perched on the front edge of his desk had piped up. Her name was Fern, and she was head of the pack's coven. She proceeded to tell him about the condition he'd been in when he'd arrived—near death—how they'd helped him get better—using a mix of medicine and magic to boost his healing—and how a blood test had shown traces of antibodies associated with viral infections.

"A virus almost killed me?" he'd asked, skeptical.

She'd shaken her head, sending her strawberry blonde waves flying. "No, not the virus. It was only used as a delivery system. What almost killed you was the magic it was altered with."

Someone had dosed him with a magical virus that nearly killed him. Oh, and erased his memories. And now, Liam Amato was drilling him like he was caught stealing pack secrets.

Before she'd left, she'd told him the amnesia was a surprise, but she agreed with Pops that his memory would probably come back. Since they had been able to counteract the magic and help his body heal, she believed whatever was causing it would go away as his body continued to heal from the effects.

"Was it the virus or magic that took his memories?" Alpha Amato had asked her, stopping her before she could slip out past a frowning Cash.

She'd shrugged. "It's hard to say for sure. And it might not be either. His brain could be protecting him from something extremely traumatic."

What a troubling thought that had been.

She'd given him a sympathetic grimace and added, "It was probably the magic though."

"What was the point in stealing my memory if the spell would kill me anyway?" he'd asked.

"It might not have been meant to kill you. Or it was an unintended side effect."

As far as he could figure, they didn't really know anything. And since he couldn't remember where he'd been or who had done it, he had no leads to figure anything out. He could have flown in from anywhere. There was no telling how long he'd been traveling either.

Until he started getting his memories back—assuming he did—they were at a bit of a standstill. He knew that was the main reason Alpha Amato was questioning him for so long. He was trying to determine if it would be safe to let him stay until he was fully back to himself or if he posed too big of a risk. Considering Pops had told him the pack was pretty isolated and wary of strangers, he wouldn't be surprised if he was given a generic *sorry we can't help* and shown to the edge of the territory.

Just driving to the Alpha House, he'd gotten the very distinct impression he wouldn't exactly be welcome with open arms. The town the pack had created was tiny, not much more than a main street with some necessary businesses. Going down the street in the front of Cash's pickup, half a dozen people had paused to stare. Some had just seemed surprised, but a few had looked angry. He'd been so distracted by the eerie feeling of being watched that he'd barely noticed any of the businesses they'd passed.

The Alpha House was located at the end of a street just off the main road. The whole thing was lined with nice-looking houses, yards meticulously maintained, and a playground next to the Alpha House that looked brand-new. Several kids had been playing, their adults standing or stepping in front of them as soon as Ore had jumped out of Cash's truck.

Cash had ushered him inside quickly, pointing to something on the other side of the street like he hadn't wanted Ore to notice. It hurt his heart that his mere presence caused so much stress, but he couldn't really blame them. The pack wasn't used to outsiders, and he couldn't tell them *anything* about himself.

That level of unknown could cause issues for the pack or maybe even bring trouble to their door. If he was on the run, someone could be following him. If he had been sent there, he could hand over information unintentionally.

He knew, without knowing how he knew, that there were some packs out there who wouldn't have bothered to save him. So despite everything, he was grateful that he had been taken care of, but he was still worried about what would come next.

Finally, Alpha Amato relaxed in his chair and shook his head. "As far as I can tell, you really don't remember anything."

Ore forced a smile. Based on the way Amato chuckled at him, it probably came off more as a wince.

"I had to be sure."

"I understand, sir," he said, and he did. That didn't mean he had to like or enjoy the process.

"But just because you don't remember—"

"—doesn't mean I'm not still a potential threat," Ore finished for him, twisting his borrowed T-shirt around his fingers. The material over his thighs was severely wrinkled from his nonstop fidgeting. "What does that mean for me?"

"I can't just let you have free rein around the pack," he said slowly, studying Ore. He glanced at his Enforcers. "Are we in agreement on that?"

The vampire just nodded. Ore still couldn't look directly at him, his eagle getting too agitated just from quick glances. It was almost a pity. The man was *devastatingly* handsome, his whiskey eyes hypnotizing in their appeal. His animal instincts knew who the bigger predator was though.

The beautiful Black woman—a leopard, he was pretty sure

—shifted in her seat, leaning forward with a frown. "We can't just kick him out, Liam. He's helpless like this."

Ore frowned at his lap. Helpless seemed a bit harsh. Sure, he wasn't a large cat shifter, and he didn't remember things, but he wasn't some weak little hatchling.

"Agreed," said the Enforcer sitting next to her. His serious face had melted away now that questioning was over, his mischievous grin tugging at the corners of his mouth once more. A few times in the last hour, he'd glanced back at Cash, making Ore wonder if the two of them were close.

"I understand the need to protect the pack," the woman continued fiercely, "but if we remove him from the territory in this state, that'll make us as bad as whoever nearly killed him."

He forgave her for the helpless comment. Shuddering, he tried not to think about the fact that someone—or multiple someones—could be looking for him right at that moment, wanting to finish the job. Even if whatever magic they'd dosed him with hadn't been intended to end his life, he *highly* doubted he'd voluntarily signed up to get injected with whatever kind of crazy cocktail they'd come up with.

The vampire, who hadn't said a word the entire time he'd been in the room, finally spoke, startling the hell out of Ore with his smooth voice. "We could put him downstairs until he gets his memories back."

He wasn't sure what that meant. Were they going to lock him in the basement or a cellar of some sort? He glanced around the room, trying to gauge everyone's reaction to the suggestion.

Liam sighed unhappily, running a hand through his long hair and looking back at the vampire. Ore's lips parted as he stared at the scars visible above the neckline of the lion's shirt. Those were claw marks. Slashes from a canine or feline shifter, he'd guess. How had a wound like that ended up leaving a permanent mark? As far as he knew—though with his memory all messed up, he could be wrong—the only way for a wound to leave a scar on a shifter was if wolfsbane was used or if it was somehow exposed to it before it fully healed.

A pang of empathy filled him as he snapped his mouth shut and looked away, not wanting to get caught staring. He wondered if Alpha Amato kept his hair longer to try and hide the scars. Was he embarrassed by them? Had someone tried to overthrow him as alpha? How long ago had it happened?

He had so many questions, but he doubted he'd get any answers.

"I don't like it, but it might be the best option." Amato turned back to Ore, fingers drumming on his desk. "We'll make you as comfortable as we can."

Well, that sounded ominous as hell.

He supposed it was still better than having to fend for himself without memories or resources.

Before Ore could thank him for letting him stay, Cash stepped forward, drawing his attention. His sharp eyes caught a muscle flexing in the Enforcer's jaw, even though the rest of him appeared completely composed. "He can stay with me. I'll keep an eye on him."

Ore jerked in his chair, grateful beyond words that the panther was saving him yet again, this time from what he was sure would've been a miserable few days—if not weeks —locked in some cell in the basement.

"What if you have pack business you need to attend to?" Liam said, eyebrows raised.

Ore could read between the lines: What if Cash had to do something they didn't want Ore to know about?

"Then I can watch him," the cheerful tiger said. "And if I'm busy, Rachel can. Or Finlay." He nodded at the other two Enforcers. "Or we can grab a beta. There's enough of us that we don't have to keep him locked up."

Neither Finlay nor Rachel protested, and gratitude filled him, his eyes burning at the intensity of the emotion. These

53

people had no reason to give him special treatment and yet were going above and beyond to accommodate him.

He smiled at each of them, trying to express his thankfulness. Cash, though, wasn't looking at him at all. His gaze was locked on his alpha, waiting for his answer. Annoyance rippled through him, and he nearly stood just to grab his damn attention, wanting it focused solely on him.

Which was… weird.

"I don't want this to disrupt the pack," Alpha Amato said, attention still on Cash. "If it does—"

"It won't," Cash assured him calmly.

"If it does," Amato repeated firmly, "we'll revisit the discussion on the room downstairs."

"Yes, Alpha."

Ore bit his lip to try and rein in his glee. Not only was he getting to stay, but he was going back to Cash's house with him. And it had been Cash's idea!

"I'll bring you some actual clothes tomorrow," Rachel said, standing and shooting a glare at Cash.

"Oh. Thank you." He glanced down at his attire. He'd almost forgotten he was only wearing one of Cash's shirts in front of all of them. Back at the house, he hadn't minded, but it was kind of embarrassing for them to see him in something that was so enormous on him.

"I can bring my gaming system over," the tiger said, staying sprawled in his chair. "Cash doesn't have much for entertainment beyond books."

Ore saw the look of distaste that flashed across the panther's face before it disappeared once more. "That's so kind, thank you. But I don't need anything special like that."

"He's supposed to be resting, Saint. Didn't you hear Fern?" Rachel asked, crossing her arms under her rather impressive bosom.

The tiger—Saint, apparently—rolled his eyes and pushed to his feet. "You all are no fun. Can he have a phone, at least?"

Ore stood as well, not wanting to linger any longer than he had to. He turned hopeful eyes on Alpha Amato. He was sure he could keep himself entertained with a phone…

"Not yet," he said, accepting his own from Finlay. He read something on it, then threw it down on the surface in disgust. He turned to Ore and locked him in his gaze, eyes glowing barely perceptibly. The cats might not have even been able to see it, but Ore could. The man's lion was just beneath the surface, poised to strike. "The second you start remembering things, I want to know."

"Yes, sir," he said softly, intimidated despite his best efforts.

"We'll start piecing things together as they come. As soon as we know where you belong, we'll get you taken care of. Understood?"

Ore nodded, trying not to take offense at the fact he'd be shipped off as soon as they knew where to address the package. "Yes. I understand. As soon as I start remembering anything, I'll let everyone know. I promise."

He wanted to know what had happened to him even more than they did. He hoped he wouldn't have to wait long before the memories started to come back, filling in not just what had led him to the Silver Oak Pack but who he *was*.

Although… He glanced over at Cash, his heart sinking a little. Once they knew where he belonged, he'd have no reason to stay with Cash and Pops. No reason to keep wrapping himself in those good-smelling sheets. No reason to see Cash at all.

He reminded himself that he could have a family out there he would want to return to. Maybe even a mate…

But his eagle rejected that idea, protesting vehemently inside him. He had to agree. It was hard to believe that, even if he didn't remember his life from before, he would have such a strong, visceral reaction to someone if he was already in a relationship.

"In the meantime, while you're here, you're our guest," Liam continued, rising from his chair and coming around his desk to lean against the edge in front of where Ore was standing. He smiled good-naturedly. "People will treat you with kindness, but they're not used to strangers. You may run into some wariness. After everything that's happened the last year, there are a lot of members of the pack who aren't comfortable with new people."

Ore raised his brows, then glanced at the others. When no one said anything, he asked, "What's happened in the last year to scare them so much?"

"Oh man," someone—Saint, he was pretty sure—muttered behind him.

Apprehension started trickling down his spine, and he looked to Cash. The Enforcer's jaw was tight as he glanced at his alpha.

Ore turned back to Amato. "I'm sorry. Should I not have asked?"

"No, it's okay," he said, sighing and threading his fingers through his hair. "I should have realized you wouldn't know what had happened."

Goddess, they were really starting to make him nervous. Had there been a damn apocalypse that he'd forgotten about?

"About a year ago, a pack up in Michigan decided to change the parahuman world."

"And it's been a fucking mess ever since," Saint added cheerfully.

Well, okay then.

CHAPTER 6

C ash scowled, but Pops just chuckled and kept packing.
"This isn't necessary. I can keep sleeping on the cot."

Pops shook his head, adding another pair of underwear to his bag. "Don't be ridiculous. We don't know how long this young man will be staying with us. You should be able to relax in a real bed."

He couldn't exactly argue with that since they had no idea when Ore's memories would return enough for him to remember where he came from or what happened to him, but it didn't sit right with him, putting his grandfather out of his own house.

"Still," Cash grumbled, "we can make it work. You don't have to leave."

Pops finally stopped and turned to face him. Cash studied his wrinkled face, loving every single laugh line next to his eyes. This man had raised him like his own son when he'd needed him the most, taking him into his home and doting on him. Showing him what unconditional love really meant.

And now, he was kicking him out of his own damn house.

It wasn't right.

Pops's face softened. He shuffled forward and clasped the sides of Cash's face. He had been nearly as tall as Cash in his prime, but his shoulders were beginning to stoop, and he had to look up to meet Cash's eyes now. But when he touched his face like that, just like he had when he was a frightened and angry cub, it made him feel eight years old again. But in the best possible way.

He had never gone unloved in this house with his nan and pops. They had taken care of him in a way his parents never had. He would literally do anything for his grandfather.

"Don't look so upset. It won't be forever." Pops patted his cheeks lightly. "Besides, I wouldn't mind some extended alone time with Martha."

Cash grimaced and looked away. He knew that his grandfather still missed his mate, but it had been years since she'd passed, and he had grown lonely. Still, it was difficult for Cash to think about his grandfather and his *special friend* like that.

"And she's okay with you staying indefinitely?" he forced himself to ask.

"Oh, yes." Pops chuckled, releasing his face and turning back to his suitcase. "She was rather excited, I'd say. Told me she would get dinner going and expected me at 6:00 p.m. sharp if I expected to eat with her."

There was such fondness in Pops's voice when he spoke about Martha. He was glad that she brought happiness toward the end of his grandfather's life. He deserved it more than anyone Cash knew.

Once Pops had everything packed that he thought he would need, they took everything out to his sedan and loaded it in the trunk. "If you think of anything else," Cash said, closing the lid, "just let me know, and I can bring it to you."

"Or I can come and get it," Pops said with a wry grin. "I'm

not going to be held hostage. It's not like we won't see each other at all."

Maybe. Cash wasn't sure how much he'd be getting into town while Ore was under his supervision, but he decided not to point that out. He did glance back at the house though, the upstairs windows glowing against the backdrop of the dark sky. Ore had been horrified at the idea of Pops leaving and tried to offer to sleep on the cot or couch too. When Pops just kept refusing, Ore had retreated upstairs, scent full of guilt.

"Of course you can," Cash said, smiling softly. "What was I thinking?"

Pops squeezed his biceps. "That you'll miss me?"

A lump formed in Cash's throat, and he nodded. "It won't be the same here without you."

"Different can be good." He peered at Cash in a way that made him think he was trying to tell him something. Considering the unsubtle way he'd reacted to the bird, he could guess the kind of *different* Pops was referring to.

It wasn't going to happen.

"I prefer for things to stay the same," Cash reminded him.

It had actually become a bit of a problem for him when he was a cub.

The therapist Nan had found for him back then had let him know it was completely normal after what he had experienced with his parents. Their volatile moods and constant arguing leading up to his abandonment would make anyone fearful of change.

Even as an adult, it had persisted. He liked knowing exactly where he stood in the world, how his days would go, and what to expect in any given situation, but all of that was getting turned upside down. He had a strange shifter staying in his house. His Pops was leaving, and he would be restricted from some of his Enforcer duties while he played babysitter.

Things were going to be very different for the foreseeable future, and it made him question—and not for the first time since Liam's office—why he had volunteered. Why had he stepped forward and made an offer that would turn his world upside down? Why was he helpless against those big, dark eyes?

He knew the answer though.

It had been... *difficult* for him to stand there and watch as his alpha asked Ore the same questions over and over again, trying to see if he could catch him in a lie. For the protection of the pack, they had to do it. They had to be sure he wasn't dangerous.

But as the interrogation had gone on and on, it had become more and more obvious that Ore really couldn't remember anything about his life. Worse yet, the longer it went on, the more upset Ore had gotten, even though he'd tried to hide it.

It hadn't mattered though. Cash's panther could scent it on the air, and it had driven his instincts haywire. The drive to protect the little bird warred with his need to do what was best for his pack.

So when Liam had been about to tell Ore he'd be staying in the magically sealable room in the basement, Cash had lost his head for a second and offered up his own place, unable to stand the idea of the young man with such sad eyes being forced to stay locked up, even if the room was quite comfortable. It wasn't like it was a cement jail cell, but he had a feeling it would be especially difficult for a bird to be forced to stay in a basement. Unable to spread his wings, unable to see the sky.

And now, everything was changing.

"I will miss you," Cash said softly as Pops carefully lowered himself into his car.

"And I you, son." Pops grinned up at him.

"Let me know when you get to Martha's."

"I will. Be a good host and listen to your cat," Pops said with arched eyebrows and a tap to his chest.

Cash frowned at him. "I always listen to my cat."

He just didn't always do what his panther wanted.

Pops gave him an exasperated look but didn't respond, simply shut the door to the car and started down the driveway. Cash watched him go, the feeling of disorientation growing at Pops's parting words. It wasn't that he didn't trust his cat's instincts, but he refused to be ruled by them. His panther had one speed: go. It didn't matter if it was about protecting his family, scentmarking the pack cubs, or running full tilt through the woods.

And it would be the same with Ore if he wasn't careful. Already, the tug to return to the bird's side was growing inside him. Instead, he scrubbed at his face and turned to the silent figure on his front porch.

"I'll be back in a bit."

Finlay nodded as he faced him, thumbs tucked into the pockets of his jeans. "Take your time. I don't have anywhere to be."

Cash appreciated that the vamp had pretended not to overhear his conversation, keeping his attention on the yard and not him and his grandfather. He appreciated even more that he'd been willing to come and hang out while Cash did one final patrol before his duties were relegated to somebody else.

His hackles rose once more at the thought. He knew Liam hadn't done it as a punishment, but it was still infuriating to have his responsibilities limited, even for a short time. Logically, he understood the reasoning. It simply wasn't doable for him to continue his daily patrolling and border checks while also keeping a close eye on their guest, but he didn't have to like it.

And he was going to miss it.

There were other aspects of being an Enforcer, obviously,

but the nightly patrols were his favorite. He walked—or sometimes ran as his panther—through the wooded areas that made up a large portion of their territory. No matter which route he took, he always ended at Silver Oak Lake so he could spend a few minutes there before heading back home. Other than his and Pops's house, it was his favorite place.

He and the rest of the pack spent a lot of time at the beach, playing in the water, but at night, with the moon reflecting off the still surface, he felt at peace in a way he usually didn't.

He reminded himself that it wouldn't be forever.

The sun was just beginning to set as he stood at the edge of the lake, staring into the calm water and listening to the steady approach of another person. Saint's scent was as familiar to him as his Pops's, but his appearance in that moment annoyed him. He didn't bother turning to look at his friend as the big tiger came up right next to him, shoved his hands in his pockets, and sighed dramatically.

Cash looked at him out of the corner of his eye but then went back to staring at the water without saying anything. Saint, never one to be able to hold still, fidgeted next to him and bumped his arm against Cash's.

Still, he ignored him.

After a minute or two of silence, Saint sighed again. Louder.

"Are you okay?" Cash asked without looking over.

"I'm fine. I'm not the one moodily staring into the lake."

"I'm not staring *moodily*," Cash grumbled, throwing him a scowl.

Saint nudged his shoulder with his own, and Cash realized he had his arms crossed tightly over his chest.

He let out a breath and dropped his arms. "I'm fine."

Saint snorted. "Even if I couldn't hear your heart, I'd know that was a lie. How about you try again?"

Cash resisted the urge to growl at his closest friend. "How

62

about not. I just finished my patrol. I'm going to head back home so Finlay can take off."

Stepping in front of him and blocking his view, Saint held his gaze, his own unusually serious. "Listen, brother, you know you can tell me anything, right?"

Rather than coax him into spilling his guts, Cash's defensiveness only grew worse. No matter what Saint thought, there was nothing to share, no secrets to bond over. They weren't twelve anymore with a stolen nudey mag hidden in their tree house. Cash didn't need him to tell him everything would be okay like he had when he'd been too nervous to look.

"Nothing to tell."

"Okay, fine. You want to pretend that it's totally normal for *you*—Mr. Grumpy-For-Three-Days-If-My-Routine-Is-Even-Slightly-Messed-Up—to invite a strange shifter to stay in your house with you?"

Cash curled his lip at the description but otherwise ignored it. "It'll only be until he gets his memories back."

"*If* he gets his memories back," Saint corrected softly. "If he doesn't, is he going to stay with you forever?"

His panther practically purred at the idea, but Cash squashed that down and shook his head. "No, of course not. If that happens... Well, we'll figure it out then."

"So he's just going to stay with you for the foreseeable future. Your whole life—your responsibilities as an Enforcer —put on hold while you wait for his brain to heal up, and you don't have anything you want to talk about? You think that's completely normal behavior for you?"

"Drop it, Saint."

Saint hummed and studied him, and Cash refused to look away. "You know you can tell me anything."

"What's that supposed to mean?" His mouth was suddenly drier than it had been a second ago.

Saint raised his dark brows. "It means... you can tell me

anything," he said slowly. "As in, if there's something you'd like to talk about, you can with me."

Cash shrugged. "I'm fine."

Saint threw his hands up in the air and stomped a few feet away before spinning around and stomping back. "You're not fine. Goddess, being your best friend can be a real pain in the ass."

Cash rolled his eyes at his theatrics.

"You looked like you were about to rip Liam's head off while he was questioning that bird. Don't think we didn't—"

"His name is Ore," Cash snapped and then immediately regretted it.

"See? That," Saint said, pointing in his face in a way that was about to get him one less finger. "Talk to me, man. What's with you and this eagle? Have you met him before or something?"

"No, of course not. It just... It didn't seem right to keep him cooped up in the basement when he'd already been staying at my place."

"While he was unconscious."

"Either way—"

"Is he your mate?"

Cash's heart jumped into his throat, his eyes widening at the blunt question. "What?"

Saint smiled and clasped him on the shoulders. "You heard me. It's the only thing that makes sense. You being so weird and disrupting your whole life for someone you don't know and we can't be sure we can trust. You'd never risk the pack unless you had a damn good reason."

He stared at his best friend. The words were on the tip of his tongue. It was too early to know for sure—or at least that was what he kept telling himself even though his panther vehemently disagreed—but it wouldn't be the worst thing to talk to someone about it.

Except...

"It doesn't matter," he said softly, shifting his gaze to the water just behind Saint and trying to find his inner peace once more. "As soon as he's better, he's leaving."

"Cash..."

"Don't."

But because Saint was Saint—and maybe had a death wish —he grabbed the sides of Cash's face and forced him to meet his eyes. "No, you listen to me, you stubborn feline. Don't give up before you even try."

"Pack law says—"

"Then we'll change pack law."

Cash shook his head and sighed. "If it were that easy, Liam would already have done it. The pack doesn't want to change. They don't want people who are different moving here and messing with their perfect little lives."

Saint blinked at him, clearly surprised at the bitterness in his voice. "Whoa. Been holding on to that for a while, huh?"

"Am I wrong?"

Shrugging, Saint dropped his hands and shoved them into his pockets. "No. But what I'm saying is that sometimes leaders have to lead."

Cash scowled at him. "We do lead. But we can't lead people where they don't want to go."

Saint moved around him and started heading back up the way he'd come. "Can't we though?"

What the hell was that supposed to mean?

He watched his friend walk away, leaving him even more confused than before.

It wasn't like they hadn't talked about changing things before. Hell, when Liam had first taken over, he'd talked a lot about what he wanted to do, adjustments he thought they should make as a pack, but the more resistance they received, the less he talked about it. Now, it was just something he, Saint, and Rachel talked about when they were alone. Their worries about the sustainability of their pack.

But after what had happened last year, keeping everyone safe from the current volatility of the parahuman world had become their number one priority. Maybe once things were more settled and the new shifter Council—sorry, *Guardians*—was officially up and running, Liam could once again work on opening their pack up to the possibilities of growing and expanding.

As for Ore?

It didn't matter what his panther wanted from the little bird. Once he recovered his memories, he'd know where he belonged and leave the Silver Oak Pack behind.

Until then, Cash had to live with a stranger in his house, watching him with big, dark eyes and smelling so fucking good it tempted him in ways he'd never experienced before.

What could go wrong?

Cursing under his breath, he kicked a stone into the water and then walked away.

CHAPTER 7

O re couldn't sleep.

He'd been tossing and turning for close to two hours and was no closer to falling asleep than he had been when he'd first lain down. It wasn't that the bed was uncomfortable or that he wasn't tired—Goddess, he was *exhausted*— he just couldn't seem to settle his mind.

He stared up at the ceiling high above him, dimly lit by the soft moonlight coming through the large glass windows on the back wall of the room. There weren't any curtains to pull over them, which would probably be annoying first thing in the morning if he wanted to sleep in, but in that moment, he appreciated it. He was glad that he could look straight out and see nothing but open sky and treetops. It beckoned to him, calling to his overwhelmed eagle to come and fly. To feel the cool night air rushing through his feathers and clearing out the mess in his head.

If he'd been somewhere where he felt a bit more... *welcome*, he probably would've gone for a flight around the territory to exhaust himself physically. But even though no one had said he wasn't allowed to leave Cash's house, the implication had been clear that he was to stay put. That way, they'd always know where he was and what he was doing.

A prisoner of sorts. There might not be bars on the windows, but Alpha Amato didn't want him around his pack any more than was absolutely necessary.

His eagle already felt restless, his skin a little too tight. He may have only been *awake* for a day, but it was obvious to him he'd been unconscious for several. Considering he was already dreaming of open air whipping around him, he had to wonder if he was used to shifting every day or two.

Though he supposed it could also be the stress—mental and physical—that he'd gone through after being injured. Maybe before then too, depending on what had happened to him. He could have been held for weeks for all he knew, with his flight into the Silver Oak territory being his first after a long captivity.

Either way, he didn't think he'd last much longer without getting the chance to spread his wings. He'd wait to bring it up with his babysitter until they got to know each other a bit better. Maybe then he could convince the serious panther that it wouldn't be a risk to come play in the trees with him.

He couldn't imagine they'd actually be upset if he simply flew away, but it wasn't as if he had anywhere to go. Not yet. Maybe not even after he got his memories back. What if no one was looking for him? What if the family that was supposed to love him had been the ones to hurt him?

Shuddering, he turned onto his side and tugged one of the pillows down so he could wrap his arms around it. It wouldn't do him any good to start spiraling and thinking of every worst-case scenario his brain could come up with. He'd just have to wait and see.

And the fact of the matter was, as much as the idea of staying cooped up in the cozy house with a cat shifter who stared at him a little too long and a little too intently didn't sound like a terrible thing, he knew he would go stir-crazy within a couple of days.

Despite the staring, Ore had wondered when Cash had left earlier if he'd come back. The thought had crossed his mind as he'd sat on the stairs to the loft, listening to Cash help his grandfather pack and try and convince him to stay. He'd felt so guilty about displacing the sweet old man that he'd almost volunteered to go back to the Alpha House. But he was too selfish and couldn't get the words out. The idea of staying inside this cute house for days on end was uncomfortable. The idea of being stuck in a basement all by himself?

Unbearable.

So he'd stayed out of sight, eavesdropping on the other two until they'd gone outside together. He'd kept expecting Cash to walk back in after he heard Pops's car leave, the headlights flashing across the downstairs through the large front windows, but he never did.

After almost half an hour, Ore had forced himself to stand from the stairs and go over to the door to peek out. The vampire from Alpha Amato's office was still standing there, unnaturally still and silent as he surveyed the front yard, but there hadn't been any sign of Cash anywhere in the shadows of the lowering sun.

"Do you need anything, Ore?" The vampire's voice had been smooth with just a hint of an accent—something European, he thought. He hadn't actually turned to look at him when he'd spoken, keeping his attention on the gravel driveway and trees beyond.

"Um, no. I just… I didn't know where Cash was."

That had caused the vamp to turn and glance at him for a moment before going back to his perusal of the yard. "He went to patrol. He'll return soon."

Cash had left. Without saying anything to Ore.

The pain that had hit him at the news had been unexpectedly severe, taking him by surprise. The vampire's shoulders

69

had tensed, like he felt it as well, but he didn't acknowledge it, thank the goddess. After clearing his throat, Ore had asked if the man needed anything or if he wanted to come and sit inside, but he'd politely declined. Ore had been more than a little relieved. The pack's second-in-command was extremely attractive, but he made Ore's eagle nervous. Like they were all prey to the vampire, but he was just choosing not to hunt them.

Ore had ended up curled up on the big, soft couch in the living room, not sure what else to do but wait for Cash to come back. He'd ended up dozing a little without meaning to, waking when Cash returned over an hour after Ore's brief conversation with the vampire outside. He'd had a bag that smelled delicious in one hand as he'd paused to stare at Ore for a long moment before going into the kitchen.

Feeling as uncertain as ever, he'd followed, his stomach rumbling embarrassingly loudly. Cash didn't say anything, just sort of grunted as he set the grease-stained bag on the kitchen table and then headed into the bedroom at the back of the house that had been Pops's.

Ore had wandered over and peeked inside to find a cheeseburger and french fries that had been exceptionally good, even though they'd been lukewarm. The fact that Cash had bothered to bring him dinner, despite obviously being annoyed at Ore's presence, had struck him as sweet and made him feel better about being left alone without so much as a warning glare not to go anywhere.

But Cash never came back out after disappearing into the back of the house. After a while, Ore had simply turned off the lights and wandered up to the loft, climbing into the lavender-scented bed in the same enormous T-shirt he'd been wearing all day.

But sleep wouldn't come.

Curled into a ball, the extra pillow doing a very poor job of making him feel less alone, Ore stared at the moon. It'd be full in another week or so. Would he still be there? Unsure of who he was or where he belonged? Would Cash still be mostly ignoring his presence?

Would whoever had hurt him come looking for him?

He shivered and squeezed his eyes shut. Part of why he couldn't settle was because he was already starting to remember things, but it didn't make sense. It was like his mind was healing itself out of order. He would get random blurry images, a scent, or a feeling without context, but nothing concrete. No clear faces. Nothing that he could use to figure out what had happened to him. It all just confused him more, and a part of him was concerned it would never solidify into anything real.

He'd be stuck in limbo, haunted with flashes of a life he could never remember.

Did he have a family out there worried about what had happened to him? Did he have... a mate? Someone he loved and cared about, who was waiting on him to come back home to them?

Something told him that wasn't the case. He might have parents or siblings out there somewhere, sick with fear over him, but would his eagle react to the big panther if they had a mate?

Seemed unlikely. Even without memories, he trusted his eagle.

But should he say something in the morning to let Cash know things were already starting to trickle back into his brain? Would he bring Ore back to Alpha Amato's house to be interrogated again?

He wasn't sure he'd be ready to do that again so soon. And unless he woke up in a much clearer state than he was now, he wouldn't be able to answer anything more than he had already.

No, he wouldn't say anything until he knew something for sure. Something *helpful*.

There was no reason to get anyone's hopes up about being able to send him on his way with a clear conscience before it was a reality. His stomach turned at the idea of being cast out, but he tried to ignore it. It wasn't fair to feel rejected. This wasn't his pack. They weren't his people, his family. Liam Amato wasn't his alpha.

He didn't belong.

A tear slipped out of the corner of his eye, wetting his pillow. Groaning softly, he swiped hurriedly at his face. He was wallowing, and he had to stop. He had more important things to focus on than hurt feelings over not getting invited to join a pack he really knew nothing about.

Like, what kind of monster used a magically modified virus to try and kill someone?

Sniffling, he flipped over, turning his back on the cheery moonlight and facing the full bookcases lining the front edge of the loft. Before curling up on the couch, Ore had taken a closer inspection of Cash's collection. There was quite the variety, though it seemed like he enjoyed autobiographies and thrillers the most. Neither was Ore's favorite, but he wondered if there was a bookstore nearby for him to have such a collection or if he ordered all of them online.

He sighed and shut his eyes. Not that it mattered. He didn't have any money to buy himself some books he would like. He didn't even have clothes or a phone.

An aching loneliness spread through his limbs. He tucked them in close to his body, making himself into a ball as small as he could. The house was so quiet it was almost as if he were all by himself again. Left to stew in his fear and worries.

For a moment, his mind convinced him he *was* all alone, abandoned by the cat who didn't really want him there.

His heart rate spiked, and his breaths turned choppy, even as he told himself it wasn't true. He would've heard Cash leave if he'd taken off again. Logically, he knew Cash was right below him, but he couldn't shake off the idea after it took root in his mind.

Maybe he could go and check just to be sure?

If he laid eyes on him, Ore was sure it would settle his anxiety. Maybe while he was up, he could get a glass of water or warm milk, something to try and help him fall asleep. He eased the covers back from his body, his feet landing lightly on the floor beneath him. He crept as slowly as he could across the loft and down the wide, wooden steps.

Taking a sharp turn around the banister, he followed the wall all the way back to the closed bedroom door. He hesitated just outside, his ears straining to hear anything on the other side. His hearing just wasn't as good as other kinds of shifters though, so all he could pick up was a soft tick of a clock somewhere in the living room.

He was going to really piss Cash off if he woke him up. He just knew it...

His anxiety kept bubbling in his veins, whispering at him that he was on his own. That the person who'd nearly killed him would come and get him, and no one would be there to help him. He'd end up getting dosed again. He'd end up in pain, locked in a basement or dumped in the middle of nowhere. He'd never find his way back to Cash—

Heart pounding in his ears, he gripped the door handle and turned it as silently as he could with his shaking hand. He only pushed the door open far enough to stick his head past it.

The inside of the room was a lot darker than the loft had been. The curtains pulled closed over the windows, blocking out all of the moonlight. His eagle eyes adjusted quickly though, and he spotted Cash's enormous body sprawled on the bed, one arm flung out to the side.

He let out a long breath, trying to settle his pulse. He wasn't alone. Even if Cash didn't want him here, he hadn't just left him to fend for himself.

Whoever had done those terrible things to him wouldn't be able to take him back.

"What are you doing, Ore?"

Cash's deep voice, thick with sleep, called out to him before he could pull the door all the way shut. He bit his lip and pushed it back open.

"I-I'm sorry," he stuttered out, not sure how to explain.

"Are you okay?" Cash asked, sitting up in bed.

Ore's eagle trilled in his chest at the site of all of that bare skin as the covers dropped to Cash's waist. There were tattoos covering a lot of his white, lightly tanned skin. Both biceps, a shoulder, and his forearms were decorated with black ink. Now that they weren't hidden, he could see the faintest glow coming from a handful.

It was on the tip of his tongue to ask what they were for, but he held it back. They weren't actually friends. No matter how much his eagle liked the way Cash smelled or looked or took care of him. It didn't change the fact that as soon as Alpha Amato said the word, Cash would be taking him to the edge of the territory and sending him on his way.

Like a stray dog nobody wanted.

"You need something?" Cash asked, scratching at the stubble on his face.

He started to say no. He didn't *need* anything, but there was something he wanted.

Desperately.

"I can't sleep," he whispered, rubbing his toes on the floor as he averted his eyes.

Cash didn't say anything for a long moment. The silence twisted up Ore's insides, and he waited to be told to go back to his own bed.

"What do you need?" Cash said again. There wasn't a trace of anger or frustration in his voice. He was rock steady as he continued to wait for Ore's response, seemingly unfazed at being woken up in the middle of the night.

He was waiting for Ore to tell him exactly what was going on so he could fix it.

At least... that's what Ore hoped.

"Can I stay with you, please?" He chanced a glance up and found Cash studying him carefully, a small frown between his brows. Ore held his breath.

"I suppose," he said slowly and pushed to his feet. He wasn't wearing anything; not a stitch of clothing covered his body, and even though Ore knew it was completely natural, that shifters didn't get embarrassed by their bodies, heat flooded his cheeks, and he turned his face away.

But not before he'd seen the very large size of... *all* of Cash.

"I'll grab the cot."

"Oh no," Ore said quickly. "You don't have to do that. I can just..." He glanced around the room, holding back a grimace. "I can just sleep on the floor."

Cash sighed and rubbed at his face again. "You don't need to sleep on the floor."

"Well, I don't want to make you sleep on a cot."

"It's not that big of a deal," Cash insisted.

"This is silly," Ore said, taking a half step back. "I'll just go back upstairs."

"Stop." Cash's voice rumbled across the dark space, cascading down Ore's spine. "Get in the damn bed."

Ore nibbled on his lip for half of a second and then darted across the room and burrowed beneath the still-warm covers. Pops's scent was strongest in the room, but when he pushed his face into the pillow Cash had been using, he found that lavender-and-leather scent. He sucked it in deep, filling his lungs as much as he could before he could stop himself.

Cash cleared his throat next to the bed. "Scoot over."

Ore's pulse tripped as he made room on the king-sized bed. He was swimming in it by himself. Settling on the other side, he ran his eyes over the tall, broad form of Cash and shivered in excitement.

He tried to tamp it down, knowing it didn't really mean anything. Cash probably just wanted to go back to sleep, and this was the fastest way to accomplish that. It didn't matter. Ore already felt safer than he had since he'd woken up. As soon as Cash eased onto the mattress and tugged the covers up to his waist, most of the tension that had built up in his neck and shoulders as Ore had fretted upstairs for hours began to melt away.

He sighed happily.

"Go to sleep," Cash grumbled, turning on his side to face away from Ore.

Ore stared at that mile-wide back, his eyes tracing the black edges of the tattoos there. How he could be so beautiful and fearsome at the same time Ore didn't know, but he had a feeling he would stay awake all night looking at the big cat if he wasn't careful.

He waited until Cash's breaths evened out and he was pretty sure he was asleep, then scooted forward an inch at a time. It took forever to close the foot of space between them, but finally, he was almost close enough to touch his nose to the skin between Cash's shoulder blades. He could feel the heat radiating off his larger body, creating a cozy little nest under the soft covers.

The rest of the tension oozed out of his body, and his eyes started to get heavy. So much better than lying upstairs all alone. In the dark and quiet, he felt safe. It didn't matter that Cash had given him his back. He'd take whatever he could get.

Would he have said no if Cash had offered to wrap him up in his thick, muscly arms?

Goddess no.

He didn't know if there was a damn thing he would say no to if Cash offered. But this was enough. It had to be.

He drifted off to sleep, praying that his memory stayed away for a while longer.

CHAPTER 8

"He was sobbing so hard I could barely understand him, but then he shoved the thing right up to my face and said, 'Why isn't it healing, Papa?'" Pops grinned at him from across the table before turning back to Ore and continuing to regale him with a story from Cash's youth. It wasn't the first, but it may have been the most humiliating. "He used to call me Papa until he got too old and too cool. That's when I became Pops. It stuck, and now, pretty much everyone in the pack calls me that."

Ore smiled widely, his eyes dancing as he glanced between the two of them. "I like Pops. It fits you."

Cash grumbled under his breath and took another bite of spaghetti, pretending like he wasn't embarrassed by his grandfather doing the verbal equivalent of bringing out his baby pictures. He wasn't sure why he hadn't expected it since Pops loved telling stories about Cash as a cub to all of his friends—or really anyone who would listen. But it felt different, sitting there and listening to the familiar retellings of the time Cash had gotten into a fight with Saint over a favorite toy or when he'd spent a week pretending to be a frog, as Ore laughed in delight and gasped in all the appropriate spots.

Not bad different. Just… vulnerable different. Like Ore would judge him as unworthy. Unworthy of what exactly? He wasn't letting himself think about that.

"So anyway," Pops continued, waving his fork in the air, "I had to try and explain to four-year-old Cash that not every animal in the world was a shifter, and sometimes when they got hurt, they didn't get better."

Ore's face dimmed. "Did the bird die?"

"Oh, no," Pop said, grinning, "not with my special little helper assisting me as I worked to keep him alive and healthy until his wing was better." He turned a softer smile on Cash. "I'd never seen Cash cry like he did when that bird flew away."

"Alright," Cash muttered, taking a swig of his beer. "Let's change the topic."

Ore snickered under his breath, daintily eating some of his own spaghetti. He'd cut up the noodles into tiny pieces and was using a spoon to scoop them up. In response to Cash's staring at the process at the beginning of the meal, Ore had just shrugged and claimed he didn't like getting messy from the long noodles.

It was oddly endearing to Cash, but he did his best to ignore the way his body warmed with affection. After the last few days of the two of them being holed up together, it was getting more and more difficult.

"Whatever you say, son," Pops said, still grinning like the devil he was. "I heard yesterday that nobody's seen you since Ore here arrived." He raised his bushy gray brows at him. "Are you keeping this young man under lock and key?"

Cash bit back a groan. That was not the change in subject he'd wanted, considering Ore had barely made it a single day before starting to ask when they could get out from inside the four walls of Cash's house. He claimed it wasn't natural for birds to be cooped up like that, and while Cash empathized —since he was going a little stir-crazy himself—his orders

80

were to keep an eye on the eagle until he was ready to go on his way. Letting him wander around the rest of the pack in their tiny town just seemed like a recipe for getting people upset.

Ore gave him a look before staring down at his plate once more, pushing his food around instead of eating. His uncertain scent poked at Cash's panther, urging him to make everything better.

Cash sighed. "The door isn't locked, but I thought it'd be for the best if we stayed here."

His grandfather huffed at him, setting his utensils down and pointing a finger bent with arthritis at him. "Cash Lawson, you listen to me. This man is not a prisoner. He is our guest. Now, you take him somewhere that isn't this house. Let him stretch his dang legs, son."

Ore beamed at the old man.

His panther didn't appreciate the scolding. No matter how old he got or how high he rose in the pack, he'd always see his grandfather as the head of their family. Disappointing him was almost as bad as disappointing his alpha.

"I'll check with Liam," he said and turned back to his pasta. "We should visit with Fern anyway. Have her check you over."

Ore nodded. "Whatever gets me outside."

Pops beamed at him with pride, easing his panther's agitation. They finished eating without any more embarrassing stories, Pops filling him in on pack gossip instead. He'd already heard most of it from Saint and Rachel, but Pops liked to put a dramatic flair to the way he shared things, so he didn't mind. Ore seemed happy and entertained as well, despite not knowing who Pops was talking about.

After dinner, the three of them sat in the living room for a bit, the evening news on in the background. Pops turned a bit nostalgic, telling Ore about his late mate. Cash didn't contribute much, his heart aching at her loss even after all these years. It didn't take long before Pops started wearing out, the pauses in his stories growing longer.

Cash offered him his room back for the night, not liking the idea of him driving back to Martha's while he was so tired, but he waved him off. "I'm not so old yet I can't drive in the dark. Stop your fussing."

He hugged Cash tightly, running his palm down his neck in a quick scenting. Then, he surprised Cash and Ore by pulling the eagle into an embrace as well.

"Don't let Cash be too grumpy," he stage-whispered, planting a hand on the top of Ore's shoulder. It was as close as he could get without actually scenting him, something usually reserved only for packmates.

Ore swallowed and nodded, standing a little straighter under the light touch. "I'll do my best, Pops."

Cash rolled his eyes and followed him outside, Ore lingering next to the couch. As soon as the front door was shut, he muttered, "I'm not grumpy."

"I know," Pops said, slowly descending the porch steps. "You're just too serious for your own good."

Frowning, he watched as Pops used his cane to navigate the uneven ground. "I have a serious job and—"

"No one is saying you don't." Pops opened the door to his sedan but turned to Cash before climbing in. "But protecting the pack can't be your whole life."

Cash reared back. "I've worked hard to become an Enforcer. I don't want to give that up."

Pops cupped the side of his face, his smile soft and a little sad. "I'm not suggesting you give it up. I'm suggesting there is *more* to life. Don't miss out on something wonderful because you think you can't have both."

He stared at his grandfather, not sure what to say. It was no secret what—or rather, *who*—Pops was talking about, but he was wrong. Cash couldn't have both. Even if Ore wanted to stay once his memories were back, that didn't mean he'd be able to.

And then where would that leave them?

He stood on the front porch, watching until the taillights disappeared, and then took a steadying breath. It was getting late, around the time he and Ore usually headed to bed. A shiver of heat ran down his spine, and his cock twitched in his pants.

He tried not to think about what happened at night during the day. Neither of them brought it up, and he'd convinced himself that if he acted like it was normal, then it wasn't a big deal. But he knew, without a doubt, that if he let himself think about the fact that the bed in the downstairs bedroom now smelled like both of them, then he'd be walking around with an erection all day.

The first night hadn't been that bad. He'd figured that Ore was just scared and disoriented and needed another body nearby, so he'd let him get in bed with him. He'd still been awake when the little bird had scooted up behind him, but he hadn't actually touched Cash. He'd been surprised that his cat had been okay with having a stranger so close to his back, but if anything, his panther had been *too* pleased with the development.

The second night, he'd felt the tips of Ore's toes and the brush of his nose, but that was it. Those were the only places they touched, so he'd told himself it was fine. Maybe Ore got cold and needed the extra body heat from Cash.

He should have known the sweet little bird was just biding his time.

Last night, Ore hadn't even bothered to wait until he thought Cash was asleep to move closer. The second he'd slid into bed and turned so he was facing the door, Ore's small body was plastered against his back, his face smooshed between his shoulder blades. He'd sighed like it was the best feeling in the world and passed out almost immediately.

It had taken Cash *a lot* longer to fall asleep.

Their weird game of snuggle chicken was bad enough, but what was worse was the fact that each morning, Cash woke up wrapped around Ore. That morning, he'd had Ore flattened on his stomach on the mattress, most of his considerably larger bulk thankfully off to the side. One of his legs had been thrown over Ore's and one of his traitorous hands trapped under him. His fingers had been right over Ore's delicate collarbones, and Cash just knew that if he didn't figure out how to stop his sleep groping, he was going to wake up soon with his palm cupping Ore's throat possessively.

Thank the goddess, he always woke first and was able to slip from the bed before Ore realized how handsy he got with him while unconscious.

He told himself they needed to stop, that Ore needed to sleep upstairs by himself, but he knew he'd never actually tell him that. Fuck, a part of him was excited to see how far Ore would push that night. Would he wrap an arm around Cash? Would he ask him to turn around?

Would Cash have the strength to say no?

Snorting, he turned to face the door, the glow from the lights inside welcoming.

If he turned over in the bed to face Ore while they were both wide-awake and his alluring floral scent spiked with citrusy arousal, he knew he wouldn't be able to stop himself from reaching over and getting his hands all over him.

His panther was growing more frustrated by the day, demanding he take action and growling in annoyance every time Cash turned away when Ore smiled up at him. Or lightly touched his arm while they were on the couch together. Or softly thanked Cash for every tiny thing he did for him.

Goddess, those thank-yous slayed him every time.

Cash had to stop his chest from vibrating with a loud purr

every time he did the most basic stuff for the little bird, his cat so pleased with them for taking care of him.

He knew what these things meant. He wasn't an idiot, and he wasn't oblivious, but he also knew it couldn't mean anything. He'd dedicated his entire life to his pack, had worked hard to become an Enforcer and someone his alpha could trust.

They didn't allow non-cats to join. That was it. End of story. So there was no reason to acknowledge the pull between them out loud. It was in both of their best interests if they never acted on the feelings because the fallout... it would be catastrophic.

There was no point. Not unless he was willing to leave everything behind and go with Ore once he remembered where he belonged and was asked—politely but firmly—to vacate their territory.

A week ago, he'd have snarled in the face of anyone who'd even jokingly suggested he'd consider giving up everything he'd ever worked for.

But now?

He couldn't say he wasn't at least a little tempted. As he lay in bed next to Ore, he'd let himself imagine the future they could have, the images playing in his head as Ore's heat and scent sank under his skin and wrapped around his heart.

He imagined a million more of Ore's sweet smiles. A hundred more meals with him and Pops teasing him. A thousand nights sprawled on the couch together as Ore watched his silly reality TV and Cash scented every inch of him.

Except... what if Ore already had a mate? Or a family he was close with who missed him terribly. Cash didn't know the most basic things about the little bird—so why should he consider even for a second throwing away his own life. The one he'd worked for since he was a kid.

More importantly... how could he risk being anything like his parents?

Everyone said that a fated mate brought out the best in you, that you were two sides of the same coin, that you were soul mates destined for one another…

But Cash knew differently.

He knew that just being fated for another didn't make either one of them a good person. It didn't mean there was anything good inside them to be brought out. The sides of the coin could be ugly and hateful just as easily as loving and kind.

His parents had been fated, and yet they'd made themselves, each other, and Cash miserable every day right up until they'd taken off to goddess knew where.

Despite what everyone claimed, he knew that just because somebody was supposedly picked for you by the goddess, it didn't mean your life would be perfect and rosy after you met them. People were still people, and they could hurt each other and be disappointments with or without the help of a deity.

When he was a kid, he'd promised himself he'd never let what happened to his parents happen to him. He'd never allow himself to become so consumed by another person that he'd lose piece after piece of himself until there was nothing left.

His pack had become his family, his stability and grounding force, after they left, packmates helping his grandparents without hesitation or needing to be asked. All he'd ever wanted to do was return the favor, protect them like they'd protected him.

He wasn't going to give up everything he'd worked for just because sad eyes and an inviting smile made his panther stir inside him.

He needed to stay strong and stick to the plan. He'd watch over Ore until he was ready to leave, and that would be it. Nodding to himself, he stepped back inside, finding Ore in the kitchen, cleaning up the dishes. He kept reminding himself of that as they quietly worked together to put the kitchen back in order, the silence between them soft and easy.

It was shocking how easily he'd grown used to having Ore there with him. He liked living with his Pops—helping him when he needed it and keeping each other company—but having Ore stay with him was different. No matter where he was in the house, Cash could feel him, an electrical presence that pulled at him until he'd go to find Ore. They would gravitate toward one another without thinking, ending up at the kitchen table or the couch, each doing their own task but close by each other.

Cash tried not to let himself like it too much, knowing how temporary it was, but his panther ignored him, reveling in having Ore nearby all day and night.

"Cash," Ore said softly as they finished putting the last items in the dishwasher.

He grunted a reply, setting it to turn on so that they would have clean utensils in the morning.

"Are you really going to ask Liam if I can leave the house?"

Cash glanced over his shoulder and studied the hopeful look on Ore's face. He was wearing another of Cash's T-shirts, even though Rachel had brought a stack of borrowed clothes over that would fit him better.

Ore had thanked her, brought them up to the loft, and then never touched them, continuing to pilfer shirts out of Cash's drawer instead. Neither one of them acknowledged it. Cash liked it too much to even pretend to force the issue. Ore just looked so delicate in his enormous shirts. And he smelled like Cash's, something his panther couldn't get enough of.

The look on his grandfather's face when he'd seen Ore had been like a bucket of ice water to the face though. Ore *didn't* belong to him. Confusing his panther about it wasn't a good idea.

"I said I would." He ignored how good it made him feel when Ore beamed at him.

"Thank you! I promise not to be any trouble."

Cash narrowed his eyes and took a step closer. "I'm not worried about you being any trouble. That's not why we've been staying here."

Ore shrugged like he didn't really believe him and glanced away. "I know it's a pain for me to be here with you, keeping you locked down as well, so I just appreciate you being willing to bend the rules for me."

Cash stared at him. "You aren't a pain," he said clearly.

Had Cash somehow made him feel like he was? The thought made him uneasy.

When Ore didn't look up, he did something incredibly stupid. Gently, he gripped Ore's chin, tilting his face up so he had to meet Cash's gaze. Fuck, he was so tiny, so delicate. Cash wanted to wrap himself around the tiny bird and keep him safe.

He also wanted to do some not-as-nice things to Ore's perfect little body, but he shoved those thoughts away.

"Listen to me," he said, his voice huskier than it had been a moment ago. "This pack can be wary of outsiders. I just didn't want anyone getting upset. That's the only reason we haven't gone anywhere, okay? You're not a pain or an inconvenience. I volunteered for this, remember?"

Ore licked his lips, staring into Cash's face. Goddess, those full lips might be the death of him.

"I remember," Ore murmured. "Thank you for that. I would definitely rather be here than in the basement of Alpha Amato's house."

Cash nodded, releasing his hold on Ore's face slowly and trailing the backs of his fingers down the front of his throat before he could stop himself. Ore sucked in a breath, pupils blowing wide. A low rumble began to grow in Cash's chest, but he coughed and took a step back.

"You're welcome. I'll text him in the morning, but I'm sure he'll say it's fine." Shit, his voice was raw, his pants getting tight as Ore's scent intensified in the cozy little kitchen.

Ore held his eyes a moment longer, running his teeth over his bottom lip. "Thanks, Cash."

He watched him walk out, heading toward the front of the house so he could go upstairs. Cash couldn't look away until he was out of sight, the drive to stalk after him so strong he had to grip the counter to stop himself.

Running a hand over his short hair, he turned off the lights and then headed to his temporary bedroom. Ore was going to stay upstairs or pretend to try and sleep up there. Every night, he went up to use Cash's shower and grab a new shirt to sleep in before coming down and getting into Cash's bed. He was usually already in there by the time Cash finished his own routine in the downstairs bathroom.

He was standing under the hot spray, doing his best to will his dick into cooperating, when he heard the faintest of creaks, his head jerking up to face the door that led into the bedroom. Ore was in there already, the sound the same one he heard every night when they climbed into the bed.

So much for stroking one out to take the edge off. It felt... wrong to touch himself like that while Ore waited for him just a door away.

Fuck, what were they doing?

He dried off, doing his best to will away his arousal and steady himself. If they were going to keep sleeping in the same bed, they might as well sleep upstairs in his loft. Pops's bed was a little firmer than he liked, and he figured Ore would prefer being up higher off the ground. He'd wait to invite Pops back though—there was no way for him to believably convince him there was nothing actually going on between him and Ore.

Hanging up his towel, he stepped into the bedroom. The lights were already off, and Ore was curled up in the middle of the bed, facing the door. Or Cash's side of the bed, depending on how you looked at it. His eyes were already shut, breathing even, so Cash decided he'd bring up sleeping upstairs in the morning.

He'd barely settled the covers over him before Ore's skin was pressing against his own.

Just his skin.

Cash sucked in a breath. The thin material of one of his T-shirts usually separated them, covering Ore's tiny body from neck to knees, but he'd apparently decided to go without for the night.

He lay there, tense as a board, as he tried to figure out what—if anything—he should do. He had to bite his lip to stop a groan from breaking free when teasing fingers trailed down his back next to his spine and then over his hip.

Fuck, he was temptation personified, and Cash didn't know how he'd make it through the night.

"Cash?"

That was new. They'd never spoken in bed before beyond that first night when Cash had told him to go to sleep. It helped them pretend they weren't crossing major lines every time they got under the covers—or at least it did for Cash.

"Yeah?" he rumbled, his hands fisting in the bedding in front of him. He wasn't going to turn around. Ore could sleep naked if he wanted to. It'd be hypocritical of Cash to demand he put on a shirt when he never wore anything.

"Can I ask you a question?"

If it was "Why do you smell like arousal?" Cash was going to go sleep on the front porch.

"Yeah," he said again, not moving a muscle even as Ore snuggled in closer, languidly rubbing his soft cheek against Cash's shoulder. *Scenting him.*

"The stories that Pops told," he said softly, tentatively, like he wasn't sure if it was okay. "He never mentioned your parents."

Cash stiffened in a hell of a lot less fun way.

That wasn't what he'd been expecting. It also wasn't a question, so he felt just fine not saying anything.

After a moment, Ore's fingers twitched where they rested on his hip. "Why is that?"

"I spent a lot of time with Pops and Nan growing up, and then I moved in with them." He kept it simple, straight to the point. He was hoping that would be the end of it.

He should have known better.

"Are they still alive?" Ore asked delicately.

"Probably."

There was a loaded silence after his snarled response. That would *definitely* put an end to things. But then Ore ran his fingers down his back again, comforting him even after his rude answer.

"They don't live around here?"

Cash ground his teeth together. He took a deep, steadying breath and let it out slowly. He was a grown man. He could talk about his parents without turning into a surly asshole.

"Scoot back, Ore," he said. The scent of shock and then hurt burned at his nose, but Ore moved without hesitation, murmuring a nearly inaudible apology.

When Cash flipped over onto his other side, he saw the little bird was practically falling off the other edge. He raised his brow and then lifted his arm, gesturing him forward. "Come here, hatchling."

Ore's cute little nose wrinkled in annoyance even as he dove forward, burying himself against Cash's chest. "I'm not a hatchling. You're just enormous."

He chuckled, running his rough hand down Ore's smooth spine, stopping at the small of his back before sliding back up. He used the small movements to soothe Ore until the scent of his pain had faded from the room.

"My parents left when I was eight."

"They left the pack?" Ore clarified, wiggling even closer so that the tip of his nose was pressed to the hollow of Cash's throat. He fit with Cash perfectly.

"Yes, they left the pack and me," Cash said simply, keeping his voice steady by force of will.

Ore's anger filled his nose. "They left *you*? You didn't choose to stay or come back later?"

"No," Cash said, stroking Ore's back once more to calm him. "One day, they dropped me off here, which was normal. They pawned me off on my grandparents more often than not anyway, but they never came back that night." He stared at the dark wall behind Ore, remembering that day and the one that followed clearly, even after all the years that had passed. "That wasn't unusual either, so I stayed the night, and the next morning, Pops drove me back to their house."

Cash could clearly recall the way his stomach had churned as they'd gotten closer to the dilapidated one-story house they'd lived in near the edge of the pack's territory. He had known that something was wrong, off. The way his mother had hugged him before leaving the day before had been strange. She usually barely looked at him when he got out of the car before driving off, but she'd held him tightly for a long couple of seconds before sending him inside the house and leaving.

"When we went inside, I could tell something had happened," Cash said carefully, keeping his voice as even as he could. "Things were overturned. Other stuff had been emptied. Pops must have realized what had happened before I did because he asked me to go wait out in the car, but I ignored him and went down the hall to my parents' room."

"What did you find?" Ore asked quietly when he paused.

"All their shit was gone."

"Oh, Cash," Ore said, rubbing his fingers back and forth against Cash's chest. "I'm so sorry. How could they have just done that?"

"They weren't good people," Cash said clearly, an edge to

his tone that he couldn't stop. "Pops and I packed up my stuff, came back here, and never really talked about it after that."

"He didn't talk to you about what had happened?"

Cash shook his head. Though, with the way Ore was buried against him, there was no way he could see it. "Not really. Every once in a while, he or Nan would make a comment about their daughter, but they never called her my mom, not after that day."

"And they never came back?"

"No, Ore, they never came back. Good fucking riddance."

Ore slipped an arm around Cash and gave him a squeeze. "Goddess, you were just a cub. I'm so sorry you had to go through that."

He was too, but it had taught him valuable lessons about how love didn't necessarily mean sunshine and rainbows. That it could bring pain and anger. Darkness and despair.

In the end, he knew that they had done him a favor, leaving him to be raised by two people who loved him more than anything, but the damage had already been done.

CHAPTER 9

"How is your fatigue?" Fern asked, not opening her eyes.

Ore eyed her glowing hands warily, but she just kept moving them over his body without touching him. "Um. It's basically gone."

"Good."

She hovered over a spot above his left hip, a furrow between her brows, then continued down his legs. Ore wasn't sure he liked having to lie on his back on her couch as she "examined" him, but he kept that to himself. At least he'd been able to keep his clothes on for it. Still… he felt oddly vulnerable as his skin tingled wherever she moved her hands.

"Have you shifted?"

"A couple of times," he said softly, though he wasn't sure why he felt like it was a secret. Alpha Amato hadn't told him he couldn't shift—heck, he'd probably be relieved if Ore just flew away and took his problems with him—but Ore had felt a bit guilty when he'd done it, staying in the upstairs bathroom at Cash's house. He couldn't fly in there, but he could stretch his wings a bit. "Not for very long though."

"That's fine," she murmured, moving to the end of the

couch. She held her glowing hands to the soles of his feet for a long couple of minutes, and then the light began to dim, her eyes opening. "I can't detect any foreign magic anywhere in you. Your healing did its job."

He sat up and shrugged. "With your help."

"With the coven's help," she corrected, plopping onto the coffee table right in front of him. Her big hazel eyes were a bit intense up close, and she reeked of magic so strongly it was making his nose itch.

"Still... thanks for not letting me die," he said. He hadn't thought to thank her the other day in Liam's office, over-whelmed by everything she'd told him and the intimidating group in the room.

She grinned and waved a hand at him. "I don't make a habit of letting folks die just because they weren't born in the same place I was. How are your memories coming along?"

He made a face, and she laughed. "Terribly. All I've gotten is... I don't know how to describe it. Impressions? Feelings? I'll get like a blurry flash and a strong reaction, but it doesn't make any sense. I still can't remember any people or events of my life."

"You need to be patient with yourself. You're rebuilding the bridge to those memories, and that takes time. They're in there though."

"That's what Pops said," he admitted, sighing and running a hand through his hair. "It's just really frustrating."

"That's understandable. I don't know if this will make it worse or better," she said, resituating into a crossed-leg posi-tion on the table, nearly knocking over an unlit candle. "I finished analyzing what I could of the spell that was used on the virus, and I believe your access to your memories was severed on purpose."

Ore's heart lurched in his chest, his eyes widening. "For real? Why would they do that and then try and kill me?"

She shrugged. "I have no proof of anything, but my suspicion is that they weren't trying to kill you. They were testing you for something."

"Testing me?"

"The use of the virus to deliver the spell is something I've never seen before, but it makes me think someone in some lab somewhere is doing some pretty fucked-up experiments on parahumans. For what end? I couldn't say." She glanced away, appearing lost in thought as her fingers tapped on her knees.

Ore tried to digest that information and the implications of it. "So you think there are others. That I wasn't just a one-off."

She met his eyes once more, anger flashing over her cherubic features. "I know you're not. I don't have any way to prove it yet, but I think you escaped the same place Liam's brother's mate did."

His eyes just about bugged out of his head. "Wait, what?"

A throat cleared, and they both looked over to find Cash standing in the doorway of the living room, a scowl etched on his strong face. "Fern—"

She stood and threw her hands up. "Don't you *Fern* me. Tell me I'm wrong."

"I'm not saying—"

She cut him off before he could answer, her fury burning his sinuses. "If he and Caden were being held at the same place, he deserves to know. And so do Caden and Quinten."

Ore climbed to his feet but stayed back, not wanting to get in the middle of whatever fight was happening between the two. Caden had to be Liam's brother's mate. Had he been dosed with the virus thing too? Or just had his memories wiped?

"We don't know that they were," Cash said harshly. "And it isn't our place to share what happened to him with an outsider."

Ore stumbled back a step, devastation hitting him like a

physical blow. Cash didn't want her telling him about this Caden, sharing the details of what had happened to him.

Because he didn't *trust* Ore. He would always just be an outsider to him.

Ice-blue eyes darted over to him, and Cash took a step into the room, inhaling deeply. "Ore, don't—"

"Don't what? Don't get upset?" He shook his head, tucking his chin into his chest and wrapping his arms around himself. "Cool, sure. No problem. I'll just ignore the fact that you don't trust me. Oh, and how there is apparently another person out there who may have gone through the same hell as me, but that's not my *business*, is it, Enforcer Lawson?"

Cash's irises began to glow faintly, and he moved farther into the room. Without taking his eyes off Ore, he said, "Fern, will you give us a minute alone, please?"

"Yup. Good luck, big guy." She headed for a different door than where Cash had come in, glancing back at Ore. "When you start getting some memories back, come and see me. I think I'll be able to help find the rest once your mind gives us the roadmap."

He nodded, not saying anything as she stepped out of the room and into what he assumed was the kitchen, closing a swinging door behind her. Once it was just the two of them, Ore had the urge to flee. The room, the house—maybe even the territory.

He felt… stupid. For days, he and Cash had spent nearly every moment together. While Cash wasn't the chattiest person in the world, he'd shared things with Ore, like the story about his parents the night before. Not to mention the fact that they slept together each night.

Ore had thought those things meant something.

He was such a fool.

Cash prowled forward, closing the distance between them. Ore wanted to move back, but he refused to shrink away. He wasn't some prey animal to Cash's predator. Lifting his chin, he met that faintly glowing gaze.

"You don't have to explain," he said tightly. "I understand."

"No, you don't," Cash growled at him. "If it were just up to me, I'd tell you, Ore. You have to know that."

He wanted to believe that was true, but the *protect the pack* excuse didn't really work. "I thought that was true, but this Caden person isn't even a part of this pack, and you're still refusing to tell me about him." He shrugged, trying to look less upset than he truly was, though he knew his scent had to still be spewing his emotions everywhere. "So no, I don't think you'd tell me. I'm surprised you've shared anything with me since you trust me so little."

Cash's teeth ground together. "He's Liam's family. That makes him off-limits."

"It's not like it's a secret!" Ore exploded, waving a hand toward the kitchen door. "Fern knows about it. You obviously know. This isn't some deep, dark secret only the family knows about to protect him. You just don't want *me* to know. You don't trust *me* with the information."

"Ore—"

"Let's just go," he said, all his anger from before already starting to drain away. It hurt that he would trust Cash with his life, but the panther didn't feel the same. "You can just drop me at the Alpha House. I'll wait out the rest of my amnesia there."

Cash darted forward, and Ore jerked back, his instincts pointing out that cats ate birds all the time. His back hit the wall, but Cash kept coming until there was only an inch of air left between them. His body filled with a syrupy heat as he craned his head back to look up, and up, and up into Cash's face.

"That's not happening, little bit," he rumbled, planting his forearms on the wall above Ore's head. "You don't fly away the second you get pissed at me."

Ore tried to slow his breathing, his pulse thumping in his ears. "You hurt my feelings."

"I know," he said, leaning down and running his nose up the side of his face. "I'm sorry. I know you aren't some spy, but until you get your memories back, I *can't* share certain things with you. It doesn't matter how I feel. I have to protect my pack."

Ore swallowed. "How do you feel?"

A soft noise filled the air around them, almost too quiet for Ore's ears to pick up. It took him a second to realize what it was, and then his damn heart melted, all his frustration and bruised feelings drifting away.

Cash was purring. For *him*.

"Terrified, little bit. You terrify me in the most exhilarating way possible."

"I'll only be fifteen minutes," Ore pleaded, giving Cash his best smile.

His big cat pressed his lips together in that way that meant he wanted to smile but didn't want Ore to know how adorable he found him. "Fifteen, and then home."

Home.

Ore nodded and raced inside the bookstore, floating on a cloud of happiness. Cash's words from Fern's house were still echoing in his ears, and he couldn't wait to see if he could get him to purr for him again. Maybe without Fern listening from the next room. The wink she'd thrown him as they'd gotten ready to leave had made him blush like a teenager.

He knew all their problems weren't magically solved just because he *terrified* the big, bad Enforcer, but they didn't feel as scary as they had before their cozy little chat. He didn't have answers to any of his questions, but he felt less alone than he had before.

Because he was Cash's *little bit*.

Sighing happily, he nearly skipped through the store, looking for the romance section. The woman behind the counter smiled at him, so he waved but didn't stop. He wondered if she was the owner. She looked like she was in her forties or fifties, despite her graying hair being braided into pigtails. Big square pink glasses took up most of her face and matched her lipstick perfectly.

He saw a man in his sixties in the historical fiction section —yuck—and a guy his own age bent over to check some books near the bottom along the back wall of the whole store that made up the Research and Spellwork area. On the far side of the store, he finally found the shelves dedicated to romance novels and began searching for something to occupy him in the afternoons when Cash was usually busy on the phone or his computer with pack stuff.

Cash was next door getting something to drink and would want to go as soon as he was finished, so Ore knew he didn't have time to read the backs of all of the books. Instead, he searched for authors he knew and picked a few to look at more closely.

He had it narrowed down to two when he felt someone moving closer to him. Glancing up, he found the young guy from the research area grinning at him. He was maybe only a couple of inches taller than Ore, his loose curls styled in a way that looked effortless. What grabbed and held Ore's attention, though, were his striking violet eyes. They were beautiful.

And full of humor.

"You're new," the guy said, propping an elbow on the shelf next to him and planting his head on his fist. "I didn't think they got new people here."

Ore inhaled subtly, surprised to find not only was the man

human but there wasn't a trace of magic on him. "I'm just... visiting."

Dark, perfectly shaped brows arched at him. "Visiting who?"

"Um. Who are you?"

"Oh shit." The guy laughed, slapping the shelf he was leaning on and straightening. "Sorry. I'm Robbie Amato."

Ore cocked his head. "I didn't realize Alpha Amato had a mate." The lion's scent was barely perceptible to his nose, but it was there. "I'm Ore. I... Well, it's hard to explain actu—"

"Wait, hold on." Robbie stepped closer and waved his hands. "We're going to get back to you in just one sec, but I need to have a little freak-out first over the fact you thought I was mated to my uncle Liam." Robbie shuddered exaggeratedly, turning in a tight circle and shaking his arms out. "Ew, ew, ew."

Ore couldn't hold in his laughter. "Sorry. I just assumed."

"Since I'm human?" Robbie nodded. "You really are new here. My dad is Uncle Liam's older brother, but they're technically only *step*brothers."

"So your dad is human too?" He hoped Cash wasn't about to pop up and catch him talking to someone about Liam's family again. If he did, Ore would be able to at least defend himself since Robbie had approached him. He was just an innocent bystander.

"Yup. My mom is too, but I don't actually know her." He shrugged like that wasn't a big deal, but Ore didn't really buy it. He didn't say anything though, figuring that'd be a fantastic way to end a conversation that could potentially get him some answers.

"Fern was just telling me a little about your dad's new mate," Ore said, subtly checking to make sure there was no sign of his big, scowly panther. "About what happened to him before he met your dad, I guess."

Robbie's face wrinkled in confusion. "Why?"

"She thinks I might have been at the same place he was," he admitted. "That's why I'm here, actually. When I got here—"

"Oh my god, wait." Robbie held up both hands, nearly slapping Ore across the face. "Whoops, sorry. But you can't just drop something like that and expect me not to react! You were held by those people who made Caden fight like a damn gladiator?"

Ore's jaw dropped. "What? Seriously?"

"I thought you just said you were there too!"

"I can't remember anything," he explained quickly, setting his books aside. "I flew into the territory about a week ago, and when I woke up, I had no memory of who I was or what had happened to me. I only knew my name and that I was an eagle shifter."

Robbie's violet eyes went huge at his speedy explanation. "Holy shit. You don't remember anything about your life or family?"

Twisting his lips, Ore shook his head. "Nothing. Fern and Pops say it'll come back, but nothing yet."

"That's crazy," Robbie whispered, studying Ore like he'd told him he could sprout a second head. "Why does she think you were in the same place Caden was then?"

He shrugged. "I guess because she thinks this virus they gave me that almost killed me was done by someone experimenting? She didn't really get a chance to explain before we were interrupted."

Robbie grabbed onto Ore's arm and gave it a shake. "Oh fuck, that's right. He told my dad they would bring him into a room and experiment on him. My dad only gave me the bare minimum of details about what happened, but I sweet-talked one of his men into telling me more. They injected him with a bunch of different stuff, but none of it took, I guess. He's perfectly healthy now."

"Now?"

103

Robbie shook his head. "Whole other story. I'll tell you later."

Ore smiled. He liked the idea of them talking more, maybe even becoming friends. Other than getting interrogated by Alpha Amato, no one had exactly been outright hostile to him, but Robbie was the first person his age who seemed actually interested in getting to know him. Well, other than Cash, but his interest wasn't friendship based.

At least Ore hoped not.

"I am kind of surprised Uncle Liam is just letting you wander around by yourself though," Robbie added. "Everyone is usually pretty—" He leaned closer and whispered. "—*uptight* about strangers."

Ore snorted. *Understatement.* "Oh, I'm not allowed out by myself. Cash is next door grabbing a drink, and then we'll head back to his house."

"Cash Grumpypants Lawson?" Robbie's eyebrows shot up. "And you're staying at his *house*?"

Cheeks heating, Ore nodded and smiled. "Yeah. He volunteered so I wouldn't have to stay in the basement of the Alpha House."

A huge grin spread across Robbie's face. "You're blushing!"

"Shh!" Ore slapped his hands to his face to try and cover the evidence. He hurried to the end of the shelf and glanced around to see if anyone was paying attention to them, and the older man who'd been on the other side of the store was now examining a display on a table near the front. His eyes were on the books, but there was a sneer on his face.

Stomach dropping, Ore ducked behind the shelf. He highly doubted the man was disgusted by the display that appeared to be featuring books written by authors from Kansas.

Robbie was watching him, smile fading. "Sorry."

Ore shook his head. "No, it's fine. I just don't want anyone to get the wrong idea and think badly about Cash. He's just helping out while I'm here."

Did he raise his voice a smidge when he said that? Yes.

Did his stomach sour at the words? He wasn't telling.

Robbie grabbed his arm and gave it a squeeze, his face sympathetic. When he stepped back, his voice was completely normal as he said, "Did you find anything good to read?"

Thankful, Ore grabbed the two books he'd been debating and showed them to him. They slowly made their way toward the front, talking books and authors. He got so caught up in the conversation and Robbie's funny reactions to things he somehow missed the way one of the front table displays had the end of a stand sticking out over the edge.

One minute, they were walking along, debating the believability of alien races being biologically compatible with humans in sci-fi romances, and the next, he'd whacked his hip on the wooden corner, a sharp pain shooting through him as the large stand wobbled.

"Shit!" Robbie yelled, jumping forward to help and slamming into Ore.

He tried to regain his balance, arms windmilling, but with Robbie's extra weight, he couldn't get his feet firmly beneath him. In what felt like slow motion, he fell backward, Robbie's violet eyes huge and about three inches from his face, and crashed into the unstable book display.

He grunted as his back hit the top of the table, his stomach swooping as it wobbled beneath them. Thank the goddess, it held. The wooden display stand?

Not as lucky.

Robbie pushed himself up, somehow kneeing Ore in the thigh in the process, and they both turned to stare in horror at the broken pieces of wood and strewn-around books. Some of them looked fine, but others had landed under the stand or at odd angles. He saw at least three with torn dust jackets.

"Oh my goddess!" a female voice shouted. The woman

from behind the counter hurried over to them, her eyes enormous behind her pink glasses. "Are you alright?"

"We're so sorry, Ginny," Robbie said quickly, dropping to his knees next to the mess.

"So very, very sorry," Ore reiterated, a little slower getting up as his hip and back still ached. "I'm not sure what happened…"

He was, but he didn't want to blame her display for the mishap. If he'd been paying attention to where he was going—

"Fucking hind toe." The snarled words were dripping with disdain. The older man from before was staring at Ore, his eyes glowing and lips curled back from his teeth.

The bookstore owner—Ginny—gasped at the slur, but Ore just stared at him in shock, nausea rolling through his stomach. Robbie, still on his knees as he sorted through the mess, jerked his head up to look back and forth between the shifters around him.

"What did you call him?"

Ginny held up her hand. "Do not repeat it, Billy. You need to get out. Right now."

"You're kicking me out?" Billy snarled, eyes still locked on Ore. "What about him? His kind isn't welcome here! I don't care who he's fucking for special treatment. I'll drag him out of our territory myself if I—*mph*!"

Ore jumped, eyes darting up to the looming Enforcer behind Billy. Cash's hand firmly planted on his mouth, he dragged Billy back until he was pressed against his wide chest. His mouth lowered next to Billy's ear, a low, dangerous rumble filling the air.

"What the fuck did you just say to him?"

106

CHAPTER 10

B illy Fucking Mittin.

Cash did his best to rein in his panther, but his anger was boiling inside him, looking for an outlet. How *dare* he talk to Ore like that? He'd known there would be some wariness from pack members who weren't used to strangers in their territory. But this?

Calling Ore that slur and then threatening to drag him out of their territory?

He wouldn't stand for it.

Billy struggled against him, and Cash growled louder, his panther right beneath his skin, ready to break free at the slightest provocation.

"Alright, let's everyone take a breath."

Cash looked over at Saint, confused for a second as to why he was there. As Billy stopped fighting to be free, his rage started to settle a bit, and he remembered how he'd been talking to his friend next door at the café. Someone had opened the door, and the scent of Ore's pain had trickled in on the air, pulling him away without a second's hesitation. He hadn't even realized Saint had followed him into Ginny's bookstore.

His friend's eyes were locked on him, but he was calm, completely in control. His scent was spiked with anger, but Cash knew it wasn't directed toward him. He wanted to tell him to back off, that he'd handle Billy, but he couldn't get the words out. His panther was too close to the surface, his fangs and claws fully on display. If he opened his mouth to speak again, all he'd let out would be a roar of anger.

Unlike Saint, he was the furthest thing from in control.

Ginny took a step forward, straightening her glasses as she tiptoed around the mess on the floor. "I'm glad you two are here," she said. "I asked Billy to leave, and he was refusing."

"We heard," Saint assured her, his eyes darting over to Ore, and Cash's attention followed.

Ore was still standing next to the now empty table, one hand rubbing at his hip. All of the color had leached out of his face, giving him a pale, sickly look as he stared at Cash with wide eyes. Fuck, his fear was still scenting the air, eating at what little grip Cash had left on his cat.

Liam's nephew, Robbie, was kneeling on the floor, looking confused and pissed as hell. "I don't know what just happened exactly, but that guy was being a real douchenozzle."

A hysterical giggle popped out of Ore's mouth before he slapped a hand over it. That, more than anything, began to lessen the rage boiling inside Cash. The sound was a reminder that while he was freaked out, Ore was fine. He wasn't hurt, and he was safe.

"Cash," Saint said, drawing his attention away from his little bird and back over to him. "Why don't you let Billy go, and I'll bring him to Alpha Amato?"

He quirked his eyebrows in a way that said, "Let me handle this before you accidentally rip this guy's throat out," and he wasn't completely wrong. If Billy said one more hateful thing, made one more threat against Ore, then Cash didn't know what he would do, and that was a little terrifying for him.

Where was his legendary discipline now? He didn't let his cat control him, and yet the more he was around Ore, the looser his grip on his panther seemed to get.

Saint nodded at him once when he saw that Cash was hesitating and took a step forward. "I got this, brother."

Reluctantly, Cash removed his hand from Billy's mouth and then shoved him unceremoniously into Saint. The older lion stumbled and fell against his chest, quickly righting himself.

He whipped around and glared at Cash. "How dare you put your hands on me like that. You really are just like your awful parents, aren't you?"

He spat the words at Cash, hands fisted at his sides, but he didn't make a move to challenge Cash. Billy knew where he fell in the pack, and it wasn't anywhere near the top, but the words were like a blow to Cash's gut. Not being like his parents had been one of his few goals in life, the reason he kept such a tight hold on himself.

Instead of showing that he'd struck a nerve, Cash bared his teeth and released a low, menacing hiss, taking a single step forward.

The lion jerked back so fast he bumped into Saint, who grabbed his arms and turned him toward the door.

"Let's go, Mittin," Saint grumbled. "Before you can get yourself into even more trouble."

As they went out the door of the bookstore, Billy's raised voice could be heard, complaining about the fact that he was in any trouble at all, claiming he'd done nothing wrong and that he had every right to—

The door shut behind him, muffling the sound. Thank the goddess. He'd never liked the man that much before, but he'd had no idea just how awful of a person he really was. Now that he'd shown his true colors, it would be up to Liam to decide what to do with him.

Cash forced himself to take a deep breath in and let it out slowly before he turned back to the trio. Ginny was staring at him with big eyes, her hands wringing in front of her. Robbie had stepped back next to Ore, his stance protective, and it eased a little more of the tension inside Cash, knowing that others could see what a good person Ore was and would be watchful around him.

Though he wasn't sure what the little human thought he would do against a shifter. Knowing Robbie's father, he supposed the kid probably had a few tricks up his sleeve.

"Your dad know you're here?" he asked, his voice barely more than a rumble still.

Robbie rolled his eyes at him, hands on his hips and sass in full swing. "Of course not. He thinks I'm visiting Yosemite with a couple of friends."

Cash shook his head but didn't comment. It wasn't his business why Liam's nephew visited their pack regularly without letting his father know what he was doing. It wasn't his family. It wasn't his human to take care of. And he definitely wasn't going to tell Quinten Amato his kid was mixed up with their coven doing who knew what.

He valued his life a little too much.

He ran his eyes over Ore's body once more to check for injuries, but he appeared to be all in one piece, a little of the color returning to his face.

Taking in the knocked-over display, he looked over at Ginny. "Any books that are damaged, I'll pay for."

"Oh, no. That's fine," she started to say, waving a hand at him. Her scent was nervous still, making him realize that despite how often he came into the shop, she was intimidated after she'd seen him nearly lose his shit.

He hid his grimace. "No, I insist."

"Well. Then, you should at least take them with you," she

said, crouching on the floor and picking up a few of the books that look untarnished, stacking them on the table.

Robbie dropped back down and started helping her, the two making quick work of separating the books that had tears or bent covers and pages from those that seemed fine. Cash left them to it, stepping around the mess and over to Ore. He put a hand on his elbow and guided him a few feet away.

When Ore wouldn't meet his gaze, he dipped his head to catch his eyes and said softly, "Are you alright?"

Ore nodded, glancing away. "Yeah, it was just an accident. I'm fine."

Cash cupped his chin and tilted his face up so that he couldn't avoid him. "I don't care about the fucking books. Are *you* okay?"

Ore sucked in a shuddery breath, his eyes glistening for a second before he blinked a few times. He cleared his throat. "I'm fine, Cash. I just wasn't expecting to hear that."

"You shouldn't have had to hear that shit," Cash said, his panther getting riled up all over again. To soothe himself and Ore, he shifted his hand to the side of his neck and rubbed his scent into his skin. Ore's eyes got wide, but he didn't pull away. "I'll make sure that Liam deals with it."

He didn't know what his alpha would do. It wasn't exactly a banishable offense, especially not for someone like Billy, who had lived in Silver Oak his entire life. But if he was that comfortable throwing hateful slurs toward someone just because they weren't a feline shifter, Cash couldn't see Liam tolerating shit like that long term.

Either way, he'd be following up with Billy and making sure he understood he was never to go anywhere near Ore again.

Or he wouldn't live to regret it.

"I CAN'T BELIEVE you had to buy all these books because of me," Ore said, setting down the stack he was carrying on the kitchen table.

Cash set his own next to him and shrugged. "They'll get read."

Ore shot him a smile and shook his head. "That's not the point. I can't even repay you. I don't have any money."

Silly little bird.

Clasping the back of his neck, Cash gave him a squeeze. "Even if you did, I wouldn't let you. You heard Ginny. She told her wife that display was too wide for that table and warned her something like this would happen."

He wasn't sure that was completely true, but he'd appreciated her making the effort to lessen Ore's guilt. The display had been a bunch of viral books, so even though most weren't his preferred genres, he knew he'd still read them.

Ore shrugged casually, but he leaned into Cash's touch a little. "Still, if I'd been paying attention instead of focused on talking with Robbie…"

"I'm glad you two are becoming friends," he said, changing the subject as he rubbed a small circle in the dip just behind Ore's jaw. "He can be a little wild though, so be careful. I don't want you two getting into more trouble every time you're together."

He'd meant it as a tease, but Ore was solemn as he said, "We won't. I'm usually much more careful, I'm sure."

Shaking his head, Cash gave him one more squeeze and then headed out of the kitchen. "I'm sure you are. Now, quit worrying."

He dipped into the back bedroom and changed into a pair of worn sweats, not bothering with a shirt, before going straight for his favorite spot on the couch in the living room. Grabbing the remote, he flopped into the corner of the sectional.

After getting so worked up at the bookstore, he needed to

just chill for a while. Usually he'd go for a run, stretch his legs until he was exhausted and his head was clear, but he knew he wouldn't be able to get very far with Ore upset and alone.

He told himself that he could trust his pack, but after what had happened, he wasn't so sure about that anymore. Most of his packmates, sure, he knew Ore would be perfectly safe with them. But he knew Billy wasn't alone in his beliefs, and while it'd be easy to spot most of the ones who weren't okay with Ore's presence in their territory, it was the ones who he couldn't guess felt the same way that had him worried. If given the chance, how many of his packmates would try and drive Ore out just like Billy had?

Not being able to answer that question meant he'd be relaxing in front of the TV, not gallivanting through the woods.

A voice in the back of his head reminded him that as soon as Ore had his memories back, he'd be leaving anyway, but Cash ignored it, flipping on reruns of some old sitcom and settling deeper into the corner of the big couch.

If some mindless TV didn't help, he'd shift and go lie on his pallet upstairs to catch some afternoon sunshine. The soft sounds of Ore moving around were even more soothing than the show, and Cash ended up focusing on that instead of whatever had the laugh track going off every ten seconds. Ore muttered to himself as he carried some books upstairs about how disorganized his shelves were, and he grinned, wondering how long it would take before he went up for a new batch of clean clothes and found everything rearranged.

His eyes were mostly closed, his panther content with Ore safe in their home, when Ore's whisper-soft tread came into the living room. His lids were heavier than he expected, making him wonder if he'd actually dozed off for a minute.

Ore came around the other end of the couch, and Cash bit back a groan. Fuck, he'd changed back into one of Cash's shirts when he was upstairs, his legs bare beneath it. His

113

panther rumbled happily, and his dick took notice. He probably should have left his jeans on. If he started sporting a hard-on, there would be no way to hide it in his sweats.

The line he'd been straddling for days, reminding himself over and over again that Ore was only there temporarily and yet drawn to him in a way that grew harder to withstand with each passing minute, disappeared the second Ore climbed onto the couch right next to him, legs folded beneath him and the scent of arousal wafting off him. After their fight at Fern's and then how fiercely he'd reacted to Billy's threat had broken down the minuscule amount of resistance left inside him.

"What are you watching?" Ore asked, scooting forward a little more so his knees pressed against Cash's hip.

"Nothing, really," Cash said, mouth drier than it had been a minute ago. He offered him the remote. "You can change it if you want."

Ore bit his bottom lip, looking uncertain. Goddess, it took everything in him not to lean over and sink his own teeth into that plump little lip. Clearing his throat, he sat up straighter. He should go and do something, anything. Sitting there with Ore right next to him—draped in his fucking scent and arousal—was pure torture.

"I wanted…" Ore hesitated, looking away.

Instead of scrambling away like he should, he snagged one of Ore's hands from where it was twisting wrinkles into the fabric over his thighs. "Whatever it is, you can tell me."

Clutching at him, Ore sucked in a breath and blurted out, "I want to suck your dick."

A dull roar filled Cash's ears as he blinked at him, clearly having misheard. There was no way he'd heard Ore say—

"Please? I can't stop thinking about it. I wanted to drop to the ground right there in the bookstore."

"What?" Cash finally croaked out. What was happening?

Had he fallen asleep? Was he dreaming about Ore begging to suck his cock?

In the bookstore?

"Before I even had the chance to really be afraid, you were just *there*, protecting me from out of nowhere. And I just... Goddess, that really did it for me, you know?"

He didn't know, but no matter how much his brain couldn't seem to compute what was going on, his dick had zero problems getting on board. And Ore noticed immediately, his sharp eagle eyes darting to his growing erection and staring hungrily at it.

Then, he licked his fucking lips and squirmed in place.

"You're asking to..."

"Suck your dick, yeah." A smile started to grow on Ore's face. "I feel like I might have broken your brain."

"Maybe." He scrubbed at his face and tried to actually focus on what Ore was saying beyond the dick-sucking part. "You know you don't have to thank me like that, right?"

Ore's eyes went wide. "What?"

"I don't expect you to..."

"Suck your dick," Ore supplied, giggling.

"Yeah, that. I don't expect that for protecting you, little bit. You don't have to thank me with sexual favors." He didn't think that was what this was, but he had to be sure. He wanted Ore, desperately, but not like that. Not in a gross, coercive way.

Running his teeth over his bottom lip, Ore huffed a softer laugh and climbed over Cash's leg to settle between his knees. "No, I don't think you expect this. Based on your reaction, I'm wondering if anyone's ever offered you a blowjob before."

Cash narrowed his eyes. "I've gotten blowjobs before."

"Mhm, sure. It's okay, baby. I'll take good care of you." Ore could barely hold a straight face as he crooned that at him, breaking into laughter right after.

Fuck, he was gorgeous when he was so happy.

He waited for Ore to get ahold of himself and meet his eyes once more, a smile still teasing at the corners of that lush mouth. Reclining back against the cushions, he tucked a thumb into the waist of his sweats.

That sobered Ore up in a hurry.

"You know I'll always protect you like that, right?"

A soft look tinged with sadness filled Ore's dark eyes. "I know I'm safe with you while I'm here, yes. You're so protective of everyone, I'm just grateful to get to feel it."

While I'm here.

Cash's panther snarled in protest, but he couldn't force out the words he wanted to scream. *You're not leaving me!* What would be the point? No matter how much either of them might want that, it didn't make it reality.

Shaking off the upsetting thoughts before they could ruin his mood, Cash tugged his waistband down an inch, exposing the top of a tattoo and a smattering of hair. "You want to feel more than my protection though."

A grin blossomed on his face at the cheesy line. "I really do."

"Come here."

Ore tipped forward, going straight for his groin, but Cash stopped him, grabbing his upper arm. "No, up here, little bit. I want to taste that mouth before you taste me."

Sucking in a hitching breath, Ore eased up his body to hover over him. The cocksureness was gone, leaving behind his sweet and shy little bird.

Gently, giving him plenty of time to pull away, Cash threaded his fingers through that soft, wild hair and guided him down, his other hand slipping around Ore's back to hold him steady. His rose-pink lips were just a little damp, and so fucking tempting, calling to Cash like a siren song.

He knew, without a doubt, once he got a taste of his little

bit, there would be no turning back. He couldn't have him and then give him up.

The thought would have been enough to stop him a week ago.

But now?

Cash jumped in with both feet.

He groaned as his mouth slid over Ore's, the softest of touches, and earned him a tiny little whimper. Shit, he wanted all of Ore's noises. Soft and loud. Big and small. Pleading and demanding.

He wanted everything.

Brushing against Ore's lips a few more times, he finally coaxed him into chasing Cash's mouth and then parted his lips to let his bird have a taste. His tongue was tentative, barely slipping inside before retreating, but when Cash mimicked him, doing the same thing to Ore, he got a frustrated sound.

Grinning against his sweet mouth, Cash gave a tiny nip to that bottom lip that had been tempting him for days. Ore gasped and pulled back for a second, gazing down at Cash with blown pupils, the scent of his arousal so thick in the air Cash could taste it on the back of his tongue.

He half expected Ore to scoot back down the couch and get to what he was apparently craving, but instead, he dove forward and slanted their mouths together. Pure pleasure streaked down his spine when Ore just about licked his tonsils.

Much better.

He let Ore explore and lead for a few minutes, relaxing and enjoying how good his little body felt sprawled across his much bigger one. When Ore squirmed against him and he felt a wet patch on the shirt rubbing against his skin, he let go and devoured every inch of Ore's mouth.

When he couldn't stand not touching his bare skin, he grabbed a handful of T-shirt and yanked it up, exposing Ore's perfect, tiny ass. Groaning, he slid his palm over the exquisite handful that was one of his cheeks.

Ore tore his mouth away, both of them panting heavily. "I love your hands on me."

"Me too," he rumbled and refocused on the delicate arch of Ore's neck. He ran his tongue up the slender column and then rubbed his face over as much of his skin as he could reach, wanting his scent so deep in Ore's pores no one would ever doubt who he belonged to.

"But I still want to suck that monster you're poking me with."

Cash coughed out a laugh and gave the cheek in his hand a firm squeeze. "By all means, help yourself."

He'd barely gotten the words out, and Ore was wiggling down his front to lie between his spread thighs. His shirt was scrunched up under his arms, but he didn't seem to notice, snagging the edge of Cash's waistband and tugging it down.

As soon as his cock was fully exposed, Ore seemed to lose focus, leaving his sweats tangled around the tops of his thighs as he stared at what he'd uncovered.

Smirking, Cash tucked a hand behind his head and let him have his fill of looking. He knew he wasn't a small man by any measure, both long and thick with a mushroom-capped head that looked obscene it was such a dark red and dripping with precome.

When Ore just stayed frozen, Cash decided to give him a hand. He gripped the wide base and pointed the end toward Ore's slack mouth. "What happened to all that big talk about needing to suck me?"

"That was before I saw the baseball bat you had between your legs."

He snorted and gave himself a quick, firm stroke. "Don't be scared."

Ore rolled his eyes, but there was a hint of a smile tugging at his lips. "I'm not scared. I'm... Okay, I'm a little nervous. You've got the biggest dick I've ever seen."

"How do you know?" Cash arched a brow at him.

"Statistics." Then, he opened wide and waited for Cash to feed him his cock.

Shuddering, he eased the tip past his lips, not wanting to go too far too fast, but Ore wasn't having it. With a soft moan, he latched his mouth around Cash's shaft and licked and sucked all the precome off him.

"Fuck," Cash muttered, unable to look away from Ore's dreamy face as he dropped down until he gagged himself. "Easy, little bit. Don't hurt yourself."

Sucking hard, Ore pulled back up, eyes half-lidded and cheeks flushed. He held Cash's gaze for a second with just the tip once again in his mouth, and a shot of arousal hit him like a kick to the gut at the gorgeous sight.

Ore hummed softly, then grabbed at Cash's free hand and led it to the back of his head.

Groaning, Cash gently gripped the soft strands of his wild hair. "You're so hungry for it, aren't you?"

He nodded as best he could before sinking back down. He went slower that time, taking even more of Cash's cock into his mouth before stopping and dragging his lips back up. Popping off the end, he dove down deeper between Cash's thighs, licking and sucking at his balls as best he could.

"Pull my sweats down more," he rasped out, releasing his cock and trying to tug at the material keeping his legs trapped together.

Ore made a little whimpering noise before darting backward and dragging the gray material with him, tossing them over his shoulder as soon as Cash's legs were free. His T-shirt joined the sweats a second later, and Cash let himself truly appreciate Ore's nakedness for the first time. His olive skin was flawless, his limbs soft instead of toned, and he was fucking tiny *everywhere*.

His little cock was erect but probably only about the length of Cash's thumb. He wasn't surprised—he knew bird shifters took after their animal sides in that aspect—but he hadn't known how much he'd like it. He was so much bigger in every way, and that *did it* for him.

Ore laid his hands on the inside of Cash's thighs—they looked so small and delicate against his thick, hairy legs—and gave a slight push, encouraging him to spread wider. Biting his lip, he stared at Cash's dick and sac with open hunger. "Perfect."

"You're the perfect one."

Ore flashed him a shy smile, then practically threw himself back down over Cash's groin. But he didn't make contact with anything, hovering above his weeping cock and staring up at Cash.

It took his lust-soaked brain too long to figure out what he was waiting for.

He slipped his fingers back into his hair and grabbed hold. "That what you want, little bit? You want me in control?"

Ore made a soft sound of pleasure and nodded.

"Whatever you want," he said, wondering if Ore understood that he meant it as more than a promise during sex. That he'd literally burn the world down to get Ore whatever he wanted in it.

He should probably save declarations like that until he knew what the future would hold for them. He had no right to make a promise he wasn't sure he could keep.

But that would be tomorrow's problem.

In that moment, all he cared about was how horny his little bird was over Cash protecting him. Hell, he'd bared his damn teeth at a packmate for him and would do it again.

He wasn't sure there was a single thing he wouldn't do for Ore, and that terrified him.

Focusing on those plump lips inches from his cock, Cash used his hold on his hair to guide Ore's mouth back down to his balls. "Use your tongue, but be gentle. They're really sensitive."

Ore followed his directions beautifully, licking over every centimeter of his sac and ratcheting Cash's pleasure higher and higher. When he tightened his hold unintentionally after Ore hit a particularly good spot, Ore moaned loudly, nuzzling closer. He worked Cash over until he was dripping wet, and he could feel the spit running down to his ass.

Groaning, he pulled Ore up to his shaft. He had to clear his throat before he could talk, his gut tight with arousal. "Ready to tame the monster?"

Ore snorted and grinned. "Ready to worship it more like."

Fuck. The things his bird said. He never held anything back, leaving himself vulnerable and driving Cash's protective instincts wild.

Running his thumb over Ore's lower lip, he hummed in approval. "Start at the base, and don't miss an inch. Once you reach the top, wrap that beautiful mouth around me. Understand?"

Nodding, Ore locked his eyes on his cock like it was the prize he was determined to win at a carnival. He didn't waste a second, moving forward before Cash could use his hold to direct him. Grinning, Cash leaned back and decided he'd just enjoy the visual of Ore's pert little ass sticking up in the air and his perfect lips kissing all over his cock, followed by tiny kitten licks.

He kept his hand in Ore's hair, but he let his bird do what he wanted and used the grip on the soft strands to let him know when he'd hit a good spot.

Fuck, they all felt like good spots with Ore.

It was a struggle to keep his eyes open, his bones and muscles liquefying as his desire drove higher and higher. Everything but them got hazy, nothing mattering beyond the couch. The house could be on fire, and he doubted he'd notice.

The air around them filled with heat and the soft, wet sounds Ore made as he did exactly what he'd said: worshiped Cash's cock. The scent of his bird's arousal was thick in the air, and he sucked in heaving breaths to take as much into his body as he could, wanting to be scented by it from the inside out.

The second those lips wrapped around him again, Cash cursed and struggled to hold his claws at bay, his panther just beneath the surface and wanting Ore just as much as Cash did.

He'd never felt anything so good, like he was knocking on the door to heaven or seeing the face of the goddess. It was probably sacrilegious to compare a mind-blowing blowjob to meeting a deity, but he *so* did not care. Ore was touching his damn soul as he attempted to suck his brains out through his dick.

He was just that good.

"Goddess, I fucking knew your mouth would feel like perfection, little bit."

Ore moaned and took in even more of him, hitting the back of his throat and powering through. Cash grunted, fighting back the urge to shove his hips upward and drive all the way in. He sagged back down as heat rippled up his spine while Ore dragged his lips up to the tip, flicking his tongue to hit all the good spots.

And on and on it went. Ore destroyed him, and Cash enjoyed every damn second of it.

It took him almost too long to realize he'd reached the edge and was about to teeter over, so lost to the feel of Ore's wet mouth and grasping fingers on his hips. Right as the base of his spine started to tighten, he tugged his bird off his cock and groaned at the sight of his swollen and red lips.

"What's wrong?" he asked breathlessly, swiping a wrist over his wet chin.

"I'm about to come." He sounded like he'd smoked two packs a day for the last twenty years.

"Isn't that the point?" Ore grinned at him, trying to inch closer.

Not wanting to pull his hair too hard, Cash used his other hand to grip his cute little pointed chin. "Not in your mouth. I need to scent you."

Ore's dark brown eyes started to glow with excitement. "Okay."

He guided him up over his body, stealing a lingering kiss that had Ore humping against his stomach by the end. As soon as he broke apart, he patted the couch next to him where it extended out in the other half of the L. "Lay down here."

Pausing only to nip at the edge of Cash's jaw, Ore scrambled over him and stretched out on his belly. His perfect little ass was right there, drawing Cash to it like a bear to honey. He gripped each tiny cheek and spread him apart, then gave a quick swipe over his hole, promising himself he'd devote hours there sometime soon.

Ore moaned and arched his back. "Oooh goddess."

Smirking, Cash leaned back and tapped his hip. "Another time, little bit. Flip over for me."

He whimpered in disappointment but did as Cash asked without hesitation, and then he was laid out before him like a damn buffet. With his feet flat on the cushion beneath him, he let his legs fall to the sides, running his hands up his slim torso, taking a moment to touch the sides of his neck before stretching his arms above his head.

"Leave your scent all over me, baby."

Cash snarled and dove forward, going right for one of those tantalizing light brown nipples. Clamping his lips around it, he teased him, using his tongue and teeth and not quite enough suction. Ore squirmed beneath him, gasping and moaning as he arched his chest to try and get more.

123

Tugging on the tip with his teeth, he purred with pleasure at Ore's hoarse shout. "So needy."

Ore clamped his legs around his waist and nodded wildly. "For you. Just for you."

"Fucking right." He kissed his way up to Ore's neck and ran his tongue up the side, groaning as that sweet, floral scent hit his taste buds and hit him like he'd chugged a bottle of shifter liquor.

He worked a hand between them and gripped his throbbing cock. Within a couple of strokes, he was right back at the edge, ready to soak his little bird in come. He nuzzled into his neck a little longer, not quite ready to give it up, but when his balls drew up and his release was *right there*, he forced himself to give one more lick and then pull away.

Ore was completely blissed-out, eyes cloudy with lust and pupils nearly swallowing his irises. His flush went from his cheeks down to his chest, which was heaving with his panting breaths.

He looked fucking wrecked.

Cash squeezed the base of his cock, trying to hold on until he was in position, but goddess, it was hard. Just the sight of his little bird so undone from giving Cash a blowjob and getting scented had his eyes glowing and claws tingling just under the surface, wanting to pop out.

"You're so gorgeous," Cash murmured, shuffling forward until his knees were almost touching Ore's ass. "It almost hurts to look at you, you're so beautiful."

"Cash…" Ore said softly, biting at his still-swollen lip.

"It's true, but I'm going to get you messy now."

He sucked in a breath, eyes darting down to Cash's cock, the tip almost purple. "Do it. Please."

He did. It only took another handful of rough pulls, and then his come started shooting out. He cupped his other hand over the tip to catch some before letting the rest hit Ore's dark red little cock. He groaned, long and loud, as it just kept coming, more than he'd ever released before. Every muscle in his body tensed, and he strained to get out the last few drops, pointing his dick at Ore's hole, just barely visible in the furrow between his cheeks.

Then, he went to work.

Using the pool he'd caught in his hand, he started at Ore's neck, dragging his palm down each side and leaving a trail of his seed behind. Ore threw his head back, exposing more skin for him and moaning loudly.

He spread the rest over Ore's flat pecs before focusing on where most of his spend had landed.

Meticulously, he rubbed his come into Ore's skin from hip to hip and then down the crease between his groin and thigh to his ass, working two fingers between his cheeks and stroking over his hole.

Ore's mouth fell open, his hips rising off the couch.

"Like that, little bit?"

"More, *please*."

"So pretty when you beg for me," he growled, then sank one of his thick fingers into that tiny hole.

Crying out, two thin ropes of come shot from Ore's cock. Cash snarled and ducked down, sucking a little more from his tiny dick and then licking the streams off his low abs so they didn't cover Cash's scent. Ore melted into the couch, mewling softly as Cash used the tips of his fingers to rub what was left of his seed over Ore's dick and balls.

"Sensitive," Ore whined, squirming away.

Cash grunted, but he stopped, leaning down and breathing in Ore's skin, covered in his scent. Then, he moved up his chest to his neck, sighing contentedly at how much like *his* he smelled.

"Happy?" Ore murmured, wrapping his arms around Cash and drawing him down.

He shifted to the side so he didn't squish his little bit, tugging until Ore turned toward him and snuggled into his chest. He ran his delicate fingers over the lines, ridges, and bulges covering Cash's much bigger body, hypnotizing him with the gentle touches.

"Mmm, very." His eyes got heavy, falling shut just as he realized the TV was still on, another episode of the same show playing in the background. He'd turn it off... after a nap.

He pulled the blanket folded over the back of the couch down over them, not wanting Ore to get chilly, then let out a slow breath and relaxed into the softness of the cushions.

"Good," Ore whispered, pressing a sweet kiss to his throat. "Me too."

CHAPTER 11

"Are you sure it's okay that I'm coming with you?"

Ore turned to face Cash as he drove them through Silver Oak. The little town looked so quaint and adorable, but after the incident at the bookstore the other day, he was nervous about meeting more pack members. Whereas before, he couldn't wait to get outside the four walls of Cash's house, now he considered it a sanctuary. He knew not everyone in the pack would be like that Billy guy had been, but he *knew* he would be safe at Cash's, so why risk it?

Cash reached over and laid one of his big hands on Ore's thigh, giving it a squeeze. He didn't even look away from the road as he did it, completely calm and unconcerned, but that touch ignited Ore's body and sent heat coursing through him. A problem he'd been having more and more of since the thank-you blowjob on the couch.

He'd kind of thought things would change between them after that, and they had… to a certain extent. Cash definitely touched him more—a light brush against his neck here, a grab of his ass there—but they hadn't done anything intimate since the couch, and it was making Ore wonder whether he had read the situation wrong. It seemed like Cash and his panther enjoyed having Ore around, and he'd definitely enjoyed the blowjob—especially the part where he'd finished on Ore's dick and then rubbed his come into his skin.

There was something growing between them, something that Ore and his eagle really liked and wanted to explore more of, but other than the extra touching and occasional scenting, things hadn't changed that much. Ore had waited the last two nights for Cash to make some sort of move, to press Ore into the mattress and really get his scent into Ore's pores again.

But the damn cat would just lie there like always, one arm draped casually over Ore, and fall asleep like it was nothing.

Maybe Ore really was reading the situation wrong?

But then he remembered the way Cash would purr for him sometimes and stare at him with eyes full of heat and longing. He had a feeling it wasn't that his big panther wasn't interested, but something *was* holding him back, something beyond his own feelings.

He told Ore the other day that he hadn't had a serious relationship in a long time, so he didn't think it was a recent breakup hampering things. It could be because of what had happened with his parents, he supposed. They hadn't really talked about it since the night he had told Ore about how they'd abandoned him like the pieces of shit that they were. That could definitely mess a person up—though he wasn't sure why it would affect how he felt or what he did with Ore.

The other reason—one that would be even more difficult to overcome than childhood trauma—was the possibility that it didn't matter how Cash felt or whether or not they had any sort of chance of a future together because it didn't change the fact that Ore would be forced to leave as soon as he was able.

And maybe once Ore got his memories back, he'd want to, but the more time he spent with his protective Enforcer—and the couple of people he'd met that seemed nice, like Saint and

Robbie—the less likely it seemed that he had some better life out there just waiting for him to get back to it.

Even if he had a nice life—a great job, family that was missing him, friends he enjoyed hanging out with—did that mean he *had* to sacrifice what he'd found in Silver Oak?

He knew the pack was only cat shifters, but... surely they would make an exception if someone mated with a non-cat.

Right?

"Everything's going to be fine," Cash said, giving Ore's thigh a pat and jarring him out of his thoughts.

For a second, he wasn't sure how Cash had known what he'd been worried about, and then he realized he was referring to Ore's concern about coming with him to the lake. He shook off his depressing thoughts and focused on their plans for the day.

"It's just that I don't want anyone to get upset that I'm there," Ore said, picking at one of his fingernails and gazing at Cash's strong profile.

"No one's going to get upset," Cash assured him. "And if they do, I'll deal with it."

Ore bit the inside of his cheek to hold back his response. It wasn't that he hadn't really appreciated the way Cash had handled Billy. He'd made that *very* clear, he thought. But the fact was, Cash shouldn't *have* to handle his own packmates on Ore's behalf. He shouldn't have to defend him against them either. The last thing Ore wanted was to make Cash's life and job as an Enforcer more difficult.

If his presence really was going to be that troublesome, maybe he *should* leave.

Goddess, he really, really didn't want to.

"Besides," Cash continued, unaware of the dark turn to Ore's thoughts, "it's mostly just the cubs and then a handful of adults."

Ore cocked his head. "Like... all of the cubs in the pack come?"

Cash shrugged. "All the ones that can walk on their own, yeah. Especially when the weather's nice. In the winter, we don't get to swim in the lake, but we usually either go for a run in the woods or play on the playground, something to give their parents a few hours of peace and quiet."

Ore's heart lurched, and he wasn't sure if he was going to have a heart attack or swoon. Goddess, the man was a big softy. He could be so serious—even a little grumpy sometimes —but then he did things like hang out with the pack cubs so their parents could have a break.

He wanted to throw himself against Cash and show him just how much he loved his softer side. Somehow, he managed to hold himself back, gripping the seat belt where it crossed over his chest.

"And you go every week?"

"Yeah, I enjoy spending time with the cubs. They're a lot more fun than most adults." He shot Ore a wry grin as he stopped at a stop sign in the dead center of town.

The place was so small it didn't have a single stoplight, and—Billy Mittin notwithstanding—Ore really did like it. It felt... peaceful and safe, the way it was isolated, giving protection from other packs and humans. The pack could just be themselves there—run in the woods, swim in the lake, shift when and wherever they wanted.

When they had been in town the other day, Cash had pointed out some cubbies that had been set up in a few locations around town and throughout the territory, so if somebody wanted to shift, they could store their clothes and not have to just leave them lying on the ground.

The whole place was set up for a pack full of shifters, and it seemed special to Ore. He had a feeling there weren't a lot of places like this, though he knew, based on the bits and pieces he'd heard when Cash had been talking to some of the other Enforcers, there were worries that the pack was becoming stagnant.

In Ore's opinion, that could help him with his case for staying, but he wasn't sure if it would be as easy as pointing out that his addition would count for positive growth, so he'd kept it to himself.

"It's sweet that you do this," Ore said softly.

Cash shrugged and looked away, but Ore's sharp eyes could detect the faint blush on Cash's cheeks. He was so adorable. Reaching over, he ran the back of his fingers down his stubbly cheek and the side of his neck. Scent wasn't as important to birds, but he knew felines and canines craved the close bonds that could be formed by scenting one another.

A soft purr filled the cab of the truck. A shiver ran down his spine as he grinned, full of happiness, and turned away to look out the window and give Cash a break. "Do you guys have a school here? Or do you have to send the kids to a human school in another town?"

"Most homeschool, actually, but there are a handful that get bused over to the next town. We'd talked about building our own school a couple of years ago when Liam first got here," Cash added, a thoughtful look on his face. "But Liam put the project on hold when he realized—"

When he didn't finish what he was going to say, Ore looked over at him, brows furrowed. "When he realized what?"

Cash sighed. "When he realized the pack wasn't growing as much as it should be under a strong alpha. Sure, there were some new pregnancies once Liam took over, but otherwise, things haven't gotten much better."

"That seems strange. Liam is obviously a competent and strong leader. Why isn't the pack growing, do you think?"

Silence filled the truck, and Ore figured he wasn't going to answer. His eyes caught on a For Sale sign in the window of a building on the corner across from Ginny's bookstore. It looked cute from the outside, the brick façade well taken care of, the windows big and clear of any clouding, and two huge flowerpots on either side of the entrance. The flowers inside were overgrown and needed some serious TLC, but that wouldn't be hard to fix.

Without meaning to, he pictured the place as a daycare center, something that would help the pack in the short and long term. If Liam could get more people to join—maybe even some non-cat shifters to freshen things up—Silver Oak would probably explode. The location was in the heart of town, secure with the rest of the pack all around it.

"They won't let it," Cash said softly, drawing Ore's attention back to him.

"Who? The pack?"

Cash nodded. "They're so stuck in their ways... A pack's strength comes from its alpha, but an alpha's strength comes from their pack. If they aren't fully bonded and in sync, the connection can wither and die."

He gripped Cash's forearm. "You all won't let that happen."

Everything he had seen and heard about Alpha Amato led him to believe that Cash was absolutely right: he was a strong alpha who would help his pack grow... if they let him.

"I'll fight like hell to stop it from happening." His voice was so serious and growly Ore couldn't help but grin at him.

"I know, baby."

As they finally crossed the intersection—the place was so dead that time of day no one had come up behind them or driven past—Ore's gaze was drawn back to the empty storefront. A warm feeling grew in the pit of his stomach, the hair on his arms standing up. He had the strangest sensation that if he were allowed to stay, that new daycare center would be his. It would be his way of giving back to the pack. He and his soft-hearted mate—who loved cubs so much—would provide care for the youngest and most vulnerable members of the pack.

He didn't say anything, though he suspected his longing

was spewing all over the inside of Cash's truck based on the weird glances he was getting from him. He forced a serene smile and focused on the water coming into view up ahead of them.

"This is the perfect weather for a day at the lake," he said cheerfully.

"It is. We'll probably have to drag the cubs away once it's time to head home. They never want to quit playing."

"Of course not," Ore said, smiling at him gently. "When do kids ever want to stop playing? Especially when they have someone who will play with them and give them his full, undivided attention. As I'm sure you do."

Cash shrugged, looking a little awkward, and muttered, "I guess."

Ore bit his lip to hide his smile as Cash steered the truck down a two-track lane that ran along the left side of Alpha Amato's house where it sat at the end of the cul-de-sac. They drove right past the house and found a large clearing between the rear and the lake that was half full of vehicles.

He looked around curiously, spotting what appeared to be several parents lingering with their small children. All of the kids recognized Cash's truck, some of them beginning to pull off their T-shirts as soon as they saw him, their parents' hands the only things holding them back from running straight into the water.

Ore laughed and unbuckled. "They definitely seem ready to get wet. Kind of strange for a pack full of cats."

Cash shot him a look, eyebrows raised. "Most big cats love the water."

"I was just teasing." Ore smiled at him sweetly.

Cash huffed as he pushed open his door and stepped down, surrounded within seconds by cubs demanding his attention and wanting to know where he'd been the week before and who was the guy who smelled funny in his truck.

Ore wasn't bothered by Cash's reaction to his joke. His

panther could be so serious. Ore decided to make it his mission for the day to get him to lighten up and have real fun with the cubs.

He needn't have worried.

Ore stood on the shore of the lake, his skin drying from his last trip into the water, and he watched Cash swim around the cubs in his shifted form as they shrieked and splashed like they'd been doing for nearly two hours nonstop. The entire time, Cash had been in the water with them, herding them back if they went too far, propping them up if they started to sink, pretending to be a monster as they played pirates.

Anything and everything the cubs wanted or needed, Cash gave them.

Saint, the Enforcer Cash was close friends with, had shown up not long after them, the big tiger shifting and jumping in almost as quickly as Cash had. The kids played with him too, but not as much as they did Cash. They were obsessed with the black panther as he cut through the water like an overprotective shark. Even while he was in his shifted form, Ore could tell this was the happiest Cash had been in the nearly ten days he'd known him. It wasn't that he'd been unhappy with Ore—especially the last few days as they'd seemed to naturally gravitate toward one another—but this was different.

As much as Cash enjoyed being an Enforcer, *this* was what called to his soul.

An aching longing began to grow inside Ore, one that had been there before, but the shape was growing, building in strength. Becoming something undeniable and breathtaking.

He didn't just want Cash—he wanted *this*. This life where they played with the cubs every week and then went home to their cozy little A-frame cabin. Where they got to snuggle on the big, comfy couch and read or watch movies. Where they shared meals with Pops, spent every night wrapped in each other's scents and arms, and patrolled the territory together—Cash on the ground, Ore in the air—protecting the pack that they both belonged to and loved.

"Those are some deep thoughts," a familiar voice said from just behind him, startling Ore so much he jolted, spinning around.

"You scared the shit out of me," he told Robbie, laughing, as he shoved at his arm.

Robbie laughed too, completely unapologetic. He had bright pink swim briefs on and a light blue button-up that only had a couple of the buttons done, showing off his golden skin perfectly.

Eyeing him, Ore raised his brows. "Is this for anyone here?"

"Hardly." Robbie pulled a face. "I can't help that I look good in everything."

Ore snorted, but he had to agree. Robbie was a knockout, even without the violet eyes that were arresting in their beauty. The jerk had the personality to go with it too. Open and curious, kind and sassy. The kind of person who could make friends easily, no matter where they were.

Taking a step back so they were shoulder to shoulder, Ore turned back to the water to keep an eye on Cash and the cubs. "Is there someone *not* here that you wish was?" Ore asked lightly.

They had talked a few times since the bookstore, twice on the phone, and then once he'd come out to Cash's house and had lunch with him while Cash ran into town. He knew that if Robbie didn't want to answer, he wouldn't.

Instead of laughing off the question like Ore assumed his friend would, Robbie sighed. It was long and dramatic—which was totally on-brand for him—but it still wasn't what he'd been expecting.

"The people I want to impress are not here, no."

"People?" Ore asked delicately, keeping his eyes on the water so Robbie didn't see his surprised face.

"It's so dumb," Robbie moaned, and Ore could see his hands flying in front of him out of the corner of his eye. "I keep telling myself to just get over them, that nothing will ever happen, but it's like every time I'm around either one of them, my body erupts in goose bumps, and butterflies start going crazy in my stomach, and I can feel my pulse pounding in my throat."

Ore turned to him, eyes wide. "That sounds pretty serious. Why couldn't it ever work out? You're amazing, gorgeous, and funny."

Robbie sighed again, less dramatically, his eyes dropping to the ground in front of him as he kicked at some of the longer pieces of grass that grew where they stood, farther away from the beach. "Because they'll never see me as anything more than my dad's kid, someone needing protection but not worth being protective of." Robbie glanced up at him. "That probably doesn't make any sense."

"No, I get it," Ore said, shooting a look toward the water, a sad smile growing on his face at the way Cash play growled at the cubs. "Cash is so protective of the pack that sometimes I wonder if the way he acts toward me is more than that or if it's just because I'm here it's being extended to me, you know?"

Robbie huffed. "I've seen the way he looks at you. That's not little-bird-needs-protecting eyes that he's giving you. It's one hundred percent 'I'm going to protect that little bird with my life and then lick him from head to toe.'"

Ore gasped and then started giggling, slapping a hand over his mouth. Robbie cracked a wide grin, looking more like his normal self than he had a minute ago.

"I can't believe you just said that. The cubs could have heard you."

Robbie rolled his eyes. "Those cubs have heard worse. The downside of having enhanced senses as a child, I'm sure."

"Maybe," Ore said. He looked out at Cash once more. "And maybe you're right. I do... Well... I want to drop a stone for him."

"I'm sorry, you what? Is that like lay an egg thing or what?" He narrowed his eyes. "It's not a... bathroom thing, right?"

"Oh my goddess." Ore snorted he laughed so hard and slapped a hand at Robbie. "No! It's a bird shifter thing, golden eagles especially."

Sobering, he pulled a stone out of his pocket that he'd snagged earlier, the blue flecks having caught his gaze since they reminded him so much of Cash's eyes.

"Dropping a stone is a mating ritual, I guess, a holdover from our animal sides," he said softly, running his thumb over the smooth surface. "You pick a special stone, and then you fly way up high before dropping it."

"Why do you drop it?" Robbie asked, confused.

"So you can dive down and catch it before it hits the ground and impress the person that you want to be with, show them your prowess, and then gift them the stone afterward."

"Why don't you do it?"

"Because, well, for one thing, it probably wouldn't mean anything to a feline who lives only among other felines, so the gesture wouldn't be the same."

"It would still mean something to you," Robbie insisted, poking him in the chest with his finger. "Cash is smart. He's traveled a lot for pack business. He might know what it means. And if he doesn't, you explain it to him."

Ore shrugged and slipped the stone back into his pocket. "There's also the fact that he's keeping distance between us."

"How much distance could he be keeping? You guys live together."

"No," Ore corrected sadly, "I'm staying with him temporarily. Once my memories are back, all bets are off, but I'm guessing it'll be 'sayonara, kid,' and I'll be shown the door."

Robbie chewed on his lower lip, frowning out at the water, where the screaming and laughing was still going strong. "Then he's an idiot."

"No, he's not," Ore snapped. He appreciated his friend sticking up for him, but he didn't want him bad-mouthing Cash to do it.

Robbie held up his hands in surrender, grinning. "Easy, birdie. I'm just saying, if he lets you get away, then he's not as smart as I thought he was."

"He might not have a choice."

Robbie's eyes turned sad and distant. Ore had to wonder again how someone as wonderful as Robbie felt so hopeless about love. Were the people he'd fallen for already in relationships? Maybe they were human like Robbie. Ore knew humans could be a lot more strict about sexuality—maybe they were men who identified as straight or women as gay. Or a combination.

Either way, the fact that both of them were wallowing in self-pity was dragging him out of his happy headspace that the cubs, Cash, and the lake had given him.

Robbie sucked in an excited breath and grabbed Ore's hand, giving it a quick squeeze. "Let's get out of here."

"And go where?"

"Back to Cash's. But we have to stop at the store. We need supplies."

"What kind of supplies?" Ore was a little worried about the gleam in his friend's eyes.

"The cookie dough kind."

CHAPTER 12

F ull moon runs were one of his favorite things, hands down.

In fact, there were only a handful of things—like his Pops and now Ore—that even came close to comparing. There was just something about the pull of the moon when she was at her fullest and most beautiful that called to his animal side. It was the one time he truly let himself run free, shrugging off the shackles of his responsibilities and giving himself completely over to his panther.

This month was even more special, and the little bird walking next to him and gripping his hand with both of his own was the reason.

Ever since he'd come home from the lake the other night and found cookies burning in his oven while Ore and Robbie sat on the floor up in the loft, completely oblivious, thanks to the stringent scent of nail polish and the blaring music coming from the sound system in the living room, he hadn't been able to keep his hands off his bird.

Not because Ore had almost burned his house down but because he'd overheard what Ore had said at the lake when he'd been talking to Robbie on the shore. He hadn't meant to eavesdrop, but his panther was so in tune with the eagle that he couldn't have stopped himself from hearing if he'd wanted to.

Ore wanted to drop a stone for him.

He'd been confused until he'd explained to Robbie the significance, and then he'd been bursting with joy. Despite Ore being afraid that it wouldn't mean anything to Cash, or that even if it did, it might not be enough to keep them together if the pack drove them apart, he couldn't help but feel overwhelmingly happy.

He wasn't sure exactly why it changed things so much for him, but it was like a switch had been flipped inside him. Before, he'd been holding himself back, not letting himself fully recognize the pull toward Ore that he'd experienced since the day he'd collapsed in the woods in front of him.

But after hearing Ore admit that he felt the same way, that he wanted the same things, Cash couldn't hold back anymore.

He didn't know exactly what that would mean for their future. He just knew he would do whatever it took to keep Ore in his life and to make him his completely. He just had to figure out how to talk to Liam about it, but he'd wait for another night. He planned on fully enjoying the pack run with his soon-to-be mate too much to bother stressing about the future.

Most of the pack met in the clearing behind the Alpha House for full moon runs. There were always a handful of people who preferred to run in smaller groups, family units or close friends, but for the most part, it was a time for them to come together, experience their animal sides in an unrestrained way as they ran through the woods, roaring and hissing and just enjoying themselves.

Cash couldn't imagine not running with the pack. He liked running with Liam and the other Enforcers, and it helped stabilize the bonds between them, strengthening them as they continued to grow as a unit. Even if the rest of the pack was being slower at bonding with Liam and letting them move away from the past and into the future.

The first full moon run they'd had after Liam had taken over as alpha and Finlay as second-in-command, he'd been surprised that the vampire had shown up. Not enough to say anything, since he'd only known him for a couple of weeks, but it *hadn't* been surprising to find out how fast he was. Vampires could move so quickly, they looked like a blur even to a shifter, their speed being their most formidable asset.

About a year ago, Pops had stopped coming, his arthritis getting so bad he couldn't keep up with Cash and the others. Cash would slow down, sticking close to him, but Pops decided it was time for him to leave the run to younger members of the pack and wouldn't let Cash convince him otherwise. It'd taken months to get used to not having Pops by his side, but they'd started doing smaller, gentler runs just the two of them.

He was sure having Ore with him would make everything even better, heightening his pleasure in the run to a level he'd never experienced before. As they walked around the Alpha House, where most of the others were already gathered, excitement palpable in the air, Cash cracked a smile at his little bird's wide eyes.

"You seem surprised."

"I just can't believe this many people are part of your pack. For some reason, I thought it was smaller."

Cash ran his eye over the crowd. They weren't even a hundred strong, which put them nowhere near one of the largest in the country, but a lot of packs were barely more than extended families, especially avians. There were only two that Cash knew of that were larger than a couple of dozen. A huge one that was very strict about only having birds in their territory on the East Coast and one on the West

Coast that had a handful of non-birds in the pack but was also maybe only fifty or sixty strong.

Birds had a reputation for liking to keep to themselves, being cold and unemotional, and rarely feeling the pull of a fated mate.

Not his Ore.

They hadn't said the words to each other, but he knew Ore felt it too. And cold and unemotional? Not even close. Sometimes he could be shy with his reactions, but he felt things deeply, showing Cash how much he loved being pressed against him and taken care of.

He had something special planned for his little bit for after the run, and his excitement for it rivaled his anticipation of the run itself. Hopefully, Ore would like his surprise.

Who was he kidding? His little bird would be beyond ecstatic.

"A decent-sized pack," Cash said, leaving it at that.

He steered Ore over to the edge closest to the woods where Saint and Rachel were leaning against a couple of trees, waiting patiently. Liam and Finlay weren't there yet, both of them probably still in the Alpha House finishing up whatever work they were doing.

"Hey, you two," Saint said, grinning at the two of them. "Cash finally let you out from under house arrest?"

"You saw him at the lake and the bookstore," he grumbled and shook his head, though he couldn't be too annoyed when Ore laughed at the absurd teasing.

"Yeah, he can be a tough warden, but I've found a few ways to get on his good side." He shot Cash a shy smile with just a hint of heat, and Cash's panther was so close to the surface with the run about to happen that he couldn't hold back his rumbly purr of satisfaction.

"Oh, gross," Rachel said, grinning. "You two are going to be sickening, aren't you?"

Ore ducked his head, stepping a little behind Cash to hide

his red face. Cash shot his friends a glare, warning them to take it easy. They both smiled but nodded. Rachel could be particularly feisty on full moons, a soft glow already showing in her amber eyes, but he knew they would respect his wishes and not tease Ore too much.

Luckily, before they even got another chance, a hush moved its way through the crowd, and he knew that Liam was coming. Sure enough, the big blond lion made his way toward the beach, pausing to greet people or clap the sides of their necks. Finlay was just behind him, offering bland smiles to the few people who said hello to him.

When Liam got to the edge of the water—about ten feet from where Cash and the others stood—he held up his hands in a call for quiet. Immediately, everyone fell silent.

"I know we all want to get out there and enjoy the night, so I'll keep this quick," Liam said, grinning at the crowd as a few people fidgeted excitedly. His deep voice carried easily all the way to the back, using only a hint of his *alpha* voice to keep everyone focused. "Fern's going to do a quick blessing, and then we'll take off. I just want to remind everyone that we have a guest with us this full moon." Liam turned and pointed toward where Ore was still half-hidden behind Cash. "Ore will be flying with us. No one is to chase him or hunt him. He is to be treated with respect, just as we would anyone else. Is that understood?"

There was a quick rumble of agreement before Saint called out, "If anyone tries, they'll have to deal with Cash."

Face stony, he met the eyes of anyone who dared to look at him—either with curiosity or thinly veiled disgust. He made a note of anyone who looked unhappy over the fact he was protective of his bird.

Cash was glad Liam gave the order, but he'd be keeping a close eye on Ore no matter what. At least he didn't have to worry about Billy Mittin. He'd been reprimanded by Liam and warned that his bigotry and shitty behavior wouldn't be tolerated and then given three days of isolation in the base-ment of the Alpha House and banned from pack activities for two months. The only thing he was allowed to attend was pack meetings, if one happened to be called. The fact that he wouldn't be there during the run eased most of the worry Cash had been having before he found out his punishment.

He'd hoped it'd be harsher, but he knew Liam had done the best he could to rectify the situation without overreacting like Cash would have. If it had been up to him, he would have driven him out of the territory himself and warned him about what would happen if he tried to come back.

He knew Liam was trying to set an example of what wasn't acceptable, no matter people's feelings on visitors within their pack, and Cash just hoped that everyone took it to heart—and that it was a sign Liam might be open to the prospect of Ore staying.

Fern came to the front next, her curls bouncing as she skipped onto the beach, a wide smile on her adorably freckled face. Her mates—Matt and Stephanie—stood just off to the side, their arms around one another and grins plastered to their faces as they watched her.

The pack blessing was familiar. Fern did it every month on the full moon, and then on new moons, she did a cleansing, which was common for packs with covens. He wasn't sure if it actually helped anything, but it was a nice reminder of who and what they were and their bonds to each other.

Once she finished, a rush of energy flew through the crowd, washing over each person and touching not just their human form but their animals within, exciting them even further.

Liam clapped his hands, pirate smile on his face. "Let's go!"

All of the shifters in the clearing began stripping off their clothes, Cash and Ore included. He'd seen his little bird as his eagle the day he'd found him and then a couple of times in the house when he'd wanted to stretch his wings, but this would be the first time he'd really get to see him flying.

Within a few minutes, they both stood naked, staring into each other's eyes. Ore grinned, his cheeks flushed with excitement as he bounced on his toes.

"Ready?" Cash asked.

"Beyond."

They started to shift at the same time. Being an Enforcer meant that Cash was stronger than the average shifter, his bonds with his alpha, as well as his packmates, making him faster. It allowed him to fully shift into his panther within a few moments, his limbs growing and bending as fur sprouted from his skin.

He gave a quick shake once he finished, then checked on Ore. He was still shrinking, feathers starting to poke out as his face elongated into his sharp beak. He didn't have to wait too much longer, and then his gorgeous golden eagle was perched on the ground right in front of him, clicking his beak excitedly.

As his panther, Cash had less control over his instinctive impulses. He darted forward without hesitation, rubbing the sides of his mouth and chin over as much of Ore as he could reach before he ruffled his feathers in annoyance and snapped warningly at him.

It was alright though—his scent was already all over Ore; he'd only needed to add a little extra before they took off after everyone else.

He waited for Ore to take flight, watching with open admiration as he spread his long, dark brown wings and shot into the air. His squeaky screech was loud, and Cash was pretty sure that if he spoke bird, it would be an exclamation of pure joy. He let him swoop around over the water a few times before growling and drawing his attention and then leading away from the shoreline and into the trees where the rest of the pack had gone.

Ore followed, swooping down low and brushing the tips of his primary feathers against the top of Cash's head before lifting back up above him, darting in and out around the trees.

Bursting with happiness, Cash let out a roar and took off at a sprint.

HOURS LATER, Cash trotted over to where they'd left their clothes piled among the rest of the pack's. Most were already gone, but he and Ore had stayed out longer, wanting to savor as much of the full moon—and each other—as they could.

He'd been right about how the run would be even better with having Ore there with him. His eagle had flown above him for hours, swooping down occasionally to caress Cash's fur with his feathers or circling around him teasingly before shooting into the night sky once more.

No matter how many times Ore flew far up above the trees, he always came back, giving Cash his squeaky little shriek before flying off again.

Thanks to the strength of the moonlight and Cash's increased eyesight as his panther, he never lost sight of Ore's dark form, even as he darted in and out of the trees around them.

Cash had kept half his focus on Ore and the rest on running through the familiar woods, catching the scents of his packmates all around him. A few times, Saint darted close to bump him playfully, his tiger nearly twice the size of Cash's panther and nearly taking him to the ground. It was a familiar game, and Cash always retaliated with a growl and head bump before racing away faster than Saint could keep up with.

Liam only ran for about an hour and a half before he settled in the middle of a clearing, let out a loud roar that carried for miles, and then collapsed on his side to take a snooze.

Lions really could be so lazy.

Others in the pack heard the call and joined him, finding places around their alpha in the grass to relax and enjoy being in their animal forms in a calm and peaceful way.

Not Cash. He kept running.

Even after Rachel and Saint had turned around and headed back, he and Ore had kept going, zigzagging back and forth, only stopping occasionally for a drink of water in a stream or the lake. But when he started to get tired, he knew his little bird probably was too.

He'd let out a roar of his own, calling to Ore to let him know, then started the journey back to where they'd begun.

As he shifted into his human skin, he pulled on his pants and threw his T-shirt over his shoulder. His muscles ached pleasantly, but there was a buzz of excitement in his veins still. Part of that was the comedown from the run, his panther still hyped up and not ready to settle yet, but the rest was about his surprise back at the house.

He heard the soft rustle of feathers before Ore landed on his shoulder, nudging at the side of his head. Cash chuckled, loving how affectionate Ore was in this form as well. "Do you want to fly home? I can grab your clothes and meet you there."

Ore shrieked, ruffling his feathers and then letting them fall flat again.

"I'll take that as a yes." He stroked the pads of his fingers down Ore's soft, silky feathers. "Go on. I'll be right behind you."

Not needing to be told twice, Ore launched himself into the air once more, his talons digging into Cash's skin through his shirt. He didn't mind though, the hint of pain gone almost before he'd felt it.

He swiped up Ore's clothes and jogged back to his truck,

hightailing it home. The drive back to the cabin seemed longer than normal though, making him antsy. He was sure Ore had made it there fine, but Cash didn't like not having his eyes on him or at least knowing exactly where he was.

When he finally pulled into the driveway, he got a gut punch of desire at the sight of Ore sitting on the front porch steps, leaning back on his hands, completely naked.

That was a welcome home he could get used to.

He stalked toward his mate, only one thing on his mind, but as he reached the bottom of the steps, he remembered his surprise, coming to a jerking halt before he could maul his little bird. Ore looked at him with glowing eyes, his eagle just beneath the surface.

He'd never looked as predatory as he did in that moment, and Cash fucking loved it.

"Hold that thought, little bit," he said, rushing up the stairs. "Don't move."

Right before they'd left for the run, he'd let Ore go outside before pretending he'd forgotten something and gone back in. He found the stone that Ore had picked for him the day at the beach tucked under his pillow up in the loft. He'd had a feeling he was keeping it close by as he worked up the courage to use it.

Cash had hidden it behind the bowl that sat in the entryway for keys and other pocket junk.

Snagging it, he returned outside and flopped down next to Ore.

"I want you to do something for me," he said as he held out his closed fist, the rock's smooth edges pressing into his palm.

Ore looked at him with wide, hungry eyes. "Anything."

He smiled and unfurled his fingers, revealing the dark gray stone with blue flecks.

Sucking in a breath, Ore glanced back and forth between Cash and the stone. "How did you…"

"I overheard you at the lake the other day."

Ore groaned and covered his face, the scent of his embarrassment burning the back of Cash's throat. "I didn't think you were paying attention."

He used his free hand to grip Ore's chin, tugging him free of his hands, and then turned him so he was facing Cash once more. His cheeks were flushed, but he held Cash's gaze as he said clearly, "I'm always paying attention to you. It's hard to ignore your heart when it lives outside your body."

Tears welled in Ore's eyes. "What do you want me to do?"

He held up the rock higher. "Drop this for me."

Breath shaky, Ore gave a wobbly nod and climbed to his feet.

Once he was in the grass, he turned and looked at Cash for a long moment. He didn't say anything as the air became charged around them, full of unspoken promises and possibilities. When he dropped the stone into the grass, Cash sat up straighter, watching avidly as he shrank back down into his eagle, stretching out his wings as he leaned down to pick up the rock with his beak.

Goddess, he was beautiful.

No matter which form he was in, Cash could barely drag his eyes away from him.

Ore jumped into the air, wings flapping, as he climbed higher and higher. He kept going until he was barely a speck in the sky. Everything froze for a moment, and then Cash's breath caught in his throat as he saw him start to dive.

The stone was too small for him to make out in the dark, but he could see Ore.

His wings were tucked in close as he shot down at an amazing speed. Cash was on his feet without realizing it. He wasn't afraid for Ore. He knew his bird's eyes were much better than his own, and he could see where the ground and stone were.

His heart still lurched behind his ribs when the tips of

Ore's wings skimmed the ground as he caught it at the last second, screeching triumphantly. He was still trying to calm his pulse and his ragged breaths when Ore landed on the ground and started to shift back.

As soon as he had fingers again, he picked up the rock, walked determinedly over to Cash, and held it out on the flat of his palm. "Cash Lawson, will you accept this stone from me?"

Emotions bubbled up inside him. He'd known the moment would be special, but he'd had no idea it would hit him like this. He knew it was because they were taking their first steps toward their future as mates.

Cupping his hands around Ore's, he slowly slid the stone out over his fingers. He gave it a firm squeeze, then pressed it into his chest right over his heart. "I'd love nothing more."

The somber expression on Ore's face broke, a wide grin spreading across his tempting mouth as he threw himself into Cash's arms. He caught him without dropping his prize, gripping him on his ass to hold him up. Ore wrapped his arms and legs around him with a surprisingly tight hold and then pressed a flurry of kisses to his cheeks, nose, and mouth, covering Cash with his uncontainable happiness.

"You let it get pretty close to the ground before you caught it," Cash muttered around another kiss.

Ore laughed delightedly, throwing his head back and releasing a sharp call of wildness into the darkness. He tipped his chin back down and met Cash's gaze. "Goddess, that was *exhilarating*. I haven't dropped that fast in years. The last time was probably when I—"

His dark eyes widened with shock, and Cash's stomach tightened, the wonderment of the moment seeping away.

This was it. Time was up.

"You're starting to remember things."

CHAPTER 13

"Are you sure this is safe? What kind of risks are we looking at?"

Fern rolled her eyes at him. "Your sweet little birdie is perfectly safe in my very capable hands. But I need *silence*. Go wait in the other room with Liam, please."

She shooed him away, herding him with her hands and body and not actually giving him a choice. He backed out slowly, keeping his eyes on Ore for as long as possible. He didn't like the idea of leaving him alone. Things were unsettled between them, and he *hated* it, his panther getting even more possessive. It wasn't that he hadn't wanted him to start getting his memories back, but he wasn't ready. They'd been living in a bubble, neither one bringing up the future or talking about a plan, and now they were out of time.

His bird smiled at him. "It's going to be fine."

He even sounded like he believed it, but there was a thread of uneasiness in his scent that matched Cash's own. For better or for worse, with Fern's help, they were hopefully going to be getting Ore's full memory back. No more waiting. No more limbo where they played house together, ignoring the fact that everything was going to come crashing down eventually.

He closed the door behind him when Fern cleared her throat loudly. As soon as he did, he couldn't hear a single thing through it, not even their heartbeats. Scowling, he eyed the solid wood etched with runes. Sound blockers.

The room on the other side was half greenhouse, half meeting space their tiny coven used on the back side of Fern's house. He understood the need for privacy, but he didn't like not being able to at least hear if Ore called him for help. If he was in there with basically anyone other than the most powerful witch he knew, he'd storm back in and drag him out.

Cash took a couple of deep breaths to try and calm his panther and then made his way back to the front of the house, where Liam and Saint were both waiting in the living room. Liam because he wanted to know as soon as Ore remembered what had happened to him. And Saint because... Well, as he put it, it was his job as Cash's best friend to be there for him *during hard times*.

While he appreciated the sentiment, he didn't like the fact Saint was anticipating the worst.

He looked between the two of them where they sat on opposite ends of Fern's couch, both with their phones in their hands. He could tell from the way Liam was frowning that he was reading his emails, whereas Saint was grinning and tapping at the screen manically. Definitely playing a game.

"She said it might be a while," Cash let them know, lowering himself into a recliner near Saint. Fern had warned him and Ore that the process could be lengthy, depending on how much rebuilding Ore's brain had done on its own.

That's what she called it: rebuilding the bridge. She said she might have to do more work if it wasn't sturdy enough. He didn't really understand what that meant, but considering he barely understood half the things she did with magic, he didn't argue with her. He just prayed that once they finally knew the truth, it wouldn't devastate him and his little bird.

Hours passed without a single peep or sighting of Fern or Ore. At one point, one of Fern's mates, Matt, came into the room and offered them beverages and snacks, insisting on bringing them at least water when they all declined.

Every twenty minutes or so, Cash would get up and pace for a while until Liam growled at him in annoyance, and then he'd sit back down. He didn't take it personally. Saint couldn't stop fidgeting either—though for a different reason than Cash's anxiousness. He just couldn't handle sitting still for too long.

Cash wished he was in the room with Ore, maybe holding his hand or talking to him if he got scared, but Fern had made it very clear she needed to be able to completely concentrate if they didn't want her to possibly fuck up his brain. Which he definitely did *not* want. He wanted his little bird exactly the way that he was: sweet and loving and perfectly filthy.

"This is ridiculous," Saint finally said, almost three hours in. "How long can this possibly take? What is she doing to him back there?"

Cash shrugged. "Rebuilding the bridge."

Saint narrowed his eyes at him, like he wasn't sure if Cash was fucking with him or not. "I don't even know what that means."

"It means be patient," Liam cut in, typing something on his phone. "If anyone can do this, it's Fern."

Grunting, Saint sagged back against the couch, drumming his fingers on his thighs a second later.

Cash had to agree with Liam. She was not only powerful but clever, constantly coming up with new ways to do things to help their pack. When Jorge had first come across the idea of magically infused tattoos, she had helped him with the formula until he could start testing. Whenever he got stuck on something, she was the first person he turned to.

Cash glanced down at the symbol just below the inside of his left elbow. It was glowing faintly like it always did, but it was one he never used and prayed he'd never need to.

The others came in handy sometimes, even if just for fun with the cubs. There was a tattoo just beneath his collarbone that silenced his footsteps. He used it when he was pretend stalking the cubs through the woods, teaching them to use not just their ears but their eyes and noses.

Another could give him a boost of strength temporarily. And one on his thigh, that hurt like a bitch when he activated it, increased his healing capabilities—but at a price. That one left him exhausted after he used it, his body becoming whole but then passing out for twelve hours afterward.

So far, Jorge hadn't offered those tattoos to anybody else, but he'd concocted one for Riggs, a beta in the pack, and his human mate, Myles. After they'd bonded a few months ago, Myles had started looking for a way to fully bond with his mate without spontaneously growing fangs. Jorge's solution had been pretty ingenious, using a mixture of magic and Myles's blood to bind them together and giving Myles the same ability to feel Riggs's emotions that his mate had gained after biting him.

Jorge was still fiddling with the rune tattoos, wanting them to be perfect before offering them to other packmates. Once he tried them out on a few more volunteers, he could then start selling the service to those outside the pack. He'd confessed to Cash a while ago that he was worried about strangers having to come into their territory to get to his shop.

Considering how much business it would bring into their pack, Cash had told him that if anyone had a problem with it, he should send them to him, and Cash would tell them where to shove it.

The only other person Cash knew with tattoos like his was Liam's brother. Jorge hadn't done those; he'd only shared the initial concept with one of Quinten's witches. She'd been concerned that her very human leader was too vulnerable without some sort of magical protection. Cash was sure some of the spells she had come up with for him were similar, but he knew for a fact there were some on Quinten that Cash would never need.

Things that had grossed out Liam when his brother had let slip what some of his runes could do.

When Saint started getting more fidgety and Liam's jaw tense, Cash reached over and shoved at his knee. "You don't have to stay. I'll let you know once we know anything."

Saint leaned back, rubbing his palms against his thighs a few times. "No, I'm fine. I can hang with you guys."

He and Liam exchanged a look, and then their alpha turned to Saint. "Go make yourself useful somewhere else, please."

Saint sighed at them but pushed to his feet. "Fine, but text me as soon as she's done with him." He stopped next to Cash's chair, gripping the side of his neck and giving him a brief scenting. "It's going to be fine, brother."

Cash forced a smile and nodded. He wasn't so sure about that, but he knew the only way for things to be alright was for the man still patiently waiting with him to do something.

He waited until he was sure Saint was gone, and then he leaned forward, bracing his forearms on his knees and dropping his gaze to the floor between his feet. "I was hoping to talk to you about something."

Liam rustled around, shoving his phone in his pocket and scooting closer on the couch, then mimicked his pose, his loosely clasped hands coming into his line of sight. "Let's talk, then. What's going on?"

"Ore and I…" He wasn't sure how to finish that. What he was going to ask for wasn't something easy. Did he even have the right to ask?

Maybe not, but he had to anyway. He couldn't live without his little bird, and he'd rather stay with him and

Pops. Luckily, he didn't have to try and figure out how to spit the words out.

"You're mates." It wasn't a question, and there wasn't a hint of surprise in Liam's voice or scent.

Cash nodded, squeezing his hands together until they ached. "Fated. I knew it the moment I saw him. Eventually, I just couldn't fight it anymore."

Liam didn't say anything, and Cash could only handle the silence for a few seconds before he had to glance up. Liam had a thoughtful look on his face, his eyes distant as he nodded slowly. His scent was fluctuating a lot, like Liam was working through some intense emotions.

"You want him to stay," he finally said, turning his azure eyes on Cash. "You want him to become a part of the pack."

"I do." Cash sat up straight. "I think he'd be a valuable member. He's smart and kind and generous—"

Liam held up a hand, stopping him before he could continue to list the other hundred wonderful qualities his bird had. "I'm sure he is and more, but you know that isn't the issue."

Cash swallowed. "I know the issue, and I know you can change it." Liam's eyes sharpened, a thrum of power surging in the room, so Cash tacked on a belated "sir."

The crackling in the room eased back down as Liam sighed heavily and leaned against the couch, running a hand through his shoulder-length hair and looking tired in a way Cash rarely saw. "You know it isn't as easy as that."

Cash moved forward on his seat, eager to convince his alpha differently. "It can be though. You're the alpha. What you say goes."

"If I want to *stay* the alpha, then I can't run the pack that way," Liam reprimanded softly. "If I go too far too fast, people will leave, weakening us further. Or I could be forced out, maybe even killed in a challenge."

Cash doubted he'd actually be taken down by anyone in

their pack. Whether as a human or a lion, Liam was fierce as hell and a well-trained fighter, unlike a lot of shifters who simply relied on their superhuman strength and speed. Liam had been taught from a young age how to fight, how to use all of his advantages to the best of his ability and how to mitigate any disadvantages he had.

The few times Cash had sparred with him, he'd gotten his ass kicked within minutes.

But he understood what Liam was trying to say. A lot of alphas were basically dictators, and what they said went. It often ended up killing a pack. Members left, and the ones that stayed didn't trust their alpha. That disconnect between alpha and pack weakened their bonds, which in turn weakened all of them, including the alpha. That was no way to be an effective leader.

"I think most people would be with you," Cash insisted, not willing to give up just yet.

"Maybe, but the loudest voices will be the Billy Mittins of the pack."

Cash scowled fiercely. "Then they can leave, and Billy can be the first out the fucking door. We don't need people like that here. If we open it up and allow non-cats to join, we could grow and thrive in a way we haven't in generations," Cash said vehemently, leaning forward. "You know I'm right. How many times have we talked about this, all of us in your office? I know we're waiting for the right moment, but maybe there isn't one."

"Cash…" Liam said softly.

"Please, just think about it. That's all I ask."

Liam stared at him, studying his tense body and face. Then, he nodded once. "I will. I'll think about it, but I can't make any promises. I can't even promise that if we do try and change pack law, there won't be… repercussions we can't anticipate."

Cash heard what he was saying. Forcing a radical change

on the pack could have a backlash that put all of them in danger, maybe especially Ore. He could become a target as the "instigator" of change.

Jaw tightening, Cash glanced at the door blocking him from seeing or hearing his mate. He would never allow anything to happen to him, but he appreciated the warning.

"I understand. Thank you."

Cash wasn't sure if he'd convinced him or not, but he knew Liam would consider what he had said. He hadn't said he would just to placate him. That wasn't his style.

The question now became: if Liam decided not to change the pack law that would allow Ore to stay, would Cash stay? Or would he go?

Even contemplating staying behind while Ore went back to wherever he'd come from, felt like a knife to his gut. His panther scratched at the surface, furious at the idea. There was no way he could do it. He hadn't even fully claimed his little bird yet, and he was already fully consumed by him.

Just like his parents had been with each other.

But unlike them, Ore was the best person Cash had ever met. He brought out only the good in him. His protective instincts, his playfulness, his desire for a family.

The fear he'd had his whole life of turning into his parents seemed silly now. And like he should have known better. He'd seen other fated mates in his lifetime who hadn't destroyed each other and those around them.

So why had he been afraid for so long?

Not actually a difficult question to answer after all his years of therapy as a kid. His parents' abandonment had scarred him in a way he would never fully recover from. No matter how much logic and insight he gained as he grew older, a small, childlike part of him remained that felt like everyone he loved would leave him.

When Nan died, the idea had been reinforced. And as he'd watched Pops get older and more frail each year, the fear of being left all alone in the world had gripped him tight. Putting him in a stranglehold that only allowed him to focus on protecting those around him.

Then Ore had crashed into his life like the fiercest of windstorms, a tempest of feathers and shy smiles and pure temptation.

Suddenly, he could breathe again.

His fear didn't completely evaporate, but he could see past it now instead of drowning.

No matter what happened with his pack, he knew without a doubt that he and Ore would build a future together. He'd never have to be alone again.

Footsteps drew him out of his deep thoughts, his heart starting to race in his chest as Ore's floral scent hit him, excitement weaving through the notes. He didn't smell like pain or fear, which was good, and there was also no anger or disappointment.

Whatever happened next, at least his little bird was happy.

Ore skipped into the room, bubbling over with glee, and threw himself into Cash's lap. "I remember!"

Cash grunted at the landing, then wrapped his arms around Ore's body to hold him secure. "What do you remember, little bit?"

Liam set his phone next to him, all of his attention on Ore, but he didn't seem to notice their audience. He pressed in close and dragged his face up Cash's neck before shivering and releasing a soft sigh.

"My parents," he whispered, voice thick with emotions and the salt of his tears tickling Cash's nose. "I remember my parents. Can we call them?"

CHAPTER 14

"I can't believe we're doing this."

"You don't have to whisper," Cash said, laughing. He pulled his shirt off over his head and tossed it toward Ore. "We're miles from town."

"Okay, yes," Ore said, dodging to the side so it landed on a large boulder behind him. "But are you saying it's completely outside the realm of possibility that somebody else has decided they want to go for a midnight swim but didn't want to do it too near town?"

Cash paused where he was unbuckling his pants and cocked his head to one side. "I guess it's not completely outside the realm of possibility, no. Though I don't know how whispering will make you invisible. Are all birds embarrassed to be seen naked, or is this just a *you* thing, little bit?"

Ore's feathers ruffled at the implication, and he crossed his arms over his chest. It was difficult to stay indignant as Cash dropped his pants to the ground and kicked them away. "I'm not embarrassed. I just…" He stopped. What was he again? Goddess, Cash looked good wearing nothing but moonlight. "I just don't want anyone sneaking up on us when we're not expecting it," he finished with a flourish, planting his hands on his hips.

Cash grinned at him, slow and easy. "Whatever you say. Now, get naked."

Ore sucked in a breath, his heart tripping in his chest as his blood heated. He held Cash's gaze as he slowly stripped off his borrowed T-shirt and the pair of jeans he'd snagged after Cash woke him up and told him to get dressed. He'd been a little surprised, not sure if he should be worried about a middle-of-the-night trip after everything that had happened that day. But he should have known that his grumpy cat was looking to reconnect.

As much as they'd both been waiting for Ore's memories to come back, the fact that they finally were was a devastating blow. Unless something changed with the Silver Oak Pack within the next couple of days, Ore would be forced to leave once his parents arrived from California. He was excited to see them but, at the same time, heartsick at the idea of leaving Cash behind.

The call with them had been both a relief and strained at the same time. While their voices had been familiar—thank the goddess—the way they'd spoken had seemed... odd. He wasn't sure if it was his patchwork memory playing tricks on him or if he'd parted with them on bad terms and didn't remember that yet. Either way, they'd offered to come to Kansas right away, claiming they couldn't wait to see him.

He wanted that, truly. But...

Cash backed into the water, beckoning Ore with his fingers. How could he give him up?

He told himself he wouldn't think about it—not when he had a sexy panther standing mid-thigh in water that glittered with moonbeams. His ivory skin and glowing tattoos were an irresistible beacon.

Tomorrow would come soon enough; he'd let himself have the night.

The water was cooler than it had been during the day, and Ore shivered lightly, but he didn't stop, following Cash deeper and deeper. They went far enough that Ore had to start swimming, unable to keep his feet under him without ducking below the surface. Cash, still walking along the bottom, laughed at him and then pulled Ore into his arms so they were flush together.

Ore was more than happy to be skin-to-skin with Cash. He wrapped his arms and legs around him, holding on tightly. Their faces were only inches apart, the water moving gently around them as they shared breaths.

The moon was still full enough that he could clearly see every detail, but it wasn't necessary. He'd long since memorized the arch of Cash's brows and the bow of his lips.

But he couldn't look away, couldn't stop staring.

What if it was the last time they'd get to be together like this, just the two of them, before Ore had to leave? He didn't want to miss a single moment of it. Wanted to capture a million snapshots in his head so he could carry them with him forever.

The soft smile on Cash's lips faded, his scent turning heavy with worry.

"Don't think about it," Ore whispered, pressing a quick kiss to his mouth. "Just enjoy this moment while we have it."

"Ore, I'm not just going to let them take you away from me."

He pressed a finger to Cash's mouth to stop him. "Don't make me any promises right now. Neither one of us knows what's going to happen as I get more memories back. I don't want to be even more heartbroken if you have to break a promise to me later."

Cash's jaw bunched as he clenched his teeth together. "That wasn't just some hopeful wish," he said against Ore's finger. "Unless you remember having a mate already and tell me you don't want me anymore, I'm not letting you go, little bit. You're mine."

Heat rushed through him before settling low in his belly. "But what if—"

"Mine."

Something settled inside him at the sharp word, and he leaned in closer, resting his head on Cash's shoulder. "Yours. What if I can't stay though?"

Cash's arms tightened around him, one hand slipping down to his ass and giving a firm squeeze. "Then I come with you."

Ore's head shot back up. "What? No. You can't just leave—"

"Yes, I can."

"But you've worked so hard! The pack depends on you. How can you—"

"Nothing and no one is more important to me than you, Ore." He held Ore's eyes, a hint of a glow deep in his pale blue irises.

"What about Pops?" he whispered, even as his brain screamed at him to shut up. Take the win and figure out the details later.

Cash lost some of the fierceness in his face. "Depending on where we end up, I'll either ask him to join us or visit as often as I can. Would that be alright? Him potentially living with us?"

He cupped the sides of his sweet cat's face. How had he gotten so damn lucky? "Of course that would be alright. You know I adore him."

"He can be kind of cranky when his pain flares up," Cash warned him.

Ore arched his brows. "That's fine. What's your excuse?"

An evil twinkle lit up Cash's eyes, and that was the only warning Ore got before he pretended to drop him, letting him slide a few inches down before hiking him back up.

Gasping, Ore slapped at his chest. "You jerk!"

"What was that?" Cash asked, loosening his grip a little on Ore's thighs.

With a laugh that carried across the water, Ore wrapped himself around Cash as tightly as he could. "I take it back. You're always sunshine and rainbows."

Chuckling, Cash pinched his butt. "Let's not get carried away."

He pressed his smile into Cash's neck, letting himself get lost for a minute in the coolness of the water as it fought against the heat radiating from Cash. There was the softest of breezes, ruffling his hair and the leaves in the trees back on shore. Cash held him close, a rumbly purr vibrating his chest.

It was a perfect moment.

"Have you remembered anything else?" Cash asked softly.

Back at Fern's, the only thing he'd known for sure was his parents. Not all the details about them, but their faces, scents, and voices. There were other things that had popped up when Fern had finished—people and places, snapshots without much context. He still couldn't remember where he'd been or what had happened to him before he'd arrived in Silver Oak.

When he'd expressed his frustration before he and Cash had headed home, Fern had assured him that it would return in time. She'd finished rebuilding the bridge to his memories, and now they just had to ease across.

Personally, he thought she was overdoing it with the analogy, but he supposed it made sense.

"I have three sisters," he said, tracing the edge of Cash's ear. "I only remember one of their names," he added with a grimace. "Hannah. She's the youngest."

"Where do you fall in the order?"

"I'm pretty sure I'm the oldest and that they still live with our parents, but don't hold me to that."

Cash stroked up his back, then back down to his ass. "I won't. Be patient with yourself."

"I know. It's just hard. It feels like everything is right there, just behind a curtain, but the more I tug at it, the more stuck it gets." Ore sighed and snuggled closer, determined not to let his annoyance ruin their romantic night.

"Stop tugging at it, little bit."

Smirking, Ore kept his face hidden as he said with innocent confusion, "But that's not what you said the other night."

Cash snorted and gripped his cheeks tighter. "Brat."

He snickered, lifting his head and nuzzling against Cash's cheek. Birds weren't usually so affectionate, but it felt amazing when Cash gave him little touches and strokes, scenting him whenever he got the chance, and he knew his cat liked it when he returned the gestures. All he ever wanted to do was make Cash happy, ease some of the burden of all of his important responsibilities.

"What am I going to do with you, troublemaker?"

"I have some suggestions," Ore said, wiggling closer and rubbing his hard dick against Cash's belly.

Groaning, Cash tightened his hold, preventing him from continuing to grind against all his delicious muscles. "I didn't bring any supplies for that."

Ore pouted. "None of these magical tattoos can automatically lube your dick? Seems like a missed opportunity…"

Cash barked out a laugh. "I'll let Jorge know. Maybe he can come up with something."

He stroked a finger over the one that glowed right below his collarbone. They were so beautiful, but that wasn't why he liked them so much. "I'm glad you have extra protection to help keep you safe. I suppose that's good enough."

Face softening, Cash leaned close and rubbed his nose against Ore's before pressing a soft, lingering kiss to his lips. "You don't need to worry about me being safe, little bit."

"Yes, I do. That's what you do when you love someone."

The words hung in the air around them. He should probably be embarrassed he'd just blurted that out without meaning to, but he wasn't. He couldn't be. It was true, and he *wanted* Cash to know. There was still a sliver of worry inside him that things would change between them once all of his memories were back, and he needed to let Cash know how he felt before it was maybe too late.

Cash shifted one of his hands to better support him and then lifted the other to palm the side of Ore's face. It was wet and cold, but he leaned into it anyway, always so hungry for his touch.

"You love me?" Cash asked hoarsely, voice barely more than a whisper.

He held Cash's hopeful and terrified eyes. "I do. I think I fell for you that first night. When you let me into your bed without hesitation because I was scared and didn't want to be alone."

A rush of air gusted out of Cash's mouth as his eyes squeezed shut, and he bowed his head for a second. Ore stroked one of his bristly cheeks, down his neck to his shoulder, and then back up, soothing him as best as he could.

"Are you okay?" he murmured, pressing a kiss to his forehead.

Cash nodded and lifted his face, tears shining in his eyes. "Yeah. I just… Fuck, I didn't realize it would hit me so hard. Knowing you feel the same way I do is… Goddess, it's like the sun is shining in my chest, warming me from the inside out."

Ore smiled softly, brushing a thumb under Cash's eyes and prompting, "You feel the same way?"

"Yes," Cash said, grinning so widely Ore could just about count all his teeth. "I love you, my beautiful, sweet, sexy bird. I fought it so long, trying to protect myself, but loving you isn't a risk. It's… everything. I don't need anything else."

Ore's heart thumped like a bass drum, his blood heating

and spreading out from his chest to his limbs. He was hyper-aware of how close—and alone—they were, his skin becoming so sensitive every brush of water sent a shiver through him until he was a vibrating mess of excitement and joy.

"I want you to have everything though," Ore insisted. "We'll figure something out. If we need to leave, we'll find a pack that sees the value in you and your skills and will make you an Enforcer right away."

Cash grunted and shrugged, taking a few steps forward. "Maybe Kincaid needs another."

The name tickled at Ore's brain, and then he gasped and slapped at Cash's chest. "The guy who blew up the Shifter Council?"

"Remember that, huh?"

"Yes! And we're not going somewhere where you'd be in danger all the time. He has too many enemies now."

Cash stopped, the water at his waist now. "Yes, dear."

Ore huffed and rolled his eyes. "I'm serious. We'll find a nice peaceful and *safe* pack. One full of cubs for you to play with."

Brushing his thumb over Ore's cheek, Cash tipped his lips up. "What about a few of our own?"

Ore swallowed and stared at him. "You'd want that?"

"If you do."

He could picture it so damn easily. A bigger house full of hatchlings—or cubs, or pups, or whoever needed them—and noise and so much love it was bursting at the seams.

"I think I do," he whispered, then shivered. Now that some of his wet skin was exposed, he was getting cold. "Let's go home, baby. We can argue over names for our future kids."

"Not just yet." Cash planted both hands on Ore's ass and lowered him into the water.

He sucked in a breath, his mostly hard dick brushing against Cash's much, *much* bigger one. Which was *fully* hard.

He shivered for a whole new reason, peering up into Cash's softly glowing eyes.

Holding his gaze, Cash used his hold to press Ore more tightly against him and then lifted him, rubbing Ore up the entire length of Cash's cock. He moaned—loudly—and threw his head back.

"Oh goddess. *Again*."

Cash chuckled, but it was a little shaky, his fingers digging into Ore's cheeks as he did as Ore demanded. The slow grind down and then back up was just as good as the first time. He grasped at Cash's shoulders, needing to hold on to something as his mate rocked his damn world with some frottage.

In a lake.

Under a radiant moon.

Oh shit. Cash had some *smooth* moves. Ore wasn't sure if he'd survive any more.

But he couldn't wait to find out.

Cash kept the same, achingly slow pace for ages, driving Ore out of his mind. Pleasure was building inside him, but so gradually, it was more of a tease than anything else.

Whining and shifting his hips to get more friction, Ore begged, "More, *please*. I need more. Need it harder and faster."

He peeled his eyes open and found Cash staring at him with bright, glowing eyes and fangs peeking out to dig into his lower lip. "All you had to do was ask, little bit," he growled.

He adjusted his hold, tilting Ore's pelvis up and forcing him even tighter against that massive cock. Instead of shifting Ore, Cash drove his hips up with a sharp grunt.

"Fuck yes," Ore moaned, letting his head drop back. He could feel every vein and ridge, the pressure *exquisite*. "Just like that."

His mind got hazy as Cash gave him everything he'd asked for and more. All he could feel was his tight grip on his cheeks. All he could hear were their panting breaths and soft noises of pleasure. But it was Cash's scent that was driving him wild. The intoxicating bouquet was usually dominated by leather and lavender, but as they both climbed higher, nearing the peak of their mounting pleasure, the lighter, more elusive fresh air high up in the trees scent grew stronger, overshadowing the rest and filling Ore's head until he was dizzy with it.

"Cash," he groaned, digging his nails into the back of his neck and bicep. His balls drew up, a tingle crawling down his spine.

His cat growled a response, speeding up his thrusts, chasing the release that was just out of reach.

"Next time we do this," Ore muttered breathlessly, "you better be inside me and end with your teeth in my neck."

Cash's head shot up, his focus having dropped to what was happening just beneath the surface, a low, brain-melting hiss filling the air around them. Then he was jerking, his eyes squeezing shut and face twisting with a grimace. His come drifted away in the water before it could hit Ore's skin, but he could feel the throbbing of Cash's dick against him.

Fuck, he was so close.

Sucking in a breath, Cash shook his head and opened his eyes. They were still glowing a little, but his fangs had receded. Ore was a little sad to see them go. He loved watching his cat let go and embrace his panther.

He squeaked as Cash hiked him up… and up. He lifted him with such ease Ore's belly fluttered even as he grabbed at his head to steady himself. Not that Cash would ever let him wobble.

The back of his thighs landed on Cash's shoulders, and he stared down with wide eyes, his dick *right there*, a couple of inches from Cash's mouth.

"Whatcha doing?" he rasped out, licking his lips.

Cash grinned up at him, not answering, then leaned forward and swallowed Ore's cock whole.

"*Fuck!*" he yelped, arching back. His mouth was so hot and wet, providing perfect suction as he worked his short length with his tongue.

He whimpered, right back to the edge within seconds. He tried to hold back, wanting the moment to last forever.

But then Cash used his tongue to scoop Ore's sac into the furnace that was his mouth.

Crying out so loudly it scared some birds in nearby trees, he shot onto Cash's talented tongue as every muscle in his body spasmed and tightened almost painfully. His head was nothing but static for a while, the waves of ecstasy hitting him over and over again.

When he finally came to, Cash was nuzzling in next to his sensitive, limp dick. He was purring so loudly it was like the night was vibrating around them.

"That was…" He had no words. World altering? Mind melting? The best thing since the invention of the wheel?

"Me too, little bit." He nipped at the inside of Ore's thigh, causing him to shudder. "Now we can go home."

CHAPTER 15

"I think they're here," Robbie said excitedly from where he was peering out the window of the Alpha House's front room.

Cash grabbed Ore's hand, holding more tightly than he probably should, but Ore just gripped his hand back. This was it. Liam still hadn't let him know what he'd decided, and depending on how long Cash's parents wanted to stay before bringing him back home, Cash might only have a few hours to let his alpha know what he'd decided.

He glanced over at Ore's nervous face. Everything he'd said in the lake the night before had been completely true. There was no way that he'd stay behind if Ore left. Just the idea made his heart ache and his panther stir with agitation.

"Wait... Why are there two cars?"

Robbie's question drew Cash's attention, and he frowned across the room at where Liam was sitting in a chair, one ankle propped up on the opposite knee. They hadn't wanted Ore's parents to feel overwhelmed or threatened, so they'd decided to keep the group small. Liam didn't look worried, but there was a small furrow between his brows.

"Did your parents say they were going to bring anyone else with them?" Robbie asked, glancing back at Ore.

"No," Ore assured him quickly, shifting on the couch next to him. "I didn't even remember about my sisters until late last night, but even if they brought them, they wouldn't have put them in a separate car."

Robbie looked out of the window once more, holding the curtain out of the way enough to give himself a gap to peer through.

"Why don't you just go open the door? You'd have a better view," Cash said, pushing to his feet. Ore stared up at him with wide eyes, hands twisting in his lap, and he tried to give him a reassuring smile.

Robbie waved a hand at him but didn't look away. "It's just one guy in the other car. He's kind of big and beefy for a bird shifter. The other two *have* to be your parents," Robbie said, throwing a grin at Ore. "Your mom might be even tinier than you are."

"Pot, kettle," Liam muttered, studying his nails.

Robbie stuck his tongue out at him, which made Ore's half-hearted smile turn genuine.

Cash appreciated that not only was Robbie there for his mate, but he was also doing his best to remain upbeat and keep Ore from spiraling.

Striding across the formal sitting room, he headed toward the front door. He took a deep breath, straightened his shoulders, and then pulled it open before the people on the other side could knock. He pasted a polite smile on his face that didn't show any teeth.

The couple that Robbie had identified as Ore's parents looked a lot like him. His mother was small, just like him, but they also had the same olive skin, and Ore's dark eyes that Cash loved to gaze into so much clearly came from his father, along with his unruly hair.

Cash held out a hand. "You must be Debbie and Harold Whitlock."

They each took his extended hand and gave it a loose shake, pulling away quickly.

"Are you Alpha Amato?" Debbie asked tentatively.

He shook his head and stepped back, gesturing to his right. "I'm Cash Lawson. I'm an Enforcer and a… friend of your son's."

He stumbled over the word, but he didn't want to make some big proclamation before Ore even had a chance to talk to them. They slipped past and headed toward the sitting room, but Cash didn't follow, instead turning toward the man lingering on the front porch.

He could tell immediately that this was an Enforcer from Ore's family's pack, and he wondered if they'd felt unsafe coming to a pack full of feline shifters on their own. Avians weren't exactly helpless, but he knew there was a lot of misinformation spread among their tight-knit packs about canine and feline shifters being highly predatory and uncontrollable.

"Enforcer Lawson," the man said politely, inclining his head. "I'm Louie Gladstone, an Enforcer in the Barney Pack."

Cash had been a little surprised to learn that Ore's pack was the decently sized one in northern California he'd heard about. He'd assumed he was from one of the small, tight-knit ones, maybe near some mountains.

Gladstone didn't extend a hand, and neither did Cash, getting a weird vibe from the guy as he unsubtly tried to peer around him to look into the house. Maybe he was just curious, but Cash's instincts were telling him it was something else, that he was looking for Ore.

"Welcome to Silver Oak," Cash offered blandly and forced himself to let the man into the house as well, though it went against his panther's drive to bare his teeth and keep him out.

He shut the door and followed Gladstone into the sitting room, where Ore's parents still had him wrapped in a tight embrace between them. No one was really saying anything, though Debbie was crying quietly, one of her hands stroking over Ore's hair. Robbie, leaning against his uncle's chair, sniffled and wiped at his eyes subtly.

"Isn't that sweet," Gladstone said with a sneer.

Ore's head jerked up, and all the color drained from his face as he stared at the Enforcer half a dozen feet in front of him. "You," he breathed out, fingers clutching at his parents as they moved to either side of him. "I remember you."

Cash looked between his mate and the Enforcer, not waiting for an explanation before stepping between them. His hackles were raised, a low growl building in his chest. He should have trusted his panther and slammed the door in the man's face.

"I'm glad you remember me, mate. It's time you come back home."

Cash couldn't hold back his snarl, flashing his fangs. Like. Fucking. Hell.

"I'm not your mate," Ore said, voice high-pitched and frantic. "I made that very clear the last time I saw you."

Gladstone eyed Cash warily but then turned his focus back to Ore, running his tongue between his teeth and lip. He eyed Ore's slender form from top to bottom.

Cash's growl began to grow in the crowded room. If the Enforcer made a single threatening move, he was getting his throat ripped out.

"That's not how it works in our pack, darling, and you know it. Now, be a good boy and go and get your things."

"Ore, please," his mom said softly. "Let's just go."

Cash kept one eye on Gladstone but turned enough that he could see behind him, unsurprised to see Ore jerking away from his parents and closer to Cash.

"Are you kidding? This guy was *stalking* me. He wouldn't take no for an answer. That's why I had to fucking flee our pack and leave you and the girls behind." Even as he said the words, understanding dawned on Ore's face. His mouth twisted angrily as he looked at Gladstone and said to his parents, "He has the girls, doesn't he?"

"Let's not discuss this in front of strangers," Gladstone said, taking a step forward, but Cash stopped him, a hand to his chest, before he could move any closer to his mate.

"You're going to want to stop right there," he said lowly. "I don't know who you think you are, but you don't come in here and make demands like that, especially not from him."

Gladstone turned his full attention to Cash and eyed him before disgust curled his lips back. "Little slut spread his legs for you, didn't he?"

Strong arms wrapped around Cash's chest before he could lunge forward, the scent of his alpha the only thing keeping him from losing his ever-loving shit. "Watch your *fucking* mouth, or you can go home without it."

"You should leave," Robbie spoke up as he hustled around behind the couch to reach Ore's side. He was the only human in the room, and yet the look on his face was so fierce Cash just knew he'd learned it from his mobster father. "Now."

"I'll leave with my mate and not a second sooner."

"He's not your mate, asshole," Robbie snapped. "He doesn't have to go with you." He glanced at his uncle, who was still holding Cash back. "Right? You aren't going to send him with this piece of shit, are you?"

"He doesn't have a choice," Gladstone said, raising his voice. "Shifter law clearly states—"

"Shifter law is currently being rewritten," Liam said clearly, speaking for the first time. His grip on Cash didn't lessen at all though. Smart guy. Rage was still boiling inside him, and if he got the chance, he'd rip off Gladstone's arm and beat him to death with it. "If you'd like, I can get Rick Kincaid on the phone right now and ask him his opinion on the matter."

That got Gladstone's attention, wiping some of the haughtiness off his face. He held his hands up in half-hearted placation. "There's no reason to get Kincaid involved. Ore and his parents belong in our pack. You can't keep them here against their will."

"I would never dream of it," Liam said smoothly. "However, I'd like to speak to them about what it is they'd actually like to do." His voice lowered, turning deadly. "Remove yourself from my territory."

The Enforcer pulled himself up to his fullest height to look down his nose at all of them, but he was still an entire head shorter than Cash and Liam. "You'll regret this disrespect."

And then he was storming out, slamming the door behind him.

Ore's parents immediately turned to him, both trying to explain at once.

"All of the hatchlings are being kept at Alpha Barney's house," his mom said, hands fluttering around, revealing just how anxious she and her bird were.

"Right after you left," his dad chimed in, "Louie rounded them all up, saying it was Alpha's orders to keep them safe and protected under his house, and he's refused to let them leave since."

"We've only gotten to see them a couple of times," Debbie cried, tears streaming down her face. "And that was supervised by another Enforcer. We have no idea if they're okay or what's going on inside that house."

Harold put a hand on her shoulder, his eyes wet as well. Their anguish filled the room, nearly choking him.

Ore's dark gaze found Cash's, and as soon as they locked on, Cash ripped himself out of Liam's hold and darted across the room, enveloping his mate in his arms and holding him close. He was trembling, his hands clutching at Cash's shirt as his fear and anguish sank beneath his skin. His panther roared inside him, demanding they go after Gladstone and get justice for their mate and his family.

Soon.

"Are you saying he's doing all of these things without your alpha's say-so or that Alpha Barney is doing the ordering but leaving all the dirty work to his Enforcers?" Liam clarified, pulling out his phone.

"Alpha Barney is old and weak," Ore muttered against Cash's chest. "He's basically been a figurehead for years, but he doesn't have any children, so he hasn't passed the pack on to anybody else."

"And since Gladstone can run the place as an Enforcer, why bother challenging him," Cash surmised.

"Exactly," Ore whispered, arms going around Cash's waist and clinging to him.

"You're not going back there," Cash murmured into his hair, pressing a kiss to the crown of his head.

"As soon as I saw his face, it all just flashed back. All of the weeks of him harassing me and following me, trying to corner me whenever I was alone to force the issue. He just kept calling me his mate, telling me we were *destined*. Even though I kept denying it, he didn't care. He wasn't going to stop," Ore said thickly, his tears burning Cash's throat.

"He wouldn't have," his father added. "That became clear to us. No matter what Ore said or did, Louie wouldn't stop until he'd won. He didn't care what Ore actually wanted."

His rage, which had begun to temper with his mate in his arms, ramped back up. His fangs dropped, and his claws fully extended.

"Dude, chill," Robbie scolded him, and surprisingly, it worked.

He took a few deep breaths, forcing his panther back down but holding Ore tighter. He wasn't sure he'd ever be able to let him out of his grasp.

"S-so we told him to leave," his mother said haltingly, and

when he glanced up, he saw she was staring at him warily. "We don't have any influence in the pack, and even though people didn't agree with what he was doing, nobody was willing to help us stand up to him." She lightly laid a hand on Ore's upper back. "We'd hoped you would find another pack, start over somewhere safe, but then you never contacted us, and we started assuming the worst."

Ore's grip on Cash tightened. He turned his head and looked over at Robbie. "I remember that too. I was... I was there, in the white room, just like your stepdad described it."

Robbie's eyes widened, and he clutched at Ore's arm. "The place where they made him fight like a gladiator?"

Shrugging, Ore sniffed and wiped his face against Cash's chest, leaving behind a wet spot. "I guess. That didn't happen to me. I only saw the cell they kept me in and the room where they brought me to do their sick experiments. It was all white, just like Caden said. It has to be the same place."

Cash's panther rumbled in his chest, and he crushed his little bird against him so hard he grunted in protest. "Sorry," he murmured, loosening his hold.

Ore patted his chest. "It's okay. I think I was there pretty much the whole time between when I left my family's pack and arrived here. I took a bus north into Oregon and got off at a random stop. I don't know if they were following me or if I just had the worst luck in the world, but I remember going into a cafe to get something to eat, and then the next thing I knew..."

"You were in that place," Robbie finished for him.

Debbie turned into her mate's arms, weeping quietly. Harold's face was slack with shock and devastation as they listened to their son talk about what had happened to him before he'd arrived in Silver Oak.

"Yeah. But it was kind of weird. They seemed really excited about me being there," he said, glancing up at Cash. He couldn't help but wonder if Ore was deliberately ignoring his parents, if it would be too hard to talk about if he had to deal with their emotions too.

"What do you mean?"

Ore shook his head. "I don't really know. They just kept saying how close I was to something, how it was almost ready."

"It?" Robbie asked, looking over at his uncle. Liam was typing furiously on his phone, probably taking notes or texting his brother everything Ore was remembering.

"I don't know," Ore said, shrugging. "The one witch that seemed to be in charge of the experiments would check me over with magic again and again and then get frustrated. In between the checks, they would... inject me with things."

Ore's mom gasped behind him, and his little bird squeezed his eyes shut, tensing.

"Yeah, it fucking sucked. It... hurt a lot."

"How'd you escape?" his dad asked, stepping forward and placing a hand on Ore's back in comfort.

"I can't remember," he said slowly. "That part's still kind of a blur. I think they gave me something, maybe so I wouldn't remember." He jerked back and stared up at Cash. "*So I wouldn't remember*. That's what Fern said during my checkup. She thought that could be why my memories were just gone. That somebody had deliberately severed my connection to them. They must have not wanted me to be able to remember how to get back to that place."

"Maybe that memory will return too," Cash said soothingly, cupping the side of Ore's face. "Just—"

"Be patient, I know." Ore made a cute little growling sound. "I know you're right. It's just... It feels more important than ever to get them all back." He sighed and leaned into Cash's hand. "All I know is that once I got out, I followed... I don't know, like a beacon."

"A beacon?" Liam said, looking up from his phone.

"Yeah, it was like—" Ore pressed a hand to his stomach. "—a tugging on my insides, guiding me."

"And it led you here?" Cash asked, eyebrows raised.

Ore smiled up at him, placing his hands flat on Cash's chest and shaking his head. "No, it led me to you."

"Oh *damn*," Robbie whispered loudly.

"YOUR PARENTS ARE SETTLED UPSTAIRS," Liam said, strolling into his office. "They've reluctantly agreed to stay and give us a chance to come up with a plan to help."

Ore nodded, his arms wrapped tightly around one of Cash's. "I'm glad. It doesn't do us any good if we just go back and keep letting the Enforcers coerce us to do whatever they want. Someone needs to hold them accountable."

"Agreed." Liam settled himself behind his desk and surveyed his crowded office.

Rachel, Saint, Finlay, and Fern had all arrived not too long after Gladstone left. Liam had ordered Finlay to follow him and make sure he actually left the territory. He'd come back not too long ago and confirmed that the Enforcer had driven straight out of Silver Oak, past the territory line, and kept going.

Saint had already emailed the pack, letting them know Liam was calling a meeting that evening to discuss some changes that would be happening. Cash tried not to get his hopes up about what that meant since Liam hadn't filled them in yet.

The big lion leaned back in his chair and propped his feet up on his desk. "Quinten's going to send a plane and some people to help. In exchange, he'd like to be able to talk to you about everything you remember about the place you were held," Liam said, looking at Ore.

"Yeah, that's completely fine. Maybe between Caden and

I, we can figure out who these people are and where we were."

Liam nodded. "Excellent, that's what I told him." He turned to his nephew, who was perched on a deep windowsill next to his desk. "You probably shouldn't be here when those reinforcements arrive."

"Yeah, no shit," Robbie said, hopping down. He came right over to Ore and wrapped his arms around him in a quick hug. "Good luck. I'll come back once things settle down, and you can tell me all about everything that happens." He looked at Cash meaningfully and then back at Ore, waggling his eyebrows. "And I do mean everything."

Ore huffed a tired laugh at his friend. "I'll call you later."

"Definitely," Robbie said over his shoulder as he strolled out. "Don't get dead, anyone."

Cash rolled his eyes and refocused on Liam. Sometimes he had to wonder if being raised around parahumans had crossed some wires in the guy's brain.

"Our next call has to be to Kincaid," Liam said, then looked bored when there were some rumbles around the room.

No one flat out disagreed though. As much as they would like to keep things tight and in the family, Kincaid and his people were pretty much the ruling authority in the parahuman world and needed to be read in on the situation as soon as possible.

Cash knew from Liam that Rick was also providing resources to Quinten to help investigate and find who had held Caden captive. He'd want to know they had another survivor from that place.

"Great, glad we're in agreement," Liam said dryly. "As for the pack meeting in an hour..." His eyes cut over to Cash. "I'll be making a few announcements, including that we will be opening our territory to anyone from the Barney Pack who would like to seek refuge here."

Ore's grip on Cash's arm tightened painfully. "Thank you, Alpha Amato," Ore gushed. "Thank you so much. I don't know how many others will want to come, but if we can get my sisters, I know my whole family will want to get out of that place and go somewhere safe like Silver Oak."

Liam nodded in acknowledgment. "I'll also be informing the pack that we'll be replacing the member law that excludes all non-feline shifters, and if anyone has a problem with it, they're welcome to fucking leave."

Cash's panther rumbled approvingly, and he grinned at his alpha. Maybe meeting Ore's parents and hearing what was happening to them had pushed him over the edge, but he could tell that his conversation had left an impression.

"You're going to get pushback," Rachel pointed out. "People are going to argue that we're just going to open our borders and let anyone in, that someone dangerous could come who'd be a threat."

Liam waved a hand. "We all know that's bullshit propaganda. We're not opening our borders; we're opening up the process to apply to be a part of our pack. Too long, we've been sitting on the sidelines, watching as others suffer and get hurt. The parahuman world is changing right now, and we can either sit back and watch it happen or we can be a part of the outcome. We can have a say in new shifter laws *and* grow in strength and numbers." He glanced at Saint, who grinned back, eyes sparkling with mischief. "Sometimes leaders have to lead, even to places others don't want to go."

Amato looked around at the others, lingering on Cash. His heart was stuck in his throat. Saint had fought for him and Ore. There was no way Liam just happened to use the same argument Saint had when he'd talked to Cash on the beach not long after Ore had arrived.

Fuck, he'd never live it down, but he couldn't be truly upset his friend had stuck up for him and his mate.

"Does anyone disagree with this decision?" Liam asked, voice firm.

No one made a sound.

Liam nodded and dropped his feet to the ground. "Excellent. You all get to keep your jobs."

Ore pressed his face into Cash's bicep and laughed. Saint cackled, slapping his leg.

Liam gave them his pirate smile and pulled out his phone. "We're going to save this pack whether they like it or not, and we're going to go save Ore's family too. Agreed?"

"Agreed," everyone said in unison.

"Alright. Now, get the fuck out so I can call Kincaid."

CHAPTER 16

"Are you sure it's safe here?"

Ore forced himself to look away from the hideous cowboy-themed decor in the room his parents had been put in and met his mom's worried eyes. "Yes, it's safe here. I haven't spent a lot of time with most of the pack, but there's only been one guy that wasn't... welcoming. Otherwise, everyone I've come into contact with has been very receptive and kind, especially considering they're not used to having outsiders in their territory."

His dad was pacing on the other side of the bed, one hand clasped on the back of his neck, but at Ore's words, he pivoted on his heel and gave him a stern look, eyes sharp. "What do you mean some guy wasn't welcoming? What happened?"

Ore shrugged, not really wanting to tell his parents about Billy and the bookstore. "It wasn't a big deal. He said something rude to me, but Cash stepped in before anything could happen." He smiled at the memory. "I thought he was going to rip the guy's throat out." At their horrified looks, he rushed to say, "But he didn't. He made sure the guy was punished though."

His mom didn't look very relieved, making him wonder what sort of punishment they thought happened in Liam's pack. "He was that upset over some rude words?"

His dad's eyes narrowed. "They must have been pretty bad for a pack Enforcer to react so violently against his own packmate while protecting a stranger."

Ore looked away, his cheeks heating. "Cash was... sort of put in charge of making sure my stay here was uneventful."

He picked his words carefully, not actually wanting to admit to his parents that he'd basically been confined to Cash's house until he finally wore him down with Pops's help, and then the first time he came into town, he'd run into Billy. He wasn't sure his parents would understand—or appreciate—their only son not being trusted by the very same pack he was now asking them to put their trust in.

They exchanged a look, wariness clear on both of their faces and scents.

"Maybe staying isn't such a good idea," his mom said, looking back at him. "I'm sure there are wonderful people here, but we have to think about all of our safety, including your sisters'."

Ore nodded. "I get that, truly, but if Alpha Amato says we're safe here, I believe him. I don't know exactly what's going to happen at this pack meeting tonight, but I do know that he plans on telling people who don't want any of the members of our pack joining to leave. He won't tolerate people being intolerant or divisive."

"Still," his dad said, crossing his arms over his chest. "This Amato has been alpha for a few years now and hasn't done anything like this. Seems like he's being rash and that he might regret welcoming us into his pack. Where will we be then?"

Taking a deep breath, Ore stood from the uncomfortable chair covered with a weird horse-print fabric. As calmly as he could, he told his parents, "If you don't want to stay, I can't make you. You have to do what you believe is best for yourselves and the girls, but I'm an adult, and I'll be staying either way."

His mom jumped up from where she'd been perched on the edge of the bed—the quilt covering it was a patchwork of belt buckles, horseshoes, and all kinds of other cowboy paraphernalia, and he couldn't help but be distracted by the idea of Liam decorating the room that way. Hadn't Cash said he'd grown up near Chicago?

She came forward and clasped his elbows, giving him a quick squeeze. "Sweetheart, you don't have to stay here because you feel a sense of obligation after they saved your life. We'll be forever grateful for that, but we just don't know if it's the best place for avian shifters, given the attitude of some of the pack members."

"I'm not staying out of misplaced loyalty or a sense of obligation." He took a deep breath and swallowed. "Cash and I are mates. I'm not leaving him."

His mother's nails dug into his skin before she dropped her hands and took a step back. He winced at the horror on her face.

"Are you sure?" she asked quietly, glancing back at Ore's dad before refocusing on him.

His dad wasn't saying anything. His only reaction to Ore's proclamation was the furrowing of his dark brows. His stomach got a little queasy, but he straightened his shoulders and nodded. It didn't matter if they approved. He and Cash loved each other. They wanted to be a family.

"I'm positive. My bird led me here to him when I was injured and terrified, and even when I couldn't remember anything, I felt drawn to him. He's kept me safe ever since I arrived. He's been generous with his time and money and affections, taking care of me in ways I couldn't even begin to explain. We're mates, and we're sticking together." He cleared the emotion out of his throat and added, "He's worked hard to become an Enforcer in this pack. I would never ask him to give that up."

His dad walked slowly over to stand next to his mom. She still looked shocked, but his dad clasped her hand and said, "Obviously, your mother and I are very happy for you. You've always wanted a mate, and we're glad you found someone as wonderful as Cash."

His mom started to say something but stopped with a faint noise that made Ore think his dad had just tightened his grip.

"We can't wait to get to know him and personally thank him for taking care of our boy," he finished, smiling at Ore. It wasn't big, but it was there.

Tears sprang into Ore's eyes. As frustrated as he was at his mom's reaction, he knew she would come around. It wasn't that interspecies matings were unheard of among shifters, but avians could be a bit stuck up about who they believed were acceptable mates. He understood it was a shock for her.

He just hoped it didn't take too long for her to realize how amazing Cash was.

Giving them a strained smile, he headed for the door. "I've got to head out and meet Cash before we go to the meeting tonight. Do you guys need anything?"

His dad shook his head. "No, son, we're just fine. It's been a long day, so I think we'll turn in for the night."

"Okay," he said, forcing himself to ignore the fact that his mother still hadn't said anything. "I'll try to come by in the morning before we leave."

ORE WAS a little surprised that the pack meeting was being held outside in the same area behind Alpha Amato's house where they'd all met before the pack run. When he said as much to Cash, his panther informed him they enjoyed having their gatherings out in nature whenever possible. The only time they used the community center was if the weather was too bad.

He supposed it made sense. Their entire territory was set up in a way that surrounded them with nature. All woods and grass and water. It shouldn't surprise him to learn that most of the pack members preferred not being cooped up inside.

His appreciation for the wildness of the territory was soon forgotten, the meeting turning heated faster than he'd anticipated.

Liam started by briefly explaining the situation, including Ore's amnesia, his parents arriving, and the threats that his family and others back in California faced from the Enforcers in the Barney Pack. He then very clearly stated the Silver Oak Pack would be helping, and the decision wasn't up for debate.

Over the noise of discontent, he told them he'd already called his brother and Alpha Kincaid for reinforcements.

More people than Ore had expected seemed upset by that, but what really set off a handful of pack members was when Liam said, "I'll be opening the territory to any of the members of the Barney Pack who would like to take refuge here, either temporarily or permanently. And if anyone has a problem with that, they are welcome to leave my pack."

Several people, including a familiar voice near the back of the crowd that had Ore inching closer to Cash, said Liam couldn't just change pack laws and policies on his own.

"As the alpha, I absolutely can change pack law as I see fit. If you don't like it, you can leave or challenge me for my position."

When there was movement in the crowd, fear gripped his intestines. Was someone going to challenge him right then and there? What if he lost and Ore cost him everything?

But then a familiar white head of hair and hunched shoulders came into view and made their way to the front of the pack, stepping up right next to Alpha Amato and scowling out at the crowd.

"Anyone complaining about Alpha Amato offering refuge to these avians should be ashamed of themselves," Pops said, his voice ringing out clearly and silencing all of the chatter. "I remember when this pack wasn't afraid of welcoming newcomers, and I, for one, am glad we'll be returning to that way of life."

"We've always been a pack of cats," someone shouted from the midst of the crowd.

Ore couldn't tell who it was, but based on the tightening in Cash's shoulders, he knew them, and he wasn't pleased with them arguing with his grandfather.

"Yes, we have," Pops agreed, giving one quick nod. "But we welcomed new ones. We didn't shun other packs. We had alliances and welcomed emissaries."

There was a murmur of agreement, especially among the older members.

"When was the last time we allowed a visitor from another pack?" Pops went on.

The same person as before called back, "Kincaid's Enforcer was here—"

"Bah!" Pops waved his cane angrily, forcing a few people to step back. "The only reason most of you got on board with Liam agreeing to help was after he pointed out it would be beneficial for Kincaid to owe us a favor." The disgust in Pops's voice was clear. "There was a time when we would've offered assistance without expecting anything in return, but now we've isolated ourselves so completely it has become detrimental to our pack growth."

A few people in the crowd nodded, faces concerned.

"Our numbers are shrinking. We have more elders than cubs, and we haven't had a new member ask to join in two years. Two. *Years*," he emphasized, giving his cane another shake. "I don't know about you, but I'm pretty sure that means our pack is dying. It's slow because we still have a strong alpha—thank the goddess—but if we don't change things right now, we won't have a pack for much longer. Maybe a couple of generations, and that's it, folks."

There were some more murmurs from the crowd. Most agreed with nods and a few "You tell 'em, Pops," though a handful seemed to scoff at his warning.

"How much longer do you expect me to act as pack healer?" He raised his bushy eyebrows, meeting the eyes of those right in front of him. "Each year, I get older, and it becomes a little harder to move and see and hear, but there's no one in our pack even training to become a healer. No one's interested in the job, and we don't have any new people joining to fill in these very important positions. If we don't grow, we die."

With those ominous words, Pops stepped back into the crowd, planting both hands on his cane and giving Ore a wink.

Liam watched Pops with fondness, but he sobered as he addressed the crowd once more. "Pops is right. We can continue going as we are until we're so dwindled in numbers there isn't a pack left, or we can choose to change. We can *choose* to become a thriving pack once more. We can help those who need it, and we can build relationships with other packs and covens. We can offer assistance in this tumultuous time of rebuilding... or we can stand on the sidelines and hope the new world we're about to step into is to our liking."

Ore was so proud of both Pops and Alpha Amato. It didn't matter that there were people who were questioning whether what they were doing was a good idea. They both were holding firm, showing their support, not just in the pack but in Ore, in his family. He honestly couldn't be more grateful.

"If we open up our territory," someone shouted, "what's

to stop terrible people from moving here? People who would steal resources or harm our elders and cubs."

There was a small rumble of agreement, but Liam held up both hands, and the crowd silenced quickly.

"What's to stop them?" he asked, a wide grin spreading across his face. "We will. *We* will stop any bad actors who try and come into our territory. This is still our pack, our home, our *family*. Giving people a door to walk through to join us isn't the same as completely removing our borders, but if we want to survive, we have to embrace the future and forget the past."

CHAPTER 17

"Wow, that got intense," Ore said as he led the way inside the house.

Cash nodded, following close behind him, shutting and locking the door. "Yeah. I knew there'd be some pushback, but it seemed like most people were supportive of the idea."

His bird headed straight for the living room, throwing himself down on the couch and letting out a dramatic groan. "Goddess, I'm tired. This day has just been so long, and I feel like I've barely seen you."

Smiling, he sat next to him, lifting his arm when Ore immediately leaned into him to snuggle close. "How are your parents feeling?"

Ore's scent soured a little. "I'm not sure. I'm hoping after a few days of processing everything, they'll be a little more open to the idea of staying here."

He glanced down, staring at Ore's face and the tiny furrow between his brows. "They're not planning on staying?"

He tipped his head back to meet Cash's gaze. "They're not sure. I kind of get it. If I didn't have you, I wouldn't be as comfortable staying in a pack full of felines. I think they're worried mostly about feeling like outsiders or like they were only admitted to the pack out of guilt or charity. I know they're worried about my sisters too."

"They'd all be safe here," Cash assured him. "I promise you."

Ore reached up and cupped the side of his face. "I know that. You don't have to convince me. I don't know that it helped when I told them about us. They seemed pretty shocked."

A lump formed in Cash's throat. "They were upset when you told them we were mates?"

He hummed in agreement, leaning up to press a kiss to the underside of Cash's chin. "My mom was. My dad came around really quickly, told me they were happy for me, but she still seemed horrified at the idea of me being mated to a panther."

Cash scowled. "Does she think I won't treat you well? I can talk to her if you want. Even if we hadn't been destined for each other, I still would've chosen you, Ore."

His mate stretched up farther to give him a quick kiss on his mouth. "I would've chosen you too. But no, you don't need to talk to her. They'll either decide to stay or to go to another pack. Hopefully if they leave, they won't end up too far away so we can visit every now and again."

"You'll still be staying?" Cash asked slowly, voicing the worry that had gripped him as soon as Ore had said his parents might not.

Ore gave his ear a tug. "Of course I'm staying. I love them, but you're my mate. You're the one I'm going to build a life with."

"If you want to be with them, we could still le—"

"No," Ore interrupted. "I would never ask you to leave. You are an integral part of this pack, and you've worked so hard to get where you are. I would never ask you to give that up."

"I just want you to be happy," Cash said softly, leaning closer and nuzzling against Ore's temple.

"You do make me happy. So does Pops—and even Rachel and Saint are growing on me. Plus, the cute little bookstore." He tapped his lips, pretending to think. "Oh yes, and I love you."

"I love you too, little bit." He couldn't help but smile at his silliness.

Ore's sweet face turned radiant with happiness. He slipped a hand behind Cash's neck and used his handhold to pull himself up and over Cash's lap so he was straddling him and they were face-to-face.

As Ore leaned in, Cash put a hand on his shoulder, stopping him. His dick throbbed in protest, but there was one more thing he needed to say before he got distracted. "I'd rather you not come tomorrow."

Liam had let the pack know at the end of the meeting that the reinforcements from his brother's pack and Rick Kincaid would be arriving tomorrow afternoon. Then, they'd fly to California together to confront Ore's old pack and rescue anyone who wanted to leave.

It would hopefully be a short trip when they showed up with formidable backup. Their numbers should discourage Alpha Barney or his Enforcers from putting up a fight. Then, it would just be sorting out transportation and anything else the pack needed before they headed back home.

Tipping his head to the side, Ore studied him, a faint smile still on his lips. "It's my family, my former pack. I have to go."

"It could get dangerous," Cash said. "I need to make sure you stay safe."

Ore clasped either side of his face, leaning in until their foreheads were pressed together. "I know, and it's one of the many reasons why I love you, but I have to do this. I need to face what happened and the fact that I just ran instead of staying and trying to help."

"You were worried about your own well-being," Cash insisted. "I doubt anyone blames you for fleeing to protect yourself."

He shrugged. "Maybe, but the fact of the matter is my sisters and other hatchlings in the pack have suffered because of my decision. I need to be a part of the solution."

Cash sighed and closed his eyes. He understood what Ore was saying—he'd feel the exact same way. Even if Ore didn't plan on staying with his old pack, he still felt responsible for them. A sense of loyalty that didn't just evaporate because he met Cash.

"If anyone even looks at you wrong—"

"You'll rip their throats out. I know," Ore said, kissing the corner of his mouth and then the other side.

Cash growled and chased his lips, threading his fingers in his hair to hold his teasing mate still. He didn't hesitate, thrusting his tongue inside and tilting Ore's head a little so he could deepen the kiss even more. Moaning, Ore slung his arms around his neck and opened for him, letting Cash take everything he wanted.

Dragging his hands up Ore's thighs, he forced himself to pull back. One look at Ore's kiss-drunk face nearly had him throwing him down on the couch and rutting against him right there.

"Let's go upstairs," he growled, giving his little bird's ass a quick smack.

With a whimper that made Cash's dick twitch, Ore nodded shakily and carefully climbed to his feet, looking unsteady for a minute.

He recovered quickly, tossing a flirty look at Cash and then dashing toward the stairs.

His panther roared with excitement. Chasing his mate, then making him his in every way possible? No way he'd pass that up.

As he ran up the stairs behind Ore, he stripped off his

shirt and tossed it aside. By the time he caught up to Ore, right at the end of their bed, his pants were unbuttoned, but he paused his stripping to grab Ore around the waist and gently toss him on the mattress.

Bursting with surprised laughter, Ore flipped around onto his back. "You caught me."

Cash unzipped his jeans and let them drop. "I'll always catch you, little bit. But I do love it when you run."

Ore sucked in a breath, his eyes moving down Cash's body like a caress and then pausing on his hardening cock. Licking his lips, Ore asked breathlessly, "You have supplies here, right? I don't want a repeat of the lake. Actually, you know what, that was pretty amazing if you want to do it again."

"Another time," he assured him, pulling open the bedside table and grabbing the new bottle of lube tucked inside.

Ore rustled around on the bed, and then a shirt hit the back of his head, followed by a bright giggle. Struggling to keep a straight face, Cash turned around and shook his head in disappointment.

"That wasn't very nice."

Digging his teeth into his bottom lip, Ore wiggled out of his jeans and briefs, throwing them next. Cash caught them and let them fall out of his hand to the floor.

He cracked a smile. "Such a brat."

Ore held out his arms, gesturing at Cash. "Come here. I need you inside me already."

Growling, he pounced on the bed and prowled forward until he was hovering over his tiny mate. "Once I'm inside, I'm never leaving."

Ore held his gaze. "Good. I'd want you to live in my skin if you could."

A spark of an idea took hold, but he shoved it aside, focusing on his sexy little bird. Leaning down, he captured his plush lips in a deep, pulse-pounding kiss. He got lost in it for a moment until Ore started whimpering and wiggling beneath him.

Kissing across his jaw and down his neck, he flipped open the top of the lube and coated his fingers. He'd need to be extra careful with preparing his mate so he didn't hurt him with his size.

He sucked on the spot between Ore's neck and shoulder, more than ready to sink his fangs into his sweet skin. Ore grabbed the back of his head, pulling him in harder and rolling his hips.

"Faster, baby. I can't wait any longer."

Grunting, he nipped with his teeth and sank a finger inside Ore when he arched up in response.

"Ung!" Ore tore at his shoulders, spreading his legs as wide as he could. "Yes, yes, yes. Give me another."

His mate was so warm… and tight. He ignored his demand and gently worked his finger in and out, rubbing against the walls until he found what he was looking for.

"*Cash*!"

For a few long minutes, Cash licked and kissed at every bit of skin he could reach while he slowly worked his mate open, tapping at his prostate whenever he started getting pushy about Cash going faster. It took a while—forever, if you asked Ore—for him to get up to three fingers that he could plunge in and out easily.

He lingered, just a few seconds longer, until his mate whimpered and thrashed beneath him.

"I'm good. I'm ready. Just get your dick inside me, please!"

Nipping at Ore's kiss-swollen lips, he slicked himself with more lube. "You think being rude and demanding is the way to get what you want?"

"I said please," Ore argued, a smile tugging at his lips.

"Hmm." Cash held his eyes as he lined up at Ore's entrance. "I suppose that's true."

Ore opened his mouth—whether to be bratty or beg, he wasn't sure—but Cash surged forward, sinking halfway inside in one go. Moaning long and low, Ore arched his neck back and dug his heels into Cash's ass.

"Goddess, yes. More, *please*."

He eased in slowly, worried about going too fast and hurting Ore despite his desire for Cash to just pound the shit out of him. He'd never risk his little bird's health or safety—not even so he could get inside his amazingly tight heat.

"Cash, faster," he pleaded, slapping at one of his shoulders. "I'm small, not fragile. I can take it, I promise."

There was a thread of desperation in his voice that called to Cash's panther, snagging and reeling him in until he was nothing but a disciple worshiping at the throne of Ore.

He sped up, going deeper with each thrust, Ore's cries of ecstasy ringing in his ears. Soon, he was lost to the pleasure building between them, face smashed into his mate's neck to suck in as much of his floral scent as possible and hips shuttling in and out at a fast, steady pace. Just before he bottomed out each time, he'd slam the rest of the way in just to hear his mate moan again and again.

"I'm so close," Ore whimpered, wrapped as tightly around Cash as he could get.

Cash grunted in agreement, speeding up a little more.

Tilting his head to the side, Ore begged breathlessly, "Bite me, please. Make me yours forever."

He released an ear-splitting roar, his fangs descending and pricking at his lip. Giving one more lick over the spot, now salty with a thin layer of sweat, he pounded into Ore twice more and then let go. His come sprayed inside him, so deep he had to believe it would stay forever, marking him with his scent.

But that wasn't enough.

With a hiss, he bit down into the meat of Ore's shoulder,

his mouth filling with his coppery blood. Ore tensed beneath him, right on the edge, and Cash moved his hips in a circle.

"Oh shit, your dick..."

His chest filled with pride at providing even more pleasure for his mate. Now that they were bonded, his cock would be able to form ridges to give Ore more sensation.

Swirling his hips once more, he released his teeth and grinned with primal satisfaction as Ore screamed, the scent of his come filling the air. Gently, he licked over the bite mark he'd left, watching with content as Ore's skin began to heal but leaving a scar behind.

Everyone would know he was claimed.

Panting, Ore flopped his limbs onto the bed, turning into a puddle beneath him. "That was... I didn't realize... Good gracious."

Cash's chest pumped with satisfaction, and he pulled out with a groan. Ore moaned softly as well but didn't open his eyes. Filled with contentment, Cash got them both cleaned up, holding Ore up while he stripped the stained comforter off the bed and then tucking him beneath the sheet.

As he crawled in behind him and wrapped his arms around his limp little body, Ore roused just long enough to mutter, "Give me five more minutes, then I'm ready for round two."

He pressed his smile into his mate's hair. It was doubtful Ore would wake at all before morning, but he didn't mind.

They had the rest of their lives to make up for it.

CHAPTER 18

"There's no reason to be nervous."

Even without the bitter scent filling Cash's nose, he would've known Ore was anxious about meeting the people coming to their aid. Both of his legs were bouncing up and down as they sat in his truck, waiting for the plane to land. At the most northern edge of their territory, an area had been cleared right after Liam became alpha, and his brother had built his own private hangar so he and his people could visit whenever they wanted without having to drive in from the city.

The place was always locked down tight when not in use, a few SUVs tucked inside and ready for them.

Quinten rarely visited himself since he was busy running his *not* completely legit business empire, but he and Liam talked on the phone constantly, it seemed like, either through text, phone calls, or video chats. They were so close he'd been surprised to learn they were only stepbrothers. Liam's mom had married Quinten's dad when he was young, and Quinten had helped raise him.

It had taken almost two years before he'd learned that since Liam wasn't exactly a big sharer, but it did explain the tiny airport in their territory. Even if Quinten couldn't come as often as he wanted, he still had a way to send some of his people down to check on his baby brother, whom he was so protective of.

"Sorry," Ore said, throwing him a quick smile that didn't quite reach his beautiful, dark eyes. He stilled his jiggling legs and tucked his hands beneath his thighs to prevent him from fidgeting more. "I am a little nervous, but I'm also kind of excited. Do you know everyone who's coming?"

Cash shook his head. "I know the two guys that Quinten is sending, but I'm not sure who's coming from the Kincaid Pack. I only know a few of his people."

Nodding, Ore leaned forward in his seat to peer up at the sky. "I thought they were supposed to be here by now."

Cash shrugged and leaned back, throwing his arm onto the back of the seat and getting comfortable. "They were supposed to be, but I've learned that dealing with multiple headstrong alphas can cause delays."

Ore shot him a wide-eyed look. "You think one of the alphas got upset? Is there a chance they won't come?"

He thought about it for a second and then shook his head. "Quinten's guys will come no matter what. There's no way he'd let his brother down like that. And Kincaid? Well, let's just say that even if I don't agree with everything he's done in the past year, he still has a reputation for being trustworthy and fair. He gave Liam his word they would help, so I don't think he'd turn his back on us just because he and Quinten—or one of Quinten's guys—got into some sort of pissing match. It probably slowed them down a bit though."

Ore nibbled on his lower lip. "That makes sense. I still don't remember everything that happened last year, but based on what I do recall and the things you've told me about all the changes the Kincaid Pack is making to the parahuman world, and the fact that Quinten is a badass human alpha who takes shit from no one, it's not super surprising the two of them would butt heads."

Cash chuckled. "I'd say that's an understatement. Luckily, Liam seems to play mediator quite well between the two when need be."

"I can see that," Ore said. "He doesn't seem to get riled easily."

"That's the lion in him," Cash said with a grin. "They're laid-back until they're threatened, and then they can become the fiercest protector you've ever met."

Ore scooted closer to him, placing one of his small, delicate hands on Cash's thigh. "I don't know. I'd say you are the fiercest protector I've ever met."

Having his mate touching him and talking about how well he and his panther protected him was all it took for his dick to get interested. Before he could suggest a quickie in his truck, he heard the faint but unmistakable sound of an approaching airplane.

Lifting Ore's hand from where it was sliding upward slowly, he gently kissed each of his knuckles. "No time for that, little bit. They're here."

That distracted Ore immediately as he craned his head around, trying to spot the plane. "Are you sure? I don't see anything. Oh, wait." Ore started vibrating with excitement next to him. "I do see them. They should be here in a minute or so." He gave Cash a pretend pout. "Definitely no time for blowjobs."

Snorting, Cash cupped Ore's face to draw him close, pressing a sweet, lingering kiss on his lips. "Definitely not."

Ore shivered and stared at him with adoring eyes. If he didn't get out of the truck soon, he'd choose spending time with his mate over doing his duty as Enforcer and welcoming their guests.

With one more quick peck, he pulled away and opened his door. He heard a faint sigh from behind him, but Ore didn't say anything, just scooted across the bench seat and hopped down as well. It didn't take long before the plane was landing on the cleared strip, finally coming to a stop next to the single plane hangar.

Cash threaded his fingers between Ore's and led him forward. They stopped a few feet away from where the stairs landed on the ground.

The first face he saw was one he was very familiar with.

Nero was as good-looking as Finlay, which made Cash wonder if all vampires looked like they should be on the cover of magazines rather than ripping people's throats out. Unlike Finlay, Nero grinned widely, rushing down the steps and wrapping Cash in a bear hug. He was wearing a T-shirt that said, "I vant to drink your blood."

Typical Nero.

The guy was as charming and talkative as they came, though based on a few things he'd heard from Liam and some of Quinten's other people, he was pretty sure Nero's main job was killing people for Quinten.

"Cash, my man. How are things?" Nero said as he gave his back a couple of hearty slaps and then pulled back.

"A little tense now, but I think we're going to fix that."

"Hell yeah, we are," Nero said, turning his beautiful smile on Cash's mate, prickling his panther. He had to stop himself from stepping between them. "This the man of the hour?"

Ore gave him a sort of dazed smile, which Cash understood. Seeing someone that good-looking and personable could be a bit overwhelming.

"This is my mate, Ore."

"Hey, little man," Nero said, stepping over and holding out his hand. "Quinten gave us the lowdown on what happened to you. I'm glad you're feeling better."

Ore shook his hand and then blinked a few times as he accepted the handshake. "Right, yes. Thank you. Me too."

"Quit blinding them with your pearly whites and get out

of the way," a deep, growly voice said, and Cash suppressed a chuckle as Nero rolled his eyes but did as he was told.

A few steps from the bottom was a copper-skinned man Cash would recognize anywhere.

"Hey, Dare," he said, holding his hand out. As the wolf moved closer to him, he gave him a quick handshake and then pointed at Ore. "This is Ore."

He nodded at him before turning to Cash. "I'm going to get our SUVs ready."

And then he turned and walked into the hangar without saying anything else.

Cash glanced at his mate and wasn't surprised to see the barely disguised horror on his face. It wasn't over Dare's abrupt personality. It was because of the scar that ran down the left side of his face and clouded his left eye. Cash didn't know if he had any vision left in it, but either way, it didn't stop him from being a fierce and very competent second-in-command to Quinten.

Ore met his eyes, and he knew he would have questions later. But more people were coming down the stairs, so they didn't have time to focus on Dare's traumatic life. He hoped his mate didn't expect an answer on how he'd gotten scarred because Cash had no idea, just like he didn't know what had happened to Liam to leave permanent claw marks on him.

The next two to exit the plane were also people he knew.

Nico and his mate, Keegan, had spent a little time with their pack about a year ago. Keegan had been in bad shape, thanks to his fucked-up mom torturing him, and Nico had promised a favor from Rick in exchange for Liam's help and allowing Keegan to stay with them until he was better. Liam had agreed because the last thing he was was a fool. Having the most powerful alpha on the continent owe you a favor was something he couldn't turn down.

Nico was nearly as big and wide as Darius, but he definitely had more of Nero's personality, a grin always at the ready.

"Hey. Cash, right?" Nico said, hurrying down the last few steps and clasping Cash on his upper arm. "Good to see you again, man."

"And you," Cash said, nodding politely.

Nico had only been with them a couple of days before heading back to his pack, and they hadn't spent a lot of time together. He gave a soft smile to Keegan, who was a little shorter than his mate and not as bulky, his skin dark brown compared to Nico's pale white.

"You've been good?" Cash asked, and the witch nodded at him, grinning widely.

"Finally bagged this one," Keegan said, jerking his thumb at his mate. "And then got settled in with the Kincaids just before they decided to… give themselves a little more responsibility."

"One way of putting it," Cash said dryly. He turned to his mate. "Ore, this is Nico and Keegan. They visited us last year for a while."

"It's nice to meet you."

"Same," Nico said as Keegan smiled and nodded and then herded his mate out of the way.

Behind them was someone he wasn't familiar with. He had alabaster skin, freckles, red hair, and was tall, maybe even taller than Liam. He was followed closely by a stockier Latino who Cash was surprised to find was human but not a witch.

An odd choice for Kincaid to send. He didn't want to have to keep an eye on his mate and some human who didn't know how to handle himself around shifters.

"Welcome to Silver Oak," he said, waiting until they both hit the ground before extending his hand.

"I'm Marcus Rivera," the redhead said, "and this is my mate, Robson Medina."

Cash gave them a polite smile. "Thank you for agreeing to help us."

A wide grin spread across Robson's face. "Don't worry, man. I've got some tactical experience from the military and from the Kincaid Pack."

Marcus gave his mate a soft, proud smile. "Robson helps train the betas in our pack as well as any other members who want lessons in fighting."

Cash was impressed. Most humans couldn't stand a chance against even an untrained shifter. He had a feeling he could maybe even learn something from this particularly cocky one.

Two more people stepped out of the plane, and then the man he assumed was the pilot brought up the rear. The woman with wild blonde curls he knew, but the other man behind her he'd never met before. He was younger, so he was guessing a beta and either Latino or Mediterranean based on his dark tan.

"Cash," the blonde said, grinning brightly at him and coming right over to wrap him in a hug. He smelled a surge of anger from his little bit, but Ore didn't say anything.

"Ericka." He loosely wrapped his arms around her, not looking to piss off his mate. "Been a minute."

She laughed, bright and cheery, and stepped back. The lioness had come with Nico last year and then stuck around to keep an eye on Keegan and his sister since she would blend in and was less well-known than the big Enforcer.

"I'll say," she said and shot her dazzling smile at Ore. "From what I hear, you haven't been staying out of trouble."

Ore made a soft, squawking noise. "I'm not trouble!"

She laughed again and then shocked his mate by pulling him in a hug too. "I have a feeling you've completely wrecked his safe, orderly life." She leaned back, resting both hands on his shoulders. "For that, you deserve a damn medal."

Ore's brows were furrowed slightly, and he gave her a confused half smile. "Thanks, I think."

"Ignore her," Cash said. "This one's a troublemaker."

"That's slander," she exclaimed.

The young guy next to her, probably around the same age actually, laughed hard. "Nah, he's got your number for sure." He shouldered the backpack he was carrying and extended his hand. "I'm José."

"Thanks for coming," Cash said, shaking his hand and then letting Ore squeeze up against him and reach across his body to give him a handshake as well.

He slid his arm around his shoulders before he could pull away, wanting to keep his mate as close to him as possible. Looking over their heads at the older man still lingering on the steps, he noted his mostly silver hair and clearly human scent.

"You the pilot?"

The man nodded. "I'm going to hang around here. Just let me know when you all are ready to leave."

Cash thanked him and turned to the small group gathered next to him. Dare was striding toward them from the hangar and posted up next to Nero, arms crossed over his chest.

"Everything good?" Cash asked.

Dare nodded. "Haven't been tampered with."

Ore shot him a look but didn't say anything. Cash gave him a light squeeze before addressing the whole group.

"Alpha Amato is waiting for us back in town, where we'll come up with a strategy that will hopefully get us in and out of California without having to raise a claw to anyone."

A couple of people nodded, but Erica frowned at him. "But what if we want to?"

He shook his head and ignored her and the way Nero reached around a few people to fist-bump her.

"He asked me to express his thanks and gratitude as soon

as you got here, but I also want to personally thank each and every one of you," Cash said, the back of his neck heating.

He wasn't used to talking so openly about his feelings, but what they were doing had the potential for danger, and these people barely knew him. They had no real reason to put themselves on the line. But one look down at Ore's sweet face and he knew he'd ask his worst enemy for help if it meant keeping his mate safe and in his life.

"I can't express with words what this means to me, but please know I owe each of you for helping me and my mate."

CHAPTER 19

The plane ride to California was… interesting, to say the least.

Ore ended up perched on Cash's lap since the plane—while luxurious—wasn't actually made for so many people to travel in. Keegan was also on his mate's lap, the two of them murmuring back and forth to each other. Nico's big hands were clasped possessively on his witch.

The vampire, Nero, had offered his lap to Ericka. She laughed and then punched him in the bicep so hard the vampire winced.

Dare, who'd been sitting next to him, snarled at Nero and then rose and offered his seat to her before stalking to the back of the plane and closing the door behind him. Ore figured it was probably a bedroom for sleeping on longer flights, but he didn't exactly feel like Dare would welcome him going back and taking a peek.

The Kincaid Pack members mostly kept to themselves, and the same with the Silver Oak Pack, three betas having joined them along with Liam.

The small bit of tension lingering in the air during the flight kept him tense and unable to relax. Even when Cash started gently running his hand up and down the outside of Ore's thigh and encouraging him to lean back and get some rest. He did lean into his mate, but resting definitely wasn't an option. Not with so many strange shifters surrounding him who didn't seem like they really got along that well.

They were only about half an hour from landing when Nico, who'd been talking to the human, Robson, sitting next to him, raised his voice just a little and said, "I am surprised Amato only sent two guys, considering it was his brother who asked for help."

Cash tensed beneath him. "We're grateful for any help—"

Nero cut him off, eyes locked on Nico. "Considering that Dare and I are equal to about six of you, I'd say it's fair, especially since he provided the plane and financial support as well."

"The two of you are worth six of us," Nico repeated, an incredulous smile on his face. "How do you figure?"

Nero leaned forward, resting his forearms on his knees and cocking his head to the side. All of his good humor and smiles had disappeared. What was left behind was a beautiful but deadly predator.

"Because the two of us aren't afraid to kill someone. That's what we train for. Not to win a fight but to end it. Permanently. Your hesitation makes you weak."

"That's enough," Liam said firmly, shooting Nero a frown before turning to the Kincaid Pack members. "Please ignore him. My brother tends not to put an emphasis on manners, but we are very appreciative of your help."

Nico kept his eyes on Nero for a long moment and then relaxed back in his seat, turning to Liam. He waved a hand. "Yeah, of course."

"I'm also grateful that Rick let me cash in my favor on this," Liam said, face solemn. "You let him know we're square now."

Nico scoffed. "Nah, brother, this is a freebie."

Liam's eyebrows twitched. "Excuse me?"

"You did something very personal for me and my mate, and Rick promised a favor in return, but this isn't for that."

Liam glanced at Cash, who was on one side of him, and then Saint, sitting on the other, before turning back to Nico. "I just assumed it was."

"No. This is because it's what's best for the parahuman community," Marcus said, looking up from his phone. "Ore's parents mentioned they couldn't risk contacting us, worried they were being watched and spied on. I think I'll suggest to Alpha Kincaid that we set up an encrypted messaging system."

"That's a great idea, cariño," his mate said, caressing the side of his neck and drawing Ore's eyes to the bonding bite there.

How on earth…

"Exactly," Nico agreed. "It's for the good of everyone. When you need a personal favor, that's when you can cash in your chit. Got it?"

Liam smiled. "Got it."

ORE WAS a little surprised that when they landed at the private airport, there were enough black SUVs waiting for all fifteen of them.

Cash looked at Liam. "Your brother?"

"When I suggested we could just use a rideshare, he laughed at me and told me it was a good thing I had my looks since I wasn't so bright," Liam told him dryly, shaking his head.

Ore slapped a hand over his mouth to suppress a giggle. He was both curious and terrified at the idea of meeting Liam's brother one day. The other Alpha Amato seemed like he was quite the character. Definitely dangerous but also generous, especially when it came to his younger brother.

They loaded into the SUVs, making sure everyone had the location of the pack, and then set off. He and Cash were in one with Nero, Dare, and Saint. Liam had jumped into the back of the one the Silver Oak betas had claimed, and then the Kincaid Pack members had split into the remaining two.

"Have you remembered anything else?" Saint asked him as soon as they were moving.

"Not since I told you everything I could remember a few hours ago," he said wryly.

Fern had explained to him that he remembered his family first because they meant so much to him. The connection was the strongest. He'd assumed he would then start remembering his packmates, alpha, and the place he'd lived most of his life.

He did remember some things, but others were still big blanks. He had a vague recollection of what his alpha looked like, but most of the rest of the pack, he couldn't at all. But he could remember his fear as he'd fled, desperate to get away from Gladstone before he... forced the issue.

Most of the rest was still frustratingly blank.

Saint slapped him on the knee, giving it a quick shake before letting go as Cash growled at him. "Don't worry. Your parents gave us the layout of the territory and your alpha's house, so we should be okay."

"Plus, we do have the advantage of surprise," Nero chirped from the front seat, twisting around to grin at them.

"They have to know we'd come for Ore's sisters," Cash said, frowning. "When his parents stayed instead of going back with Gladstone, they had to assume we'd do something to get the girls back."

Nero shrugged. "Well, yeah, but they're probably expecting you to go about it diplomatically. Put together a formal request, go through all the red tape, yada, yada, yada.

I doubt they're expecting you to show up with force to *make* them turn over the girls."

"And anyone else who wants to leave," Dare added gruffly, keeping his eyes on the road.

"Rivera mentioned on the plane ride from Michigan that he and the rest of the Kincaid Pack contingent will be staying if everything goes to plan," Nero added, distracted by something outside the window. "I guess they're going to help whoever steps up to be the new alpha get settled and make sure better Enforcers are selected."

Ore was a little surprised at that. He'd assumed they would have to immediately get back to their own pack and their duties. It seemed like most of them were Enforcers, after all.

Cash must have read his mind because he said softly, "Kincaid's pack is a lot bigger than ours. He has more Enforcers to pick up the slack."

"And betas," Saint added. "I heard once he has like thirty of them."

Ore whipped his head around to stare. "Seriously?

"I don't know if it's thirty," Nero said thoughtfully. "But there's definitely a lot of activity at HQ there. But since so many people are coming from other packs to help get the new government set up, it can be hard to tell who's a part of his pack and who's there for that. It also benefits them if people think they have so many Enforcers and betas to protect their territory."

Ore nodded. "That makes sense."

Still, being around all of that activity sounded stressful to him, especially since Kincaid had only made his pack an even bigger target by building the new government just outside of his own territory.

He much preferred the small, more intimate pack in Silver Oak. He didn't know how long they would have that peaceful existence before new members started arriving, but he had no doubt they would. Once word got out that a strong alpha like Liam was looking for new members of any shifter species, they'd be running to apply.

It only took about twenty minutes to get to the Barney Pack territory. Ore shivered as they crossed over the boundary line, not because it was imbued with magic like the Silver Oak Pack's were, but because he wasn't looking forward to the confrontation coming up.

He had so many bad memories of Gladstone harassing him, and all of them were beating at his brain, trying to distract him. A big hand he was achingly familiar with slipped underneath his own where he was clutching at his jeans and threaded their fingers together.

He smiled up at his mate.

"It's going to be okay," Cash said firmly, no doubt in his voice or scent.

"I know." Ore nodded, looking back out through the windshield as they passed through the small human town on the outskirts of the pack's territory. Most of the pack lived clustered around the alpha's house a few minutes away from the edge of town.

"Yeah, we're going to kick ass and be out the door before you know it," Nero said cheerfully, pointing at some store and nudging Dare with his elbow. "We should stop there before we get back on the plane."

Dare grunted at him, not bothering to respond.

Saint shot Ore a grin, seeming more amused than anyone else by the vampire's weird behavior.

As soon as Alpha Barney's house came into view, Ore's hands started shaking, a trickle of sweat dripping down his spine between his shoulder blades.

Cash didn't say anything, but he did squeeze his hand harder.

That show of support helped calm him. It would be fine. They'd tell Barney what was going on, get his sisters, and then get out of there. Marcus and the others could deal with all the rest.

The three other SUVs pulled up behind them, and they all parked in a line directly in front of the dilapidated porch on the front of the house. Ore vaguely remembered it once being in good condition, but that must have been when he was a kid because it looked like a strong wind would knock it down now. The house itself wasn't in much better condition. Anger over his sisters being trapped inside helped push the rest of his fear away.

"Ready to do this?" Nero asked, turning to look at all of them in the back seat, his gaze landing on Ore and holding. "You can stay in the car if you want. Once we've handled things, you can go in and get your sisters."

Ore shook his head. "No, I'm fine. Let's go."

He tried to insert more confidence in his voice than he was feeling, but he doubted any of the parahumans in the car with him bought it. No one said anything, though, or tried to talk him out of it. Cash opened the door and stepped out, dragging Ore behind him.

The others jumped out of their vehicles as well just as the screen door slapped open and Louie Gladstone stepped out, a scowl on his face.

"What the hell do you think you're doing here?" he yelled, eyes locked on Cash.

"Cleaning house," Cash said clearly and calmly and then nodded toward the Kincaid Pack members.

Marcus stepped forward, his red hair nearly orange in the bright sunlight. "Are you Enforcer Gladstone?"

"Yeah, who the fuck are you?"

"Marcus Rivera, Enforcer in Garrick Kincaid's pack." He let that information linger in the air, Louie's face dropping in shock as he ran his eyes over the rest of their group.

"You're all from Kincaid's pack?" he asked shakily.

Nero raised his hand. "Not me and the wolf." He pointed

at Dare next to him. "Quinten Amato wanted us to come and say hi."

It was immediately obvious that Louie was familiar with the name, blood draining from his face, and he looked even more scared than he had a minute ago.

"What's going on out here?" an old, creaky voice called, and then Alpha Barney slipped past Gladstone. He squinted out at the gathered group on his front lawn. He looked even older than Ore remembered, his face so wrinkled it was hard to see where his features were. Most of his hair had been gone for as long as Ore could remember, but he looked stick thin, like he wasn't really eating.

"Louie," Barney said, looking at his Enforcer. "Who are these people?"

Before Barney could decide whether he should come clean or lie, Cash stepped forward, Ore's hand still clasped in his. As soon as he moved away from the others, his old alpha's eyes landed on him and widened with recognition.

"Forester, is that you?"

He'd only been gone a month, but he tried to remember the last time he'd actually seen his alpha in person before that, and he couldn't. That could be his memory, but now he was wondering if Alpha Barney was being kept from the pack as much as the hatchlings were.

"Yes, sir," he said clearly, lifting his chin and refusing to show any fear in front of Gladstone. "I'm here for my sisters."

Barney looked confused for a second and then nodded once. "Ah, the hatchlings that have been staying with us for a little while." He looked over at Gladstone. "Are they finished with their training?"

Training? Was that what Gladstone had told him to get him to agree to keep the hatchlings locked in his house day after day? How on earth had he believed it?

He took in Barney's appearance again, and a dark thought entered his head.

"Alpha Barney?" Ore called out. "Do you know what day it is?"

Face turning ruddy, he immediately blustered at him, "Who can keep track of the days? When you're my age, they all string together."

Maybe, but he didn't think that was the real reason, and he looked at Cash and then back at the others, the resigned faces letting him know he wasn't the only one who'd realized the alpha's mind was slipping, making it even easier for the Enforcers to do whatever they wanted.

Force matings. Steal hatchlings. There was no one strong enough to stop them.

Until now.

Marcus walked toward the porch, concern etched on his freckled face.

"Careful, cariño," his mate muttered behind him.

Marcus moved to the bottom of the steps, glancing between Gladstone and Barney. "What you've done here is *despicable*," Marcus said fiercely, surprising Ore. The whole flight over, the redhead had only really shown emotion toward his mate. "You will be dealt with, but first, I need you to release all of the hatchlings right now."

"You can't do thi—"

Marcus cut him off. "That's where you're wrong. We absolutely can and are prepared to."

He gestured over his shoulder, and Ore looked too, not understanding for a minute and then catching sight of Keegan at the end of the line. Purple tendrils of what looked like smoke were weaving around his fingers and up his arms.

He stared in shock. He'd never seen a witch with magic like that.

Gladstone's cheeks pinkened, but he swallowed and stepped aside. "Fine, take them, I don't care. They might've made it easier to control the weaklings in this pack, but I

221

don't actually need them. No one will stand up to us. This is our pack."

"Not anymore," Dare growled.

Gladstone eyed him warily as Marcus, Robson, and one of the Silver Oak betas—Riggs, he was pretty sure his name was—headed into the house. Gladstone's fists were clenched at his sides, but Alpha Barney still just looked confused.

"What's happening, Louie?" he whispered to his Enforcer.

"Nothing, sir. Go on back inside and watch your programs."

"He's been terrorizing the pack," Ore called out. "He and the rest of the Enforcers."

"What?" Alpha Barney asked, looking shocked. "What do you mean?"

"We'll explain everything," Liam said, clasping Ore on the shoulder and letting him know he would handle it. "I'm going to need you to call the rest of your Enforcers here though."

"Who are you, young man?"

"Alpha *Liam* Amato," he said with a polite smile.

Ore stopped worrying about Alpha Barney the second a familiar young face filled the doorway. Hannah's hair was as dark as his own, although her skin was lighter, closer to their dad's. She was grinning widely, racing toward him before he had time to do anything but stare at her. She hit him at full speed, and only Cash's hand on his back stopped him from tumbling backward.

"Ore, you're here!" she screamed in excitement. "I knew you'd save us."

His eyes prickled with tears as he stared over her head at his other sisters, Savannah and Holly.

Holly was the second oldest but still almost seven years younger than him. The girls were much closer in age than he was to them. She looked tired, her eyes scarily blank as she guided Savannah across the porch and down the steps, keeping herself between her and Gladstone.

As soon as they were close enough, he pulled them into his tight embrace with Hannah.

"Thank the goddess you're safe," he murmured, running his hands over their heads and backs, unconsciously scenting them after having spent so much time with Cash.

"Where's Mom and Dad?" Holly asked, a little of her stone facade cracking as she took in the group behind him.

"They're back in Kansas. I've been with a pack there." He nodded toward Liam. "His pack. For about two weeks, they've been taking care of me."

"Taking care of you how?" Savannah asked, watching him with her wide, hazel eyes.

"I was pretty hurt when I got there," he said, rubbing a hand over Hannah's head when she made a soft noise of distress.

"But you're okay now?" she asked.

"I'm okay now." He pointed unsubtly at Cash. "See that man?"

They all nodded, staring at him with round eyes.

"He saved me. And," he added in a fake whisper, "we're mates."

Hannah clapped her hands in excitement, and Holly smiled, but it was strained. Savannah ran her eyes over Cash warily. He didn't take it personally. He had no idea what they'd been going through after spending weeks and weeks locked in that house with no one but a daft, old alpha and his brutal Enforcers.

"We're going to take you to Mom and Dad," he said, meeting each of their eyes, showing them that he was serious.

"We don't have to stay here?" Hannah asked in a hopeful voice.

"We're never coming back here again."

He jerked back as Gladstone came storming down the

223

steps, scattering the other hatchlings that had come out but were lingering by the porch, unsure what was happening or where to go.

Ore pulled the girls behind him.

"You piece of shit. You've ruined everything," Gladstone seethed, eyes locked on Ore and filled with hatred. "All you had to do was fall in line like the others. Instead, now I'm going to have to—"

He didn't get the chance to finish the threat. Before Ore even saw him move, Cash's panther burst forward, shredding his clothes as he lunged at Gladstone, taking him to the ground quickly.

Unlike what Nero had said on the plane, Cash didn't hesitate.

Ore covered the girls' eyes as best he could as his mate ripped the throat out of the man that had hurt and terrorized so many of the people he was supposed to protect. Cash didn't linger over his kill, turning and trotting right back over to Ore and rubbing his bloody face against his leg.

He gave his black ears a scratch. "Thank you."

Cash looked up at him, and within a handful of heart-beats, he was back in his human skin, pulling Ore into his arms and burying his face in his neck. Ore ran his hands down his mate's naked back, doing his best to soothe him while his muscles twitched with tension.

"Whoa," Savannah whispered. "I totally get it now."

CHAPTER 20

"Martha left some food in the fridge, but if you need anything, you can go into town and get it, or shoot me or Cash a text, and we'll take care of it."

"Are you sure this Martha doesn't mind us using her house for a while?" his dad asked, eyes locked on where his mom sat on the couch, holding the girls the same way she'd been doing pretty much since Ore and Cash had gotten back the night before.

"I'm sure." He shot his dad a patient smile, even though he was exhausted and wanted nothing more than to go pick up his mate from Jorge's and go home. "She and Pops—that's Cash's grandfather—they're going to be staying at Alpha Amato's house until some other housing can be situated."

His dad dragged his eyes off the girls and looked at Ore, eyebrows furrowed. "Why aren't they staying with you and Cash?"

Ore ducked his head to hide his blush. They'd offered as soon as he'd left his parents with the girls late last night. He'd returned to the cabin to find Pops and Martha waiting with Cash. They firmly informed him his family was going to stay in her house and that she and Pops would stay with Alpha

Amato. Martha's sweet face had softened from her no-nonsense expression. She'd gripped Ore's hand and told him that a family who has been through what Ore's had needed time and space to heal and grieve together.

Cash had tried to insist Pops move back in with Martha, pointing out that he and Ore slept up in the loft, so there was plenty of space, but Pops had thumped his cane on the floor and laughed.

"Move in with two newly mated shifters? There aren't thick enough earplugs in the world, son."

Ore had thought his skin would catch fire he was so embarrassed, but Cash had just shaken his head, more exasperated than anything else.

"Um, they just said it would be nice to give Alpha Amato some company," he lied unconvincingly.

His dad raised a brow at him but didn't argue. He looked around the quaint little kitchen. It wasn't big, but it was neat and cheery. "Where are the others staying?"

"Only a few came back with us," he admitted. "But Marcus and the others will help relocate anyone else who doesn't want to stay there while they get a new alpha set up. The ones who did come, one of them is staying at the Alpha House too, and the rest are bunking with Silver Oak folks who volunteered to share their space."

His dad looked back at him quickly. "People offered up their own homes to share?"

Ore nodded, a little sad that his dad found that so hard to believe. "They did. In fact, more people offered than were needed."

He didn't share that over a dozen people were choosing to leave, packing up their houses as they spoke, determined not to stay in a pack that was diversifying their ranks. Thankfully, Billy Mittin was one of the first to announce his departure.

Once they were gone and the places were checked to see if anything needed to be fixed or updated, the former Barney

Pack members would be able to start moving into those homes.

"Well, that was nice of them." He touched Ore's arm and led him out of the kitchen, away from the others. Closing the laundry room door, he lowered his voice. "Has Holly said anything to you?"

His gut clenched. "Not really. I wasn't sure if I should ask her what had happened. I ended up deciding I would let her tell us when she was ready."

"I could kill that Gladstone," his dad muttered, his scent thickening with anger and face turning red.

He wasn't used to seeing his dad get so upset, but he understood it. Remembering his parents' kneejerk reaction when he told them Cash was his mate, he hesitated before saying, "Cash already took care of that."

His dad looked up at him in surprise once again. "He did?"

"Yes," Ore confirmed. "You don't have to worry about Gladstone anymore, and the rest of the Enforcers were removed and will be taken back to Michigan with the Kincaid Pack members to be dealt with."

Nodding slowly, his dad absorbed that information. "Good. I'm glad... I'm glad they were able to help."

"Me too." He gripped his dad's arms briefly. "I'm going to take off. But let me know if you need anything. Seriously. If you don't want to ask me, you can ask one of the Enforcers or betas here. They want to help."

"Alright, son."

Ore gave him one last smile and then headed out of the house, calling a soft goodbye to his mom and sisters. Hannah was the only one to chirp back, "Bye, Ore!"

Heading for Cash's truck, he took a few cleansing breaths. It would take time, but he had to believe his family would heal and come out of the other side of all of this. If Holly didn't want to talk to them, Ore would get her a professional to help her.

As his own memories continued to come back—sometimes in a wave that overwhelmed him and gave him a headache and other times a single moment slowly forming—he had to deal with his own traumatic experience. A part of him wished he couldn't remember anything about that *place*. The scary implements around the stark white room, being strapped to an examination table, crying and begging for them to stop, only to be ignored.

The more he remembered, the more he clung to his mate. Healthy or not, burrowing into Cash's heat made him feel safe, and he wouldn't give it up. The entire plane ride back to Kansas, he'd stayed curled in Cash's lap—the girls passed out in the back, which turned out *was* a bedroom with a huge bed —crying quietly. Not for a single minute did his cat let him go.

The next few weeks and months would be tough—for everyone in the pack, no doubt—full of grief and change and uncertainty, but he believed it would also bring an abundance of love. And acceptance.

And a brighter, safer, and more secure future.

Hefting himself up into Cash's truck, he headed toward the center of town, where his friend Jorge lived. His mate had asked him to drop him off before Ore went to check on his family so he could get one of his tattoos powered up again.

Ore could barely reach the pedals, which Cash had found hilarious, but he'd promised to get him his own car he could drive more comfortably. It would probably be a good idea. Although... he liked the idea of them sharing one, of them sharing *everything*. Of always being together, completely wrapped up in each other and their lives.

It wouldn't be practical in the long term, but he'd figure out ways to stick close to Cash. He doubted his possessive and overprotective mate would mind.

As he made his way down Main Street, he glanced at the empty storefront still for sale. He'd wait until things settled a bit and then share his idea with Cash to see what he thought. He couldn't imagine his mate would have a problem with it. The joy he got playing with and teaching the cubs was obvious even to a casual observer. Sure, he'd still have his Enforcer duties and wouldn't be available all the time, but Ore doubted he'd have an issue getting other folks to volunteer to help out.

He pulled up outside of Jorge's house, feeling lighter and more positive than he had in days. He would make a life here for himself, one he'd cherish every day.

Not bothering to knock, he walked in using the front door. He knew they'd be in what was originally probably a dining room, but the witch had converted it into a private studio to do work that was... off the books.

His formal shop was attached to his house, but Ore couldn't imagine he got a lot of work, considering how resistant to outsiders the pack had been. He was incredibly talented though, so Ore hoped he'd end up with more work than he could handle.

"Hey," he called out, getting some of the keys on Cash's ring stuck outside his jeans pocket. Moving slowly toward the studio space, he fought to get them situated. "I'm back. They're all settled at Martha's. How are things... going..."

His voice gave out as he stared at his mate, confused at what he was seeing for a second. Cash was leaned back in the chair as Jorge bent over his chest and worked on a *new* tattoo, not the one on his bicep he was getting charged up.

Blinking several times, he stood frozen in the doorway, emotions welling inside him and burning his eyes. Jorge was putting the finishing touches on a black tribal piece on Cash's left pec.

It was... an eagle.

Cash was having an *eagle* tattooed on his body.

"What… When…" He couldn't figure out what to say, his eyes locked on the new ink.

"Come here, little bit." Cash held out his hand, beckoning him forward.

Legs shaky, he stumbled across the room and grasped those offered fingers. Cash's big, familiar hand helped shake some of the shock out of his system. He tore his eyes away from where Jorge was wiping the tattoo, meeting his mate's gaze.

"You didn't have to do that." His voice was little more than a whisper, hoarse and croaky, but Cash heard him and smiled.

"Jorge needs something from you."

"From me?" He raised his brows and looked back over at Cash's friend.

The witch had light brown skin and a devilish smile, his black hair swept back from his forehead and amber eyes dancing with humor. "Just a few drops of blood."

He shot a look at his mate, who nodded encouragingly. "It'll be worth it. I promise."

Still confused, but trusting Cash, he held out his hand. Jorge spun around on his stool and ripped off his gloves. Ore couldn't see what he was doing, but when he whirled back around, he had a stone bowl with crushed herbs inside and a small knife.

"Do you want to do it, or should I?" Jorge asked, holding up the blade.

Ore looked at Cash one more time and then shrugged, offering his hand once more. "You can do it."

Without hesitating, Jorge pricked the end of one of his fingers and squeezed out a few drops before his body could heal the tiny cut.

"Thanks," Jorge said, spinning back around.

Ore turned to his mate, prepared to demand some answers, but Cash distracted him, grabbing his hand and pulling it up to his mouth. Holding Ore's eyes, he sucked the remaining drop of blood off his finger, then ran his tongue over it.

Heat pooled low in his belly, and he had to take a few deep breaths before he could form coherent words. "Are you going to tell me what this is about?"

Cash kissed the tip of his finger, then lowered his hand and pressed it against his ribs, laying his own over top to hold him in place. "Patience."

That word distracted him from the feel of his mate's warm, naked skin, and he rolled his eyes. He was sick of people telling him to be *patient*. If one more person—

Jorge muttered a few words, drawing Ore's attention back to him. The scent of magic flared in the air, and then he turned back around, a scoop of the mixture from the bowl on his fingers.

"You ready, hermano?"

Cash nodded. "Do it."

To Ore's fascination and horror, Jorge pressed the mixture right over the lines of the new tattoo. His mate healed fast, but there was no way his skin wasn't still raw from the tattoo machine. The process was way more extensive than Ore's tiny prick from the knife.

Was this how Jorge did the other magical tattoos? He'd never actually asked Cash what the process was, but he'd assumed the spell was in the ink, not applied afterward.

The witch spread the mixture over every line, then leaned back and wiped his hands on some paper towel, a satisfied expression on his face.

Ore looked between him, his mate, and the herb-crusted ink.

"Um."

Cash pressed his hand harder against him, asking once more for patience. Huffing a breath, Ore stared at the tattoo. Just as he was about to speak up again, annoyed with just standing in silence, he noticed the herbs were… disappearing. Was Cash's body absorbing them?

His lips parted as every speck vanished before his eyes, and then the black lines began to… glow. It started at the farthest edges—the talons, tailfeathers, and tips of the wings —but it quickly spread until the entire piece glowed a fiery orange, way brighter than any of Cash's other spelled tattoos.

He licked his dry lips. "What—*shit*."

He slapped a hand over his chest, and his eyes started watering as a fire poker tried to explode out between his pecs. He whimpered, and Cash was right there, sitting up and swinging his legs around.

"Try and breathe through it. It'll pass, little bit."

Whining, he squeezed his eyes shut and pressed as close to his mate as he could get, the burning growing, melting his muscles and bones and making it hard to take a deep breath. "Hurts."

"I know. I'm so sorry." His voice sharpened. "What the fuck? You didn't say it would hurt him like this!"

"I didn't know! I told you: it's never been done on a parahuman before, let alone a shifter. Maybe his eagle is rejecting it?"

His pulse was throbbing in his ears, and there was a buzzing under his skin, but he tried to focus. He felt for his eagle, ignoring the searing pain as best he could, and when he found him, he was surprised to find him… overjoyed.

As soon as the realization hit him, the heat began to dial back, slowly ebbing out of his fingers and toes, down his arms and up his legs, until it coalesced in the center of his chest. He sucked in a few deep breaths, waiting to see if the pain would get worse again or if the ball of warmth lingering next to his heart would fully dissipate.

Neither happened.

But the longer he focused on it, the more apparent it became what it was. He could *feel* Cash's horror, panic, and guilt as he continued yelling at Jorge to do something. Slipping his hand up to the side of Cash's neck, he gripped it hard, snaring his attention.

Beautiful glowing eyes locked on him. "What's happening? Is it getting worse? Talk to me, Ore."

"It's better now." He sounded raspy, like he'd been screaming for twenty minutes, but he knew he hadn't. Glancing around his giant mate, he caught Jorge collapsing on his stool, tossing aside what appeared to be an old—and no doubt valuable—book so he could bury his face in his hands. "My eagle wasn't rejecting it."

Jorge glanced at him, sliding his hands up into his hair. "I'm so sorry, Ore. I should have done more research or tried to test it somehow. I never meant—"

"I know. It's okay." He shot his mate a wide-eyed look.

Grunting, Cash turned, keeping his arms firmly around Ore. "Sorry I lost my fucking head."

"No, I get it. I'd be the same way," Jorge said, rubbing his face a few times and then standing. "Obviously, I'll have to figure out what went wrong, but I'd understand if you didn't want to try again."

"We—"

"It worked," Ore said, grinning at the both of them. Placing his hand over his chest, he met his mate's eyes, no longer glowing but just as breathtaking. "I can feel you right here, baby."

Cash sucked in a breath, then touched his own chest. "Just like I can you. We're fully connected now, little bit."

Staring into the face of the man he loved more than anything, he felt the warm spot pulse with happiness and adoration. *Cash's* happiness and adoration. Birds didn't exchange bonding bites, so he'd never thought about being connected to a mate in such a way.

He'd had no idea what he was missing out on.

To feel so close to another person, having their emotions and affections living inside him?

Worth every second of pain to get.

A shuffling sound drew his eyes back to their audience, and his cheeks flushed. How long had they just been standing there making heart eyes at each other?

Clearing his throat, he told Jorge, "My eagle wasn't fighting it, but I think I was. Once I realized he didn't feel threatened, the pain started to go away."

"Fuck." Cash squeezed his eyes shut. "I'm sorry, little bit. I thought it'd be a nice surprise, and instead—"

"It *is* a nice surprise," he assured him, then poked him in the chest with a teasing smile. "You know, minus the brain-melting, excruciating pain."

Cash ran his tongue between his teeth and lip, looking like he wasn't sure if he should still wallow in his guilt or laugh. He leaned down as he cupped the sides of Ore's face and kissed him deeply. Arousal shot through him, and his legs turned to jelly as he fought to keep up with the fierce way Cash was tasting him.

A throat cleared. "Don't you two have your own home to make out in?"

Ore broke away, laughing even as his face burned. "We do."

Staring down at Ore for a long moment, Cash finally gave his hip a quick squeeze, then strode around the tattoo chair and pulled Jorge into a hug before the witch knew what was happening.

Ore smiled and ducked his head, trying not to listen as Cash quietly told him they were good. He slipped out of the room when Jorge took a shuddering breath and whispered back, "I thought I'd killed him, Cash."

Swiping under his eyes, he waited by the front door as the two talked for a few minutes. As scary as it had been for him, it must have been just as bad for Cash and Jorge, not knowing what was happening or if he'd be okay. He was grateful their close friendship was still intact.

Cash's eyes were suspiciously red when he joined him, new tattoo covered by his dark T-shirt, but Ore didn't say anything, just smiled gently and held out a hand. "Where to next? Any more surprises I should know about?"

His mate shook his head, the side of his mouth twitching. "No, brat. We're going home."

"Fuck yes! Harder!"

Cash grunted and slammed inside him, causing the kitchen table to skid a few more inches across the floor. Ore barely even noticed as he threw his head back and moaned, lost in a sea of pleasure.

The second they'd walked through the door, he'd started tugging at the bottom of his mate's shirt, desperate to get his eyes on *his* mark again. Licking his way up Cash's hard abs, he'd made his way to the ink and groaned as he ran his tongue right over it.

That had gotten his mate moving.

Over Cash's shoulder, he could see the front door, still hanging open, but he couldn't have cared less. Even on the off chance someone came all the way out to where their A-frame cabin was located, he wouldn't have stopped. Couldn't have.

An obsessive possessiveness was driving him, turning him fucking feral. He couldn't quit running his hands over every inch of Cash he could reach or stop licking that glowing mark. As his mate plowed into him, sweat glistening on his chest and forehead, Ore whimpered and nuzzled at the ink before sucking as much of his tattooed skin into his mouth as he could and biting down.

"Shit," Cash groaned, his hips going off rhythm for a second before he recovered and found it again. He changed his angle so he was hitting Ore's prostate with every thrust and making him cry out, releasing his mouthful. "You're driving me crazy. Every time you touch it, it's like a bolt of lightning to my fucking nuts."

Giving him a break, Ore fell back onto the table, struggling to get enough strength back in his legs to prop his heels on the edge. Cash gripped his hips, making things just right, and then slowed down his thrusts, gazing at Ore with softly glowing blue eyes.

He glanced back down at the tattoo and squeezed around his mate, making him groan. "You marked yourself for me."

Eyes going bright, Cash fell over him, bracing one hand next to his head. "I'd do anything for you, mate."

He thought of Gladstone's dead, bleeding body and slid his palms up Cash's torso, over his shoulders, and around his neck. Tugging him closer, he kissed up the side of his jaw and whispered in his ear, "I know, baby. Thank you."

Then bit his lobe.

"*Shit*," Cash grunted, driving his hips forward.

"You're mine. Forever," he said, licking at the abused flesh and tracing a finger over the lines of the glowing proof.

"I always have been."

Heart soaring, he relaxed back onto the table again, settling his hands on Cash's massive biceps. "Make me come, then remind me who I belong to."

Cash flashed his fangs, a growl building in his chest as he lowered himself fully onto Ore. He gave a hard thrust, rubbing his lower abs perfectly against Ore's weeping dick and making his eyes roll back in his head.

Nuzzling into the scar on Ore's neck, Cash rumbled against his skin, "You need reminding? Was my claiming not —" He slammed into him, scooting him across the table. "—memorable enough?"

Ore moaned, biting his lip. He could feel the ridges growing on Cash's cock as he neared completion, turning his mate's large dick even bigger. But goddess, the ribbing hit every single good spot inside him at once.

When he didn't answer fast enough, Cash drove into him again. "Little bit?"

"I'll never forget," he gasped, wrapping his arms and legs around him and holding as tight as he could. "Because you're going to show me every day."

Snarling, Cash muttered something that sounded like *You're fucking right I will,* but Ore's mind whited out as he bit over his bonding mark, his fangs pricking at his skin. All of the sensations swirling inside him slammed together and then exploded.

He moaned Cash's name again and again as waves of pleasure crashed over him. As Cash chased his own release, licking at the tiny drops of blood he'd drawn, Ore's lungs seized at how *fucking* good those ridges felt, catching at his rim every time.

Just as black spots started to fill his vision and he worried about passing out, Cash sank as deep inside him as possible and grunted, his cock pulsing against his sensitive walls.

He stayed locked around his mate's huge body as he tried to catch his breath. "Holy guacamole."

Cash twitched but didn't raise his head. "What?"

"A regular curse didn't seem strong enough."

Those massive shoulders shook. "Fuck, I love you."

"That's nice, but you're squishing me." He was still struggling to draw deep breaths, but he realized it wasn't because of the mind-blowing orgasm. His mate was just *really* heavy.

Grunting, Cash pushed himself up onto his forearms. "Half my body isn't even on the table."

"Yes, but look how little I am," he said, smirking as his mate's cock twitched inside him and his eyes started heating once more.

"Let's go upstairs. You can be on top this time."

Ore threw his head back and laughed, though his own

dick was definitely interested in the idea. "I'm surprised we didn't have to go up there already, Mr. Didn't Think to Bring Lube to a Romantic Midnight Skinny Dip. Apparently, you have no problem stashing some in the kitchen though."

Cash grinned. "I'm learning."

"What if Pops and Martha had moved back in and found it?"

Groaning in a not-good way, his mate dropped his head onto Ore's chest. "Do *not* talk about my grandfather while I'm still balls-deep inside you, little bit."

He cackled.

EPILOGUE

Three weeks later

"He can really feel you the same as if he'd bitten you?" Saint asked, peering at Cash's tattoo with curious eyes.

When he lifted a hand like he was going to touch it, Cash slapped it away and tugged his shirt back down. "Yeah. And my connection to him is stronger. When we're near each other, I can feel... everything."

It had been intense the first few days, trying to sort through his own feelings and those of his sweet little mate. Who had, it turned out, a *lot* of feelings. He'd gotten used to it though. Now, unless he focused on it or Ore was feeling something really strongly, he could let it fade into the background.

His favorite moments had to be when the two of them were alone, reading or watching TV or talking quietly about everything and nothing, and he'd get a rush of affection and love from his mate.

Goddess, how could he have been scared of this for so long?

"That's seriously cool." Saint led the way through the Alpha House toward Liam's office. "Have you, uh, seen Jorge since he did it?"

He was trying to sound casual, but Cash wasn't buying it. He grabbed Saint's shoulder and pulled him to a stop, turning him to face Cash. His friend wouldn't meet his eyes, and he sighed. "You need to leave him be, brother. He told me about catching you in his backyard a few times."

A light flush colored his tan cheeks. "Did he say I was making him uncomfortable?"

Cash hesitated. That's not what Jorge had said, actually. He'd merely asked if Cash had known why his best friend was stalking him. It didn't really matter though. "He said you were following him and hanging out behind his house in the dark. He might be a witch, but he's still human."

Saint turned his face away, blowing out a breath. "Yeah, you're right. It's just… I thought maybe…"

Raising his brows, Cash clapped him on the side of the neck, giving him a quick scenting. "If you were mates, you would have known when he moved here two years ago. So either ask him out or leave him alone."

His rugged face twisted stubbornly, but then he sagged his shoulders in resignation and nodded. "You're right. I will."

Cash watched him walk down the hallway, scent heavy with guilt and a hint of anger. But was it directed at Cash… or Jorge?

Frowning, he followed him, promising himself he'd keep an eye on the situation. Jorge still felt bad about what had happened to Ore, but they'd talked a couple more times, and things seemed to be getting better. Which he was grateful for. He'd lost his head for a minute, but at the end of the day, he truly trusted the witch and considered him a good friend.

So if his best friend couldn't take no for an answer, Cash would personally beat some sense into him.

As soon as he relaxed onto the only open chair, Liam closed his laptop and focused on him. "Everyone settled?"

He switched gears in his head, sitting up straighter. Since the former Barney Pack people had moved to Silver Oak, Cash had been tasked with making them comfortable and overseeing their housing situation.

"Yes, sir. The last pair are all moved into their new homes."

"How many vacant houses do we have left?" Liam leaned back, folding his hands over his abdomen.

"A dozen." He hesitated, then added, "I've been hearing some rumblings about a few more people thinking about leaving."

Saint nodded. "I have too. At least three households."

"I've heard of four," Rachel said, crossing her legs under her cheetah-print dress. "At least two are for sure going. They're just waiting for official confirmation of acceptance from the packs they've asked to join."

They all glanced at Finlay where he stood in his usual corner behind Liam. He raised one brow at them. "No one shares things like that with me."

Liam waved a hand, unconcerned. "It's fine. I'd rather they leave now than stick around for a year knowing full well they don't plan on staying."

"Agreed," Saint said, voice hard. "If they aren't loyal to us, they don't belong here."

Cash glanced at him out of the corner of his eyes. *Us*, not *you*. Was he stewing over the Jorge conversation? Why should Jorge be loyal to him?

Liam didn't comment, but Finlay's sharp eyes were on the tiger, and then he glanced at Cash. He could only shrug. Who knew what was going on with him.

"I talked to Kincaid about an hour ago," Liam informed them casually. "He'll be here in a few months."

Rachel jerked so hard in surprise she nearly toppled out of her chair. "I'm sorry—what the hell?"

Sighing, he leaned forward, planting his elbows on his desk. "He and Quinten have been having... difficulties working together, but both agree that finding the fuckers who hurt Caden and Ore—and who knows how many more— needs to be a top priority. Alpha Kincaid has requested I host a summit and play mediator."

"If it's such a high priority, why isn't he coming now?" Cash asked.

"He's a busy man with a lot of responsibilities." Liam scratched at his beard and shrugged. "I suggested he send someone on his behalf, but he insisted on being involved, so we have to wait."

"That's ridiculous," Saint muttered.

"How many people will be coming from each pack?" Rachel asked, phone in hand.

"I don't know."

"Do we have an actual date picked?"

"Not yet."

"A timeline for the length of the summit?"

Liam didn't even bother answering.

She raised her head and gave their alpha an unimpressed look. "Okay. Where are we supposed to put these unknown number of people for who knows how long?"

"We'll figure it out," Finlay interjected smoothly, taking a step forward. "This is happening."

Sighing, Rachel tucked her phone away. "Understood. Maybe I can reach out to his assistant and get a better idea about things."

"Good idea," Liam said, then ran his eyes over each of them. "We won't just be sitting on our asses twiddling our thumbs while we wait. Our pack still needs guidance and protection. Now more than ever."

242

Cash nodded. As much as he wanted to find who'd hurt his mate, he was realistic enough to know it would take time. While they worked to find them, they still had a pack to run. He knew there would be growing pains as they expanded and changed, but he and the others would make sure things went as smoothly as possible.

"Is there anything else, sir?" Cash planted his hands on the arms of his chair, prepared to stand.

"One more thing." Liam pressed his lips together and glanced at Finlay. The vampire didn't say anything or do so much as twitch an eyebrow, but their alpha nodded. "Kincaid does have a... tip."

The three of them exchanged glances.

"What does that mean?" Saint asked.

"It means someone reached out to him through one of his pack members and claims to have information about the people kidnapping shifters."

Cash's temperature spiked, his panther pacing inside him. "Who are they? Has Kincaid talked to them?"

Liam shook his head. "All I really know is he's a Cervidae, and he has some conditions before he'll share what he knows."

"Cervidae?" Saint muttered.

"Conditions." Cash's claws dug into the arms of his chair. "How about he tells us everything he knows, and we don't rip his—"

Holding up a hand, Liam gave him an exasperated look. "Which is why you won't be going, and I need Rachel here to coordinate things for the summit."

There was a loaded silence where he and Rachel turned to look at Saint. He stiffened, whipping his head back and forth between them before turning to Liam with wide eyes. "Oh, what the hell."

"I need you to go to North Dakota—"

"North Dakota!"

"—and retrieve this man and bring him back here." Saint was shaking his head, but Liam kept going. "That's one of his conditions. He feels he won't be safe staying in his pack if anyone finds out he's talked to us."

Groaning, Saint rubbed at his face. "Fuck. I'm at least going now, right? I don't have to go to North Da-fucking-kota in the middle of winter?"

"You'll leave as soon as possible," Finlay said, pulling out his phone and typing something. "I just sent you the info we have."

"What are the other conditions?" Rachel asked, ignoring Saint's continued muttering as he read the text. "Does he want money or something?"

"He won't say until we send someone to get him," Liam said, tension in his voice. "But Kincaid's pack member thought it might have something to do with a child."

Saint's head shot up, all traces of annoyance gone. "What child? The Cervidae's?"

Liam shook his head. "I don't know."

Clapping Saint on the shoulder, Cash gave him a squeeze. "I guess you'll find out when you get there."

"But seriously—North Dakota?"

"Cash, hold up a minute," Liam said, stopping him from rising with the other two.

He nodded and sat back down, calling after Saint, "Will you—"

Saint raised a hand over his shoulder without turning around. "Yes, I'll go check on your precious mate. He at Pack Play?"

"Yeah."

Two weeks ago, he'd realized his mate stared at an empty storefront on Main Street every time they went past it. After some careful—and sexy—interrogating, Ore had confessed his idea to open a daycare center there to help out the pack.

Three days later, Cash had handed him the keys and told him to give him a list of things he needed. The building was technically owned by the pack, and since it was being used for pack purposes, they didn't even need to sign a lease or rent it. His mate had spent nearly every waking moment the last few days trying to get the space ready as fast as possible.

Once the door shut behind Saint, Liam opened a drawer in his desk and pulled out two folders. "Word has gotten out quickly that we're looking to expand our pack."

"That's great," he said honestly. He wasn't sure what it had to do with him though.

Liam lifted the thicker folder. "These are cat shifters who've applied."

Brows rising, he eyed the other folder. "And that one?"

"Everyone else. Non-cat shifters, witches, and a seer or two." He pushed both folders across his desk, closer to Cash. "I'd like you—"

Finlay cleared his throat, pulling a single sheet of paper out of his back pocket.

Liam rolled his eyes. "I told you to get rid of that."

"I didn't."

Plucking it from his fingers, Liam set the piece of paper with a list of names on top of the cat folder, then pointed at the other one. "I want you to start with this one. Do background checks, call references. Hell, if you want, you can use some of my brother's resources to dig into each candidate."

"Sir—"

"You'll work with Fin," Liam reassured him before Cash could begin to panic. "Pull out anyone you think would be a good fit, and we'll talk about it."

Swallowing, he stared at the folders. "I don't know that I'm the best choice for this."

"Yes, you are." Liam waited until he looked up, then gave him his pirate smile. "I don't know anyone who takes their duties of caring for this pack more seriously than you. This is an important job, and you're up for the challenge."

He took a couple of breaths, then reached for the folders. "I won't let you down."

"I know you won't. Everyone who came from the Barney Pack has done nothing but sing your praises."

Jerking his head up, he stared at Liam. "Really?"

Liam chuckled. "Really. Once you're done with the non-cats, you can start looking at the other folder, but I want your focus on diversifying us first."

"Understood. And the list?" He glanced between Finlay's passive face and Liam's annoyed one.

"Those are people my brother thinks we should... persuade to leave other packs and come here."

"He wants us to *poach* from other packs?"

"Make an offer," Finlay said, coming around the desk. "Nothing more. No one will be pressured to leave their packs."

Liam grunted. "He's delusional if he thinks any of those names are willing to come here."

"Why?" Cash asked, standing once more.

"Because most are Enforcers or seconds-in-command," Liam said, shaking his head. "Quinten thinks we need to beef up our defenses now that we're coming out of isolation."

Finlay walked over to the door and pulled it open, gesturing Cash out. "Call your mother."

"Leave me be, nag."

Cash left the office, confused and honored. He was still a little surprised Liam had asked him to go through the applicants, but the more he thought about it, the more excited he got. Finding the best fits for expanding their pack was important, and it would give him a chance to continue proving to those still in doubt that it would only strengthen them.

"Are you busy now? I'd like to do a quick triage if we can," Finlay said, pointing toward the room across the hall from Liam's office.

It was mostly just used for meetings with the betas since they wouldn't all comfortably fit in the office. There were tables and chairs and a small refreshment station that had coffee and water on those days.

Cash checked the time, then shrugged. "Sure, we can do that."

For the next hour, they sorted through the applicants, splitting them into *Not a Chance*, *Maybe*, and *Strong Possibility* piles. In the non-cat folder, there were only a handful they dismissed right away, which he found promising. The majority went into the *Maybe* pile, and the rest seemed like the most promising candidates.

"I'm surprised how many prey shifters have applied," he admitted as they finished.

"It's fairly common. They like packs with strong but not tyrannical alphas and predator shifters. Makes them feel safer," Finlay said absently, pulling the feline applicant folder closer. "Have time to do this one?"

"Yeah, let me grab something to take notes with though."

They worked through that stack, putting more than a third into the *Not a Chance* pile.

"It's like they didn't even bother putting any effort into the applications," Cash muttered, rejecting another that put the equivalent of *looking for a change* as their reason for wanting to join.

"Most probably assume just being a feline will get them to the front of the line."

Cash scoffed and moved to the next.

He lost track of time, not even realizing the sun had set until Saint walked into the room eating a turkey sandwich and making his stomach go crazy. Glancing out the window, he groaned and pulled his phone out, expecting missed calls or texts from his mate, but there weren't any.

"What are you two still doing here?" Saint said around a mouthful, coming closer to peer at the papers they had spread around across the table. "Applicants to join the pack?"

"Yeah, where's Ore?" He started organizing things, keeping the piles separated in their new folders.

Saint shrugged. "Last time I saw him, he and Robbie were talking about getting something to eat, then going back to your place."

"Fuck me," Cash groaned. "The last thing I want to deal with when I get home is the Chaos Cubs."

Saint and Finlay stared at him like he'd lost his mind.

"They… aren't cubs?" Saint said, but with a questioning inflection on the end like he wasn't sure if he'd missed something.

"They act like they are when they're together," he grumbled. Stacking all the folders together, he turned to tell Finlay he'd call him in the morning and they could set up a schedule and figure out how to split the work, but froze when he found the vampire smiling softly.

"What's happening?" Saint whispered.

"I've known Robbie his whole life, and he does tend to… bring the chaos wherever he goes."

Cash tried not to stare. Finlay had just shared something with them. Something *personal*.

When the silence stretched, Finlay glanced between them, a frown creasing his perfect face. "But he's a good person. Ore is safe with him."

"We know, man," Saint reassured him.

Cash nodded, shaking off his shock. "He's a great friend to Ore. They just tend to… accidentally destroy things when they're together."

Saint nodded and pointed with his half-eaten sandwich.

"That's true. Though that was probably the best sales day Ginny's ever had."

Heading for the door, Cash chuckled. "Fair enough. I'll call you tomorrow, Finlay."

Both of the incidents with Ore and Robbie had actually ended pretty well for Cash. The bookstore had led to Ore begging to suck his dick, and the burnt cookies? He grinned, jogging to his truck. That night had definitely been memorable too.

The drive home took longer than normal—or he was just overly eager to be with his sweet little bird after not being near him all day. Pulling up to the house, he was surprised to see only Ore's Prius. Maybe Robbie had ridden with him from Pack Play and left his own car downtown.

He didn't hear any smoke detectors going off, which was a good sign.

Soft music was playing—the romantic kind, not the loud pop stuff he and Robbie normally listened to—and the smell of roasted meat tickled at his nose, making his stomach growl plaintively. He pulled open the front door and paused just inside.

The kitchen table had a white tablecloth draped over it, two places set, wineglasses already half full, and a lit candle in the middle. His mate, wearing nothing but one of Cash's shirts, hadn't noticed him yet, busy muttering to himself as he pulled a roast pan out of the oven.

He softly shut the door behind him, drawing Ore's attention. A wide, gorgeous smile filled his bird's face, and then he was hurrying toward him. Leaping from a few feet away, Cash caught him, letting his momentum lean him back against the door.

"Welcome home, baby."

Unable to resist, Cash gave his cute ass a squeeze and captured his grinning mouth in a tongue-tangling kiss.

"What's the occasion?" he murmured against Ore's panting lips.

"You."

Cash lifted his head. "Me?"

Ore nodded and squirmed against him. "Robbie told me his uncle was going to give you an important assignment, so I thought we should celebrate." He pecked Cash's lips, then again. And a third time with a subtle little thrust against his abs. "You work so hard. You deserve to be celebrated."

Emotions thick in his throat, Cash nuzzled into the crook of his neck and inhaled deeply, pulling those floral notes that now mixed with his own scent deep into his lungs. "Thank you, little bit."

Ore scratched the back of his head with one hand and wrapped the other around Cash's shoulders to hug him. "Congratulations."

"I love you," he murmured, kissing the scar from his teeth just to make his mate shiver in his arms. And because he loved the visible proof that he'd been found worthy of his little bird. His tiny tempest.

"I love you too, baby." He stroked Cash's head and neck. "Now. Would you like a perfectly cooked roast served with carrots and potatoes or me?"

Laughing, Cash headed for the stairs, holding his mate securely against him.

Like that was even a choice.

*Curious about the **memorable** night Cash referenced and what happened after Ore burned some cookies?*
Fear not!
I've decided to offer that deleted scene FOR FREE to my newsletter subscribers!

Scan the QR code below or go to the Bonus Content tab on my website, www.kikiclark.com.

Want more of the Silver Oak Pack?
Preorder Saint's book, Fervor, and find out what exactly a cervidae is and why our tiger is so drawn to a certain witch. ;-)

Scan the QR code below to jump right to Amazon.

A NOTE FROM KIKI

THANK YOU. THANK YOU. THANK YOU.

Thank you for reading *Tempest*. If you enjoyed Cash & Ore's story, please consider leaving a review to help other readers find their book!

Wanna never miss a release or sale?
Follow me on BookBub or on Amazon!

To always make sure you know what I'm working on, have the opportunity to read early copies of my books, and get freebies, subscribe to my newsletter!

WHAT TO READ NEXT!

THE ALPHA AND HIS KING — where the Kincaid Pack Universe begins! It features fated mates, hurt/comfort, found family, knotting, possessiveness, loooots of scenting, an age gap, and a series-long story arc!

Available in eBook, Paperback, Audio & KU!

THE MOBSTER'S MATE — find out how Liam's human brother became an alpha! When a human mobster meets an injured jaguar shifter you get: hurt/comfort, an age gap, touch him and die, possessiveness, found family, (mild) exhibitionism, and baddies getting what's coming to them.

Available in eBook, Paperback, Audio, & KU!

ALSO BY KIKI CLARK

Leather & Chrome Series

Reckless (Tank & CJ)

Temptation (Six & Ollie)

Yearning (Houston & Kenneth)

Joyful (Rooster & Emmett)

Possession (Tomas & Mason & Vinnie)

Blue Collar Hearts Series

Out In the Cold (Coop & Beau)

Laying Pipe (John & Lukas)

Banger (Kevin & Hank)

Forever Family Trilogy

Favor (Declan & Jeremy)

Easy (Simon & Jackson)

Faker (Samuel & Will)

Collected Works — *Best deal!*

Many of my books are also available in audio! Be sure to check out
my website or Audible.com.

ABOUT THE AUTHOR

A small-town Michigan girl, Kiki has enjoyed reading since she first picked up a YA fantasy as a child. After that, she devoured everything she could get her hands on and dreamed of one day writing her own books that touched people's hearts.

In 2020, she proudly joined the ranks of authors releasing character-driven, emotionally satisfying books showcasing that everyone deserves to find love.

To keep up-to-date with Kiki, sign up for her newsletter: http://www.kikiclark.com/newsletter.

Keep in touch by following her on any of these platforms:

facebook.com/kikiclarkauthor

instagram.com/kikiclark2017

amazon.com/author/kikiclark

bookbub.com/authors/kiki-clark

goodreads.com/kikiclark

www.ingramcontent.com/pod-product-compliance
Lightning Source LLC
Chambersburg PA
CBHW051628260626
47170CB00004B/1079

* 9 7 9 8 8 8 6 7 5 0 1 4 0 *